'There is much to astonish, to disturb and to admire in this dense book, which demands the reader's fullest engagement. Ondaatje's ability to create deeply moving fictions through indirection is a rare triumph: a poet in the skin of a novelist, he makes the mysteries of silence speak with the force of his words' *Guardian*

'The story here, meticulously researched for seven years, is that of ordinary people caught up in a war not of their own making and professionals trying to keep up with their consciences. Excavation is the theme - finding out exactly who had inhabited the body of a contemporary skeleton, nicknamed 'Sailor' by Anil, unearthed at a government archaeological site. But it is Anil, too, who is being unearthed, challenged, her liberal values tested on the touchstone of terror. Each character has his or her own ghosts to come to terms with' A. Sivanandan, *The Good Book Guide* (author of *When Memory Dies*)

'Important, beautiful and profoundly moving' *Scotsman*

'There is a territory that Ondaatje is marking out as distinctively his own. It is the area of war – World War II in *The English Patient* and the civil war in Sri Lanka in his latest novel, *Anil's Ghost* – and it is war as no one else has written of it: 'war for the sake of war', war as a way of life, where the tragedy, the terrible waste and horror of war is transformed into a kind of hallucinatory poetry' Anita Desai

ANIL'S GHOST

Michael Ondaatje was born in Sri Lanka and moved to Canada in 1962. His most recent books of poetry include *The Cinnamon Peeler* and *Handwriting*. He is also the author of the internationally acclaimed prose works *Coming Through Slaughter*, *Running in the Family*, *In the Skin of a Lion* and *The English Patient*, for which he won the Booker Prize in 1992. He lives in Toronto.

ALSO BY MICHAEL ONDAATJE

Prose
Coming Through Slaughter (1976)
Running in the Family (memoir) (1982)
In the Skin of a Lion (1987)
The English Patient (1992)

Poetry
The Dainty Monsters (1967)
The Man with Seven Toes (1969)
The Collected Works of Billy the Kid (1970)
Rat Jelly (1973)
Elimination Dance (1976)
Claude Glass (1979)
There's a Trick with a Knife I'm Learning to Do (1979)
Tin Roof (1982)
Secular Love (1984)
The Cinnamon Peeler (1991)
Handwriting (1998)

Anthologies
The Long Poem Anthology (1979)
From Ink Lake (1990)
The Brick Reader (with Linda Spalding) (1991)

ANIL'S GHOST

Michael
Ondaatje

PICADOR

First published 2000 by Bloomsbury Publishing Plc, London
and in the United States by Alfred A. Knopf, Inc., New York

This edition published 2000 by Picador
an imprint of Pan Macmillan Ltd
Pan Macmillan, 20 New Wharf Road, London N1 9RR
Basingstoke and Oxford
Associated companies throughout the world
www.panmacmillan.com

ISBN 0 330 48077 4

Grateful acknowledgment is made to the following for
permission to reprint previously published material:
Garden Court Music Co.: Excerpt from 'Talk to Me of Mendocino'
by Kate McGarrigle, copyright © by Kate McGarrigle (ASCAP).
Reprinted by permission of Garden Court Music Co. (ASCAP).
Warner Bros. Publications U.S. Inc.: Excerpts from 'Slim Slow
Slider' by Van Morrison, copyright © 1968, 1971 (copyright
renewed) by WB Music Corp. (ASCAP) & Caledonia Soul Music
(ASCAP). All rights administered by WB Music Corp. All rights
reserved. Reprinted by permission of Warner Bros. Publications
U.S. Inc., Miami, FL 33014.

39 38 37 36 35

A CIP catalogue record for this book is available from
the British Library.

Printed and bound in Great Britain by
Mackays of Chatham plc, Chatham, Kent

Author's Note

From the mid-1980s to the early 1990s, Sri Lanka was in a crisis that involved three essential groups: the government, the antigovernment insurgents in the south and the separatist guerrillas in the north. Both the insurgents and the separatists had declared war on the government. Eventually, in response, legal and illegal government squads were known to have been sent out to hunt down the separatists and the insurgents.

Anil's Ghost is a fictional work set during this political time and historical moment. And while there existed organizations similar to those in this story, and similar events took place, the characters and incidents in the novel are invented.

Today the war in Sri Lanka continues in a different form.

M.O.

ANIL'S GHOST

In search of a job I came to Bogala
I went down the pits seventy-two fathoms deep
Invisible as a fly, not seen from the pit head

Only when I return to the surface
Is my life safe . . .

Blessed be the scaffolding deep down in the shaft
Blessed be the life wheel on the mine's pit head
Blessed be the chain attached to the life wheel . . .

—Miner's folk song, Sri Lanka

When the team reached the site at five-thirty in the morning, one or two family members would be waiting for them. And they would be present all day while Anil and the others worked, never leaving; they spelled each other so someone always stayed, as if to ensure that the evidence would not be lost again. This vigil for the dead, for these half-revealed forms.

During the night, plastic sheeting covered the site, weighted down with stones or pieces of iron. The families knew the approximate hour the scientists would arrive. They removed the sheeting and got closer to the submerged bones until they heard the whine of the four-wheel drive in the distance. One morning Anil found a naked footprint in the mud. Another day a petal.

They would boil up tea for the forensic team. In the worst hours of the Guatemalan heat they held up a serape or banana leaf to provide shade.

There was always the fear, double-edged, that it was their son in the pit, or that it was not their son—which meant there would be further searching. If it became clear that the body was a stranger, then, after weeks of waiting, the family would rise and leave. They would travel to other excavations in the western highlands. The possibility of their lost son was everywhere.

One day Anil and the rest of the team walked to a nearby river to cool off during their lunch break. On returning they saw a woman sitting within the grave. She was on her haunches, her legs under her as if in formal prayer, elbows in her lap, looking down at the remains of the two bodies. She had lost a husband and a brother during an abduction in this region a year earlier. Now it seemed as if the men were asleep beside each other on a mat in the afternoon. She had once been the feminine string between them, the one who brought them together. They would return from the fields and enter the hut, eat the lunch she had made and sleep for an hour. Each afternoon of the week she was part of this.

There are no words Anil knows that can describe, even for just herself, the woman's face. But the grief of love in that shoulder she will not forget, still remembers. The woman rose to her feet when she heard them approach and moved back, offering them room to work.

Sarath

She arrived in early March, the plane landing at Katunayake airport before the dawn. They had raced it ever since coming over the west coast of India, so that now passengers stepped onto the tarmac in the dark.

By the time she was out of the terminal the sun had risen. In the West she'd read, *The dawn comes up like thunder,* and she knew she was the only one in the classroom to recognize the phrase physically. Though it was never abrupt thunder to her. It was first of all the noise of chickens and carts and modest morning rain or a man squeakily cleaning the windows with newspaper in another part of the house.

As soon as her passport with the light-blue UN bar was processed, a young official approached and moved alongside her. She struggled with her suitcases but he offered no help.

'How long has it been? You were born here, no?'

'Fifteen years.'

'You still speak Sinhala?'

'A little. Look, do you mind if I don't talk in the car on the way into Colombo—I'm jet-lagged. I just want to look. Maybe drink some toddy before it gets too late. Is Gabriel's Saloon still there for head massages?'

'In Kollupitiya, yes. I knew his father.'

'My father knew his father too.'

Without touching a single suitcase he organized the loading of the bags into the car. 'Toddy!' He laughed, continuing his conversation. 'First thing after fifteen years. The return of the prodigal.'

'I'm not a prodigal.'

An hour later he shook hands energetically with her at the door of the small house they had rented for her.

'There's a meeting tomorrow with Mr. Diyasena.'

'Thank you.'

'You have friends here, no?'

'Not really.'

Anil was glad to be alone. There was a scattering of relatives in Colombo, but she had not contacted them to let them know she was returning. She unearthed a sleeping pill from her purse, turned on the fan, chose a sarong and climbed into bed. The thing she had missed most of all were the fans. After she had left Sri Lanka at eighteen, her only real connection was the new sarong her parents sent her every Christmas (which she dutifully wore), and news clippings of swim meets. Anil had been an exceptional swimmer as a teenager, and the family never got over it; the talent was locked to her for life. As far as Sri Lankan families were concerned, if you were a well-known cricketer you could breeze into a career in business on the strength of your spin bowling or one famous inning at the Royal–Thomian match. Anil at sixteen had won the two-mile swim race that was held by the Mount Lavinia Hotel.

Each year a hundred people ran into the sea, swam out to a buoy a mile away and swam back to the same beach, the fastest male and the fastest female fêted in the sports pages for a day or so. There was a photograph of her walking out of the surf that January morning—which *The Observer* had used with the head-line 'Anil Wins It!' and which her father kept in his office. It had been studied by every distant member of the family (those in Australia, Malaysia and England, as well as those on the island), not so much because of her success but for her possible good looks now and in the future. Did she look too large in the hips?

The photographer had caught Anil's tired smile in the photograph, her right arm bent up to tear off her rubber swimming cap, some out-of-focus stragglers (she had once known who they were). The black-and-white picture had remained an icon in the family for too long.

She pushed the sheet down to the foot of the bed and lay there in the darkened room, facing the waves of air. The island no longer held her by the past. She'd spent the fifteen years since ignoring that early celebrity. Anil had read documents and news reports, full of tragedy, and she had now lived abroad long enough to interpret Sri Lanka with a long-distance gaze. But here it was a more complicated world morally. The streets were still streets, the citizens remained citizens. They shopped, changed jobs, laughed. Yet the darkest Greek tragedies were innocent compared with what was happening here. Heads on stakes. Skeletons dug out of a cocoa pit in Matale. At university Anil had translated lines from Archilochus—*In the hospitality of war we left them their dead to remember us by.* But here there was no such gesture to the families of the dead, not even the information of who the enemy was.

Cave 14 was once the most beautiful site in a series of Buddhist cave temples in Shanxi province. When you entered, it looked as if huge blocks of salt had been carted away. The panorama of Bodhisattvas—their twenty-four rebirths—were cut out of the walls with axes and saws, the edges red, suggesting the wound's incision.

'Nothing lasts,' Palipana told them. 'It is an old dream. Art burns, dissolves. And to be loved with the irony of history—that isn't much.' He said this in his first class to his archaeology students. He had been talking about books and art, about the 'ascendancy of the idea' being often the only survivor.

This was the place of a complete crime. Heads separated from bodies. Hands broken off. None of the bodies remained—all the statuary had been removed in the few years following its discovery by Japanese archaeologists in 1918, the Bodhisattvas quickly bought up by museums in the West. Three torsos in a museum in California. A head lost in a river south of the Sind desert, adjacent to the pilgrim routes.

The Royal Afterlife.

On her second morning they asked Anil to meet with forensic students in Kynsey Road Hospital. It wasn't what she was here for, but she agreed to it. She had not yet met Mr. Diyasena, the archaeologist selected by the government to be teamed with her in the Human Rights investigation. There had been a message that he was out of town and that he would contact her as soon as he returned to Colombo.

The first body they brought in was very recently dead, the man killed since she had flown in. When she realized it must have happened during her early-evening walk in the Pettah market, she had to stop her hands from trembling. The two students looked at each other. She never usually translated the time of a death into personal time, but she was still working out what hour it was in London, in San Diego. Five and a half hours. Thirteen and a half hours.

'Is this your first corpse, then?' one of them asked.

She shook her head. 'The bones in both arms are broken.' Here it was, in front of her already.

She looked up at the young men. These were students who had not yet graduated, young enough to be appalled. It was the freshness of the body. It was still someone. Usually the victims of a political killing were found much later. She dipped each of the fingers in a beaker of blue solution so she could check for cuts and abrasions.

'About twenty years old. Dead twelve hours. Do you agree?'

'Yes.'

'Yes.'

They seemed nervous, even afraid.

'What are your names again?'

They told her.

'The important thing is to say out loud what your first impressions are. Then rethink them. Admit you can make mistakes.' (Should she be lecturing them?) 'If you are wrong the first time, redraw the picture. Maybe you can catch what was overlooked. . . . How did they break the arms without damaging the fingers? It's strange. Your hands go up to protect yourself. Usually the fingers get damaged.'

'Maybe he was praying.'

She stopped and looked up at the student who had spoken.

The next corpse brought in had flail fractures on the rib cage. It meant he had fallen from a great height—at least five hundred feet—before hitting the water belly-down. The air knocked out of the body. It meant a helicopter.

She woke early the next morning in her rented house on Ward Place and walked into the darkness of the garden, following the sound of koha birds busy with their claims and proclamations. She stood there drinking her tea. Then walked to the main road as a light rain began. When a three-wheeler taxi stopped by her she slipped into it. The taxi fled away, squeezing itself into every narrow possibility of the dense traffic. She held on to the straps tightly, the rain at her ankles from its open sides. The *bajaj* was cooler than an air-conditioned car, and she liked the throaty ducklike sound of the horns.

Those first days in Colombo it seemed she always found herself alone when the weather broke. The touch of rain on her shirt, the smell of dust in the wetness. Clouds would suddenly unlock and the city would turn into an intimate village full of people acknowledging the rain and yelling to one another. Or there would be an uncertain acceptance of the rain in case it was only a brief shower.

Years before her parents had given a dinner party. They had set up the long table in their parched and dry garden. It was the end of May but the drought had gone on and on and still there was no monsoon. Then, towards the end of the meal, the rains began. Anil woke in her bedroom to the change in the air, ran to her window and looked out. The guests were scurrying under the thickness of the downpour, carrying antique chairs into the house. But her father and the woman he was beside continued to sit at the table, celebrating the break in seasons, as earth turned to mud around them. Five minutes, ten minutes, they sat and talked, she thought, just to make sure it was not a passing shower, to make sure the rain would keep coming down.

Ducklike horns.

The rain swept across Colombo as her *bajaj* proceeded via a shortcut, towards the Archaeological Offices. Lights were coming on here and there in the small shops. She leaned forward. 'Some cigarettes, please.' They swerved to a halt against the pavement and the driver yelled towards a shop. A man came into the rain with three different kinds of cigarettes and she picked out the Gold Leaf package and paid him. They took off again.

Suddenly Anil was glad to be back, the buried senses from childhood alive in her. The application she had made to the Centre for Human Rights in Geneva, when a call had gone out for a forensic anthropologist to go to Sri Lanka, had originally been halfhearted. She did not expect to be chosen, because she had been born on the island, even though she now travelled with a British passport. And it seemed somewhat unlikely that human rights specialists would be allowed in at all. Over the years complaints from Amnesty International and other civil rights groups had been sent to Switzerland and resided there, glacierlike. President Katugala claimed no knowledge of organized campaigns of murder on the island. But under pressure, and to placate trading partners in the West, the government eventually made the gesture of an offer to pair local officials with outside consultants, and Anil Tissera was chosen as the Geneva organization's forensic specialist, to be teamed with an archaeologist in Colombo. It was to be a seven-week project. Nobody at the Centre for Human Rights was very hopeful about it.

As she entered the Archaeological Offices she heard his voice.

'So—*you are the swimmer!*' A broad-chested man in his late forties was approaching her casually, with his hand out. She hoped this wasn't Mr. Sarath Diyasena, but it was.

'The swimming was a long time ago.'

'Still . . . I may have seen you at Mount Lavinia.'

'How?'

'I went to school at St. Thomas's. Right there. Of course I'm a bit older than you are.'

'Mr. Diyasena . . . let's not mention swimming again, okay? A lot of blood under the bridge since then.'

'Right. Right,' he said in a drawl she would become familiar with, a precise and time-stalling mannerism in him. It was like the Asian Nod, which included in its almost circular movement the possibility of a no. Sarath Diyasena's 'Right,' spoken twice, was an official and hesitant agreement for courtesy's sake but included the suggestion that things were on hold.

She smiled at him, wanting to get over the fact that they had managed to clash in their first few sentences. 'A true pleasure to meet you. I've read several of your papers.'

'Of course I'm in the wrong era for you. But I know most of the locations at least. . . .'

'Do you think we can get a breakfast?' she asked as they walked towards his car.

'Are you married? Got a family?'

'Not married. Not a swimmer.'

'Right.'

'The bodies turn up weekly now. The height of the terror was 'eighty-eight and 'eighty-nine, but of course it was going on long before that. Every side was killing and hiding the evidence. *Every side*. This is an unofficial war, no one wants to alienate the for- eign powers. So it's secret gangs and squads. Not like Central America. The government was not the only one doing the killing. You had, and still have, three camps of enemies—one in the north, two in the south—using weapons, propaganda, fear, sophisticated posters, censorship. Importing state-of-the-art weapons from the West, or manufacturing homemade weapons. A couple of years ago people just started disappearing. Or bodies kept being found burned beyond recognition. There's no hope of affixing blame. And no one can tell who the victims are. I am just an archaeologist. This pairing by your commission and the gov- ernment was not my idea—a forensic pathologist, an archaeolo- gist, odd pairing, if you want my opinion. What we've got here is unknown extrajudicial executions mostly. Perhaps by the insurgents, or by the government or the guerrilla separatists. Murders committed by all sides.'

'I couldn't tell who was worst. The reports are terrible.'

He ordered another tea and looked at the food that had arrived. She had specifically asked for curd and jaggery. When they were finished he said, 'Come. I'll take you to the ship. Let me show you where we will work. . . .'

The *Oronsay,* a passenger liner in the old days of the Orient Line, had been gutted of all valuable machinery and luxury furnishings. It had once travelled between Asia and England—from Colombo to Port Said, sliding through the narrow-gauge waters of the Suez Canal and journeying on to Tilbury Docks. By the 1970s it made just local trips. The rooms of tourist class were broken apart to become a cargo hold. Tea, fresh water, rubber products and rice replaced difficult passengers, save for a few souls, such as nephews of shareholders of the shipping line looking for work and adventure. It remained a ship of the Orient, a vessel that could survive the heat of Asia, that still contained the smells of salt water, rust and oil, and the waft of tea in cargo.

For the last three years the *Oronsay* had been berthed permanently in an unused quay at the north end of Colombo harbour. The grand ship had now become essentially part of the land and was being used by Kynsey Road Hospital as a storage and work area. With limited lab space in the hospitals in Colombo, a section of the transformed liner was to be Sarath and Anil's base.

They left Reclamation Street and walked up the gangplank.

She struck a match, and in the dark hold, light focussed and spilled up her arm. She saw the cotton thread of 'protection' on her left wrist, and then the match went out. In the month since the *raksha bandhana* had been tied on during a friend's *pirith* ceremony it had lost its rose colour. When she pulled on a rubber glove in the laboratory, the thread was even paler under it, as if within ice.

Next to her Sarath turned on a torch he had located during the flare of her match, and they both moved forward behind the spoke of twitching light, towards the metal wall. When they reached it he banged hard with the flat of his hand and they heard movement in the room beyond, the scurrying of rats. He banged again, and again there were sounds of movement. She murmured, 'Like a man and a woman scrambling out of bed when his wife comes home,' then stopped. Anil didn't know him well enough to taunt the structure of marriages. She was about to add, *Honey, I'm home.*

Honey, I'm home, she would say, crouching beside a corpse to ascertain the hour of death. The phrase came out caustic or tender, depending on her mood, mostly in a whisper as she put her hand out and held her palm a millimetre over the flesh to take in its body heat. *Its.* Not *his* or *hers* anymore.

'Bang it once more,' she asked him.

'I'll use the claw hammer.' This time the metallic noise echoed into the dark space, and when it died down everything became silent.

'Close your eyes,' he said. 'I'll light a sulphur lamp.' But Anil had worked in night quarries alongside sulphur brightness, or in basements made naked by it. The porous light revealed a large room, the remnants of a toppled saloon counter in the corner, behind which she later would find a chandelier. This was to be their storage space and work lab, claustrophobic, the odour of Lysol in the air.

She noticed Sarath had already begun using the space to store some of his archaeological findings. There were rock and bone fragments wrapped in clear plastic all over the floor, crates roped tight. Well, she hadn't come here to deal with the Middle Ages.

He was saying something she could not hear, while unlocking boxes, bringing out the results of a recent dig.

'. . . mostly sixth century. We think it was a sacred grave for monks, near Bandarawela.'

'Were any skeletons found?'

'So far three of them. And some fossilized wood pots of the same period. Everything fits into the same time pattern.'

She pulled her gloves on and lifted an old bone to test the weight. The dating seemed right.

'The skeletons were wrapped in leaves, then cloth,' he told her. 'Then stones were placed on top of them, which slid down later through the rib cage into the chest area.'

Years after a body was buried there would be a small shift on the surface of the earth. Then a falling of that stone into the space left by decayed flesh, as if signalling the departure of a spirit. This was a ceremony of nature that always affected her. As a child in Kuttapitiya Anil had once stepped on the shallow grave of a recently buried chicken, her weight driving the air in the dead body out through its beak—there was a muffled squawk, and she'd leapt back with fear, her soul jostled, then clawed earth away, terrified she would see the creature blink. But it was dead, sand in its eyes. Anil was still haunted by what had occurred that afternoon. She had buried it once more and walked backwards away from the grave.

Now she picked a fragment of bone from the detritus pile and rubbed it. 'This is from the same place? It doesn't seem sixth-century.'

'All this material comes from the monks' burial midden, in the government archaeological preserve. Nobody else gets in.'

'But this bone—it doesn't come from that time.'

He had stopped what he was doing and was watching her.

'It's a government-protected zone. The skeletons were interred in natural hollows near the Bandarawela caves. Skeletons and loose bones. It's unlikely you'd find anything from another era.'

'Can we go there?'

'I suppose so. Let me try and get a permit.'

They climbed back up onto the deck of the ship, into sunlight and noise. They could hear powerboats in the main channel of Colombo harbour, megaphones shouting out over the crowded waterways.

On her first weekend, Anil borrowed a car and drove to a village a mile beyond Rajagiriya. She parked by a lot tucked away behind trees, so small she could not believe a house existed there. Large speckled leaves of crotons spilled into the courtyard. There seemed to be no one at home.

The day after she arrived in Colombo Anil had sent a letter but there had been no reply. So she didn't know if this would be a wasted trip, whether the silence meant acceptance or the address she had was extinct. She knocked, then looked through the bars of the window, turning around quickly as she heard someone come out onto the porch. Anil could hardly recognize the tiny aged woman. They stood facing each other. Anil stepped forward to embrace her. Just then a young woman walked out and watched them without a smile. Anil was aware of the stern eyes that were taking in this sentimental moment.

When Anil leaned back the old woman was weeping; she put her hands out and ran them over Anil's hair. Anil held her arms. There was a lost language between them. She kissed Lalitha on both cheeks, having to bend down to her because she was small and frail. When Anil let go, the old woman seemed stranded and the young woman—*who was she?*—stepped forward and led her to a chair, then left. Anil sat next to Lalitha and held her hand in silence, feeling an ache in herself. There was a large framed photograph on the table beside them, and Lalitha picked it up and passed it to Anil. Lalitha at fifty, and her ne'er-do-well husband, and her daughter, who held two babies in her arms. Her finger pointed to one of the babies and then into the darkness of the house. So the young woman was her granddaughter.

The young woman brought out a tray of sugar biscuits and tea, and for the next while the granddaughter talked in Tamil to Lalitha. Anil could understand only a few words when it was spoken, relying mostly on the manner of speech to understand what they were saying. She'd once said something to a stranger who had met her sentence with a blank stare, and had then been told that because of her lack of tone the listener didn't understand the remark. He could not tell if it was a question, a statement or a command. Lalitha seemed embarrassed to be talking in Tamil and was whispering. The granddaughter, who barely looked at Anil after the first shaking of hands, was speaking loudly. She looked at Anil and said in English, 'My grandmother wants me to take a picture of the two of you. To remember that you came here.'

She left once more, then returned with a Nikon and asked them to move closer to each other. She said something in Tamil and took one picture before Anil was quite ready. One seemed to be enough. She was certainly confident.

'Do you live here?' Anil asked.

'No. This is my brother's house. I work in the refugee camps up north. I try to come down every other weekend, so my brother and his wife can get away. How old were you when you last saw my grandmother?'

'I was eighteen. I've been away since then.'

'You have parents here?'

'They're dead. And my brother left. Just my father's friends are still here.'

'Then you don't have any connection, do you?'

'Just Lalitha. In a way she was the one who brought me up.' Anil wanted to say more, to say that Lalitha was the only person who taught her real things as a child.

'She brought *all* of us up,' the granddaughter said.

'Your brother, what does he—'

'He's quite a famous pop singer!'

'And you work in the camps . . .'

'Four years now.'

When they turned back to her, they saw Lalitha had fallen asleep.

She entered Kynsey Road Hospital and in the main hall found herself surrounded by hammering and yelling. They were breaking up the concrete floors in order to put down new tiles. Students and faculty rushed past her. No one appeared to be concerned that these sounds might be terrifying or exhausting to patients brought in to have wounds dressed or receive stabilizing drugs. Even worse was the voice of the senior medical officer, Dr. Perera, yelling to doctors and assistants, calling them devils for not keeping the building clean. It was so continuous, this yelling, that it seemed to go unheard by most who worked there.

He was a short, thin man, and he had probably only one ally in the building, a young woman pathologist, who, not realizing his reputation, had come to him for help once and thus, by startling him, was befriended. The rest of his colleagues in the building distanced themselves with a tidal wave of anonymous memos and posters. (One poster announced that he was wanted in Glasgow for murder.) Perera's defense was that the staff was undisciplined, lazy, foolish, unclean and wrongheaded. It was only when he spoke in public that he switched to intellectual and subtle arguments about politics and its link to forensic pathology. His milder twin somehow seemed to have smuggled himself onto the stage.

Anil had heard one of his talks on her second night in Colombo and had been surprised that there were people with his opinions in positions of authority. But now, in the hospital, where she had come to use some equipment, she met the roving snapping dog that was the other side of his nature. She stood there openmouthed while exhausted staff, personnel and workmen and ambling patients veered away from Perera, creating a zone between themselves and this Cerberus.

A young man came up to her.

'You are Anil Tissera, no?'

'That's right.'

'You won the scholarship to America.'

She didn't say anything. The foreign celebrity was being pursued.

'Can you give a small talk, thirty minutes, on poisoning and snakebite?'

They probably knew just as much about snakebite as she did, and she was sure that this choice of subject was intentional—to level the playing field between the foreign-trained and the locally trained.

'Yes, all right. When?'

'Tonight?' the young man said.

She nodded. 'You contact me at lunch and tell me where.' She was saying this as she swerved past Dr. Perera.

'*You!*'

She turned to face the infamous senior medical officer.

'You're the new one, no? Tissera?'

'Yes, sir. I heard your speech two nights ago. I'm sorry I—'

'Your father was . . . *this thing* . . . right?'

'What . . .'

'Your father was Nelson K. Tissera?'

'Yes.'

'I worked with him at Spittel's Hospital.'

'Yes . . .'

'Look at those *padaya*s. Look—the rubbish here in the halls. This is a hospital, no? Bloody bastards, like a latrine. You are busy now?'

She was busy though she could have changed her plans. She was eager to speak to Dr. Perera and reminisce about her father, but she wanted to do so when he was decaffeinated, calm and alone, not in the midst of a fury. 'I've got a government appointment, I'm afraid, sir. But I'm in Colombo for a while. I hope we can meet.'

'Your dress is Western, I see.'

'It's a habit.'

'You're the swimmer, no?'

She walked away, nodding exaggeratedly.

Sarath was reading her postcard upside down as he sat across the desk from her. An unconscious curiosity on his part. He was a man used to cuneiform, faded texts in stone. Even in the shadowed light of the Archaeological Offices this was an easy translation for him.

The sound in the offices was mostly that of the careful pecking of typewriters. Anil had been given the desk by the copy machine, around which there was a permanent tone of complaint, for it never worked properly.

'Gopal,' Sarath said, slightly louder than usual, and one of his assistants came to his desk.

'Two teas. Bullmilk.'

'Yessir.'

Anil laughed.

'It's a Wednesday. Your malaria pill.'

'Took it.' She was surprised by Sarath's concern.

The tea arrived with the condensed milk already in it. Anil picked up her cup and decided to push it.

'To the comfort of servants. A vainglorious government. Every political opinion supported by its own army.'

'You talk like a visiting journalist.'

'I can't ignore those facts.'

He put his cup down. 'Look, I don't join one side or the other. If that's what you mean. As you said, everyone has an army.'

She picked up the postcard and spun it between her thumbs. 'Sorry. I feel tired. I've spent all morning going through reports at the Civil Rights Movement office. There's nothing hopeful there. Do you want to have dinner later?'

'I cannot.'

She waited for some explanation but nothing more came from him. Just his eyes darting to a map on the wall, to the picture of the bird on her postcard. While he continued to tap his pencil against the desk.

'Where's that bird from?'

'Oh . . . nowhere.' She could close down too.

An hour later they were running through rain and were fully wet by the time they climbed into the car. He drove her to Ward Place and kept the car idling under the portico as she collected her things from the back seat. 'See you tomorrow,' she said, and closed the door.

Once inside, Anil emptied her bag onto the table to find the postcard. Rereading her girlfriend Leaf's message from America made her feel better. Some communication from the West. She went into the kitchen, her mind circling around Sarath once more. She had been working with him for several days and she still had no handle on him. He was high up in the state-sponsored Archaeological Department, so how much a part of the government was he? Was he its ear and eye while assigned to aid her in the Human Rights investigation and report? In that case whom was she working for?

Forensic work during a political crisis was notorious, she knew, for its three-dimensional chess moves and back-room deals and muted statements for the 'good of the nation.' In the Congo, one Human Rights group had gone too far and their collection of data had disappeared overnight, their paperwork burned. As if a city from the past had been reburied. The investigative team, which included Anil in a lowly role as a programme assistant, had nothing left to do but get on a plane and go home. So much for the international authority of Geneva. The grand logos on letterheads and European office doors meant nothing where there was crisis. If and when you were asked by a government to leave, you left. You took nothing with you. Not a slide tray, not a piece of film. At the airport, while they searched her clothing, she'd sat almost naked on a stool.

One postcard from Leaf. One American bird. She pulled some cutlets and a beer out of the fridge. There would be a book to read, a shower to take. Later she might go to Galle Face Green and have a drink at one of the newer hotels, watch the drunk members of a touring English cricket team sing karaoke.

Was the partner assigned to her neutral in this war? Was he just an archaeologist who loved his work? The day before, on a road trip out of Colombo, he had shown her a few temples and then, passing some of his students working in a historic area, had joyfully joined them and was soon collecting slivers of mica, telling them where they were likely to find fragments of iron in the ground, as if he were a gifted and natural finder of things. Most of what Sarath wished to know was in some way linked to the earth. She suspected he found the social world around him irrelevant. His desire, he had told her, was to write a book someday about a city in the south of the island that no longer existed. Not a wall of it remained, but he wanted to tell the story of that place. It would emerge out of this dark trade with the earth, his knowledge of the region in chronicles—its medieval business routes, its presence as a favourite monsoon town of a certain king, as revealed in poems that celebrated the city's daily life. He'd quoted a few lines from one of the poems which his teacher, a man named Palipana, had taught him.

That was Sarath at his most expressive, almost enthusiastic, one evening after a crab dinner in Mount Lavinia. He stood by the surf drawing the shape of the city with his hands, sketching it in the dark air. Through the imaginary lines she could see the waves, their curl and roll, like his sudden excitement moving towards her.

*T*here were police officers all over the train. The man got on carrying a bird cage with a mynah in it. He walked through carriages, glancing at other passengers. There were no seats left and he sat on the floor. He was wearing a sarong, sandals, a Galle Road T-shirt. It was a slow train, travelling through rock passes, then emerging into sudden vistas. He knew that a mile or so before they got to Kurunegala there would be a tunnel and the train would curve into the dark claustrophobia of it. A few windows would remain open—they needed fresh air, though it meant the noise would be terrible. Once past the tunnel, back into sunlight, they would be getting ready to disembark.

He stood just as the train went into darkness. For a few moments there was the faint muddy light of the bulbs and then they went out. He could hear the bird talking. Three minutes of darkness.

The man moved quickly to where he remembered the government official was, beside the aisle. In the darkness he yanked him forward by his hair and wrapped the chain around his neck and began strangling him. He counted the seconds to himself in the darkness. When the man's weight fell against him he still didn't trust him, didn't release his hold on the chain.

He had a minute left. He stood and lifted the man into his arms. Keeping him upright, he steered him towards the open window. The yellow lights flickered on for a second. He might have been a tableau in somebody's dream.

He jerked the official off the ground and pushed him through the opening. The buffet of wind outside flung the head and shoulders backwards. He pushed him farther and then let go and the man disappeared into the noise of the tunnel.

While Anil was working with the forensic team in Guatemala, she'd flown into Miami to meet Cullis. She arrived exhausted, her face and body drawn out. Dysentery, hepatitis, dengue fever, they were all going around. She and her team were eating in the villages where they were exhuming bodies; they had to eat the food they were given because it was the only way the villages could participate—by cooking for them. 'You pray for beans,' she murmured to Cullis, removing the work clothes she still had on—she had rushed to catch the last plane out—then climbing into her first hotel bath in months. 'You avoid the seviche. If you have to eat it you throw up somewhere privately, as quick as you can.' She stretched out in the miracle of a foam bath, a tired smile towards him, glad to have reached him. He knew that exhausted and focussed look, the drawl of her slurring voice as she told her stories.

'I never actually dug before. I'm usually just in the labs. But we were doing exhumations in the field. Manuel, he gave me a brush and a chopstick and said break up the ground and brush it away. We got five skeletons the first day.'

He was on the edge of the tub watching her, closed eyes, away from the world. She'd cut her hair short. She was much thinner. He could see she had fallen even more in love with her work. Tired out but also refreshed by it.

She leaned forward and pulled the plug out, lay back again to feel the water disappear around her. Then she stood on the‑

tiles, her body passive as he pressed the towel against her dark shoulders.

'I know the name of several bones in Spanish,' she boasted. 'I know some Spanish. *Omóplato* is this. Shoulder blade. *Maxilar*—your upper jaw bone. *Occipital*—the bone at the back of the skull.' She was slurring words, as if counting backwards with anaesthetic in her. 'You've got a mixed bag of characters working on those sites. Big-shot pathologists from the States who can't reach for salt without grabbing a woman's breast. And Manuel. He is part of that community, so he has less protection than the others like us. He told me once, *When I've been digging and I'm tired and don't want to do any more, I think how it could be me in the grave I'm working on. I wouldn't want someone to stop digging for me. . . .* I always think of that when I want to quit. I'm sleepy, Cullis. Can hardly talk. Read me something.'

'I've written a piece on Norwegian snakes.'

'No.'

'A poem, then.'

'Yes. Always.'

But Anil was already asleep, with a smile on her face.

Cúbito. Omóplato. Occipital. Cullis wrote the names into his notebook, sitting at the table across the room from her. She was deep in the white linen bed. Her hand moving constantly, as if brushing earth away.

She woke at about seven in the morning, the room dark and hot, and slid naked from the large bed where Cullis was still dreaming. She already missed the labs. Missed the thrill that got knocked into her when they snapped lights on over the aluminum tables.

The Miami bedroom had the atmosphere of a boutique, with its embroidered pillows and carpeting. She entered the bathroom and washed her face, ran some cold water through her hair, wide awake. She climbed into the shower and turned it on but after a minute came out with an idea. Not bothering to dry herself, she unzipped her travelling bag and pulled from it the large, outdated videocamera she had brought with her to Miami to get a new microphone part installed. It was a secondhand television camera that the forensic team used, a remnant from the early eighties. She used it on sites and was accustomed to its weight and its weaknesses. She inserted a cassette and hoisted it onto her wet shoulder. Switched it on.

She began with the room, then returned to the bathroom and filmed herself waving briefly into the mirror. A close-up of the texture of the towels, a close-up of the shower water still running. She stood on the bed and shot down at Cullis's sleeping head, his left arm out to where she had been all night beside him. Her pillow. Back to Cullis, his mouth, his lovely ribs, back off the bed onto floor level, the camera steady, down to his ankles. Walked backwards to take in their clothes on the floor, and then to the table to his notebook. Close-up on his writing.

She removed the cassette from the machine and buried it under some clothes in his suitcase. She packed the camera in her bag, then got back into bed beside him.

They were lying in bed, in the sunlight. 'I can't imagine your childhood,' he said. 'You are a complete stranger to me. *Colombo*. Is the place languid?'

'It's languid indoors. Frenetic outside.'

'You don't go back.'

'No.'

'A friend of mine went to Singapore. All that air-conditioning! He said it was like being stuck in Selfridges for a week.'

'I suspect people in Colombo would love it to be Selfridges.'

Their life together was best in these brief quiet times, lazily, postcoitally conversing. To him she was clear and funny and beautiful, to her he was married, always interesting, permanently defensive. Two out of three was not good.

They had met on another occasion, in Montreal. Anil was there for a convention, and Cullis had run into her in a hotel lobby quite by chance.

'I'm sneaking away,' she said. 'Enough!'

'Have dinner with me.'

'I've got plans. I promised myself this evening with a group of friends. Join us. We've had days and days of papers. I promise you the worst meal in Montreal if you come with me.'

They drove through the suburbs.

'Do you speak French?' he asked.

'No. Just English. I can write some Sinhala.'

'Is that your background?'

A no-name plaza appeared on the side of the highway, and she parked beneath the blinking lights of a Bowlerama. 'I live here,' she said. 'In the West.'

Cullis was introduced to seven other anthropologists, who looked him over carefully and considered his posture to assess whether he would be useful on their team. They seemed to come from all over the world. Having flown to Montreal from Europe and Central America, they had escaped another slide show and were now, like Anil, ready for bowling. Bad red wine from a machine dribbled into small paper cups like the ones dentists offered and was being consumed by them at great speed, along with chips and vinegar and canned hummus. A paleontologist organized the computer-scoring panels, and within ten minutes these forensic celebrities, probably the only non-French-speakers in the Bowlerama, were goblinlike in their bowling shoes, and indeed raucous. There was competitive cheating. There was the dropping of bowling balls onto the parquet lanes. Cullis did not wish for his dead body ever to be touched by such incompetents, who committed so many foot faults. More and more, as the contest progressed, he and Anil rushed to each other to give hugs of congratulations. He felt light in his speckled shoes, he flung the ball without aiming and knocked over what sounded like a bucketful of nails. She came over and kissed him, tentatively but precisely on the back of the neck. They left the arcade in each other's arms.

'Must be something in the hummus. Was that real hummus?'

'Yes.' She laughed.

'A known aphrodisiac . . .'

'I'll never sleep with you if you say you don't like The Artist Formerly Known As. . . . Kiss me here. Do you have a difficult middle name I have to learn?'

'Biggles.'

'Biggles? As in *Biggles Flies East* and *Biggles Wets His Bed*?'

'Yes, that Biggles. My dad grew up on his books.'

'I never wanted to marry a Biggles. I always wanted to marry a tinker. I love that word. . . .'

'Tinkers don't have wives. Not if they are true tinkers.'

'You've got a wife, don't you?'

*

In the ship's lab in the harbour, one night, working alone, she cut herself badly with a surgical blade, slicing the flesh along her thumb. She poured Dettol over it and taped it, then decided to go to the hospital on the way home; she didn't want it infected—there were those rats always in the hold, scurrying perhaps over the instruments when she and Sarath were not there. She was tired and hailed a late-night *bajaj* that dropped her off at Emergency Services.

There were about fifteen souls sitting or lying on the long benches. Now and then a doctor strolled in, signalled for the next patient and went off with him. She was there for more than an hour and in the end gave up, because more and more injured were coming in off the street and her wound began to seem insignificant in comparison. But that wasn't why she left. A man wearing a black coat walked in and sat down among them, blood on his clothes. He remained there in silence, waiting for someone to help him, not bothering to pick up a number like the rest of them. Eventually there were three empty spaces on the bench and he stretched out, took off his black coat and used it as a pillow, but he couldn't sleep and his open eyes stared across the room at her.

His face was red and wet from the blood on the coat. He sat up, pulled a book out of his pocket and began reading very fast, turning pages, taking it in quickly. He swallowed a tablet and lay down again and this time dropped off, his circumstances and surroundings lost to him. A nurse approached him and touched him on the shoulder; when he didn't move she kept her hand there. Anil was to remember all this very well. He got up then, pocketed the book, and touched one of the other patients and disappeared with him. He was a doctor. The nurse picked up the coat and took it away. That was when Anil left. If she couldn't tell who was who in a hospital, what chance did she have?

*T*he National Atlas of Sri Lanka has seventy-three versions of the island—each template revealing only one aspect, one obsession: rainfall, winds, surface waters of lakes, rarer bodies of water locked deep within the earth.

The old portraits show the produce and former kingdoms of the country; contemporary portraits show levels of wealth, poverty and literacy.

The geological map reveals peat in the Muthurajawela swamp south of Negombo, coral along the coast from Ambalangoda to Dondra Head, pearl banks offshore in the Gulf of Mannar. Under the skin of the earth are even older settlements of mica, zircon, thorianite, pegmatite, arkose, topaz, terra rossa limestone, dolomite marble. Graphite near Paragoda, green marble at Katupita and Ginigalpelessa. Black shale at Andigama. Kaolin, or china clay, at Boralesgamuwa. Plumbago graphite—veins and flakes of it—graphite of the greatest purity (ninety-seven percent carbon), which would be mined in Sri Lanka for one hundred and sixty years, especially during the World Wars, six thousand pits around the country, the main mines at Bogala, Kahatagaha and Kolongaha.

Another page reveals just bird life. The twenty species of bird out of the four hundred native to Sri Lanka, such as the blue magpie, the Indian blue chat, the six families of the bulbul, the pied ground thrush with its fading hoot, the teal, the shoveller, 'false vampires,' pintail snipes, Indian coursers, pale harriers in the clouds. On the reptile map are locations of the green pit viper pala-polanga, which *in daylight, when it cannot see well, attacks blindly, leaping to where it thinks humans are, fangs bared like a dog, leaping again and again towards a now hushed and fearful quietness.*

Sea-locked, the country lives under two basic monsoon systems—the Siberian High during the northern hemisphere winter and the Mascarene High during the southern hemisphere winter. So the northeast trades come between December and March, while the southeast trades travel in from May to September. During the other months mild sea winds approach the land during the day and reverse their direction during the night.

There are pages of isobars and altitudes. There are no city names. Only the unknown and unvisited town of Maha Illupalama is sometimes noted, where the Department of Meteorology once, in the 1930s, in what now seems a medieval time, compiled and recorded winds and rainfall and barometric pressure. There are no river names. No depiction of human life.

Kumara Wijetunga, 17. 6th November 1989. At about
  11:30 p.m. from his house.
Prabath Kumara, 16. 17th November 1989. At 3:20 a.m.
  from the home of a friend.
Kumara Arachchi, 16. 17th November 1989. At about
  midnight from his house.
Manelka da Silva, 17. 1st December 1989. While playing
  cricket, Embilipitiya Central College playground.
Jatunga Gunesena, 23. 11th December 1989. At
  10:30 a.m. near his house while talking to a friend.
Prasantha Handuwela, 17. 17th December 1989. At about
  10:15 a.m. close to the tyre centre, Embilipitiya.
Prasanna Jayawarna, 17. 18th December 1989. At
  3:30 p.m. near the Chandrika reservoir.
Podi Wickramage, 49. 19th December 1989. At 7:30 a.m.
  while walking along the road to the centre of Embilipitiya
  town.
Narlin Gooneratne, 17. 26th December 1989. At about
  5:00 p.m. at a teashop 15 yards from Serena army camp.
Weeratunga Samaraweera, 30. 7th January 1990. At
  5:00 p.m. while going for a bath at Hulandawa Panamura.

The colour of a shirt. The sarong's pattern. The hour of disappearance.

Inside the Civil Rights Movement offices at the Nadesan Centre were the fragments of collected information revealing the last sighting of a son, a younger brother, a father. In the letters of anguish from family members were the details of hour, location, apparel, the activity. . . . *Going for a bath. Talking to a friend* . . .

In the shadows of war and politics there came to be surreal turns of cause and effect. At a mass grave found in Naipattimu-nai in 1985, bloodstained clothing was identified by a parent as that worn by his son at the time of his arrest and disappearance. When an ID card was found in a shirt pocket, the police called an immediate halt to the unburial, and the following day the president of the Citizens' Committee—who had brought the police to the location—was arrested. The identity of others in this grave in the Eastern Province—how they died, who they were—was never discovered. The warden of an orphanage who reported cases of annihilation was jailed. A human rights lawyer was shot and the body removed by army personnel.

Anil had been sent reports collected by the various human rights groups before leaving the United States. Early investigations had led to no arrests, and protests from organizations had never reached even the mid-level of police or government. Requests for help by parents in their search for teenagers were impotent. Still, everything was grabbed and collected as evidence, everything that could be held on to in the windstorm of news was copied and sent abroad to strangers in Geneva.

Anil picked up reports and opened folders that listed disap-pearances and killings. The last thing she wished to return to every day was this. And every day she returned to it.

There had been continual emergency from 1983 onwards, racial attacks and political killings. The terrorism of the sepa-ratist guerrilla groups, who were fighting for a homeland in the north. The insurrection of the insurgents in the south, against the government. The counterterrorism of the special forces against both of them. The disposal of bodies by fire. The disposal of bodies in rivers or the sea. The hiding and then reburial of corpses.

It was a Hundred Years' War with modern weaponry, and backers on the sidelines in safe countries, a war sponsored by gun- and drug-runners. It became evident that political enemies were secretly joined in financial arms deals. 'The reason for war was war.'

Sarath drove into the high altitudes, climbing east towards Bandarawela, where the three skeletons had been found. He and Anil had left Colombo several hours earlier and were now in the mountains.

'You know, I'd believe your arguments more if you lived here,' he said. 'You can't just slip in, make a discovery and leave.'

'You want me to censor myself.'

'I want you to understand the archaeological surround of a fact. Or you'll be like one of those journalists who file reports about flies and scabs while staying at the Galle Face Hotel. That false empathy and blame.'

'You have a hang-up about journalists, don't you.'

'That's how we get seen in the West. It's different here, dangerous. Sometimes law is on the side of power not truth.'

'I just feel I've been cooling my heels ever since I got here. Doors that should be open are closed. We're here to supposedly investigate disappearances. But I go to offices and I can't get in. Our purpose here seems to be the result of a gesture.' Then she said, 'That small piece of bone I found, the first day in the hold, you knew it wasn't old, didn't you?'

Sarath said nothing. So she continued. 'When I was in Central America there was a villager who said to us: When soldiers burned our village they said this is the law, so I thought the law meant the right of the army to kill us.'

'Be careful what you reveal.'

'And who I would reveal it to.'

'That too, yes.'

'I *was* invited here.'

'International investigations don't mean a lot.'

'Was it difficult getting the permit for us to work in the caves?'

'It was difficult.'

She had been taping his remarks about archaeology in this part of the island. Now the conversation strayed onto other subjects, and she eventually asked him about the 'Silver President'—the populace's nickname for President Katugala because of his shock of white hair. What was Katugala really like? Sarath was silent. Then his hand reached over and took the tape recorder from her lap. 'Is your tape recorder off?' He made sure it was switched off and only then answered her question. The last time she had used the machine was at least an hour earlier; it lay there forgotten by her. But he hadn't forgotten.

They turned off the road and stopped at a rest house, ordered lunch and sat outside above a deep valley.

'Look at that bird, Sarath.'

'A bulbul.'

She put herself into the position of the bird as it took off, and was suddenly vertiginous, realizing how high they were above the valley, the landscape like a green fjord beneath them. In the distance the open plain was bleached white, resembling the sea.

'You know birds, do you?'

'Yes. My wife knew them well.'

Anil said nothing, waiting for him to say more or to formally digress from the subject. But he stayed in his silence.

'Where is your wife?' she asked finally.

'I lost her a few years ago, she did— She killed herself.'

'Jesus. I'm so sorry, Sarath. I'm so . . .'

His face had become vague. 'She had left me a few months before.'

'I'm sorry I asked. I always ask, I'm too curious. I drive people mad.'

Later, in the van, to break the longer silence. 'Did you know my father? You're how old?'

'Forty-nine,' Sarath said.

'I'm thirty-three. Did you know him?'

'I've heard of him. He was quite a bit older.'

'I kept hearing my dad was a ladies' man.'

'I heard that too. If someone's charming they say that.'

'I think it was true. I just wish I had been older—to learn things from him. I wish I'd had that.'

'There was a monk,' Sarath said. 'He and his brother were the best teachers in my life—and it was because they taught me when I was an adult. We need parents when we're old too. I would meet him once or twice a year when he came to Colombo, and he'd somehow help me become simpler, clearer to myself. Nārada was a great laugher. He would laugh at your foibles. An ascetic. He stayed in a little room in a temple when he was in town. I'd visit him for a coffee, he sat on the bed, I sat on the one chair he'd bring in from the hall. Talking archaeology. He'd written a few pamphlets in Sinhala, but his brother, Palipana, was the famous one in that field, though there never seemed to be any jealousy between them. Nārada and Palipana. Two brilliant brothers. Both of them were my teachers.

'Most of the time Nārada lived near Hambantota. My wife and

I would go down to visit. You walked over hot dunes and came upon the commune for unemployed youth he'd set up by the sea.

'We were all shaken by his murder. He was shot in his room while sleeping. I've had friends die who were my age, but I miss that old man more. I suppose I was expecting him to teach me how to be old. Anyway, once a year, on the anniversary of his death, my wife and I would cook the food he was especially fond of and drive south to the village he'd lived in. We were always closest on that day. And it made him eternal—"persistent" might be a better word—you felt he was there with the boys in the commune who loved the *mallung* and the condensed-milk desserts he was partial to.'

'My parents died in a car crash after I left Sri Lanka. I never got a chance to see them again.'

'I know. I heard your father was a good doctor.'

'I should have been a doctor, but I swerved off into forensics. Didn't want to be him at that time in my life, I guess. Then I didn't want to come back here after my parents died.'

She was asleep when he touched her arm.

'I see a river down there. Shall we have a swim?'

'Here?'

'Just down that hill.'

'Oh, yes. I'd love to. Yes.' They pulled towels out of their bags and clambered down.

'I've not done this for years.'

'It will be cold. You're in the mountains, two thousand feet up.'

He was leading the way, more sprightly than she expected. Well, he's an archaeologist, she thought. He got to the river and disappeared behind a rock to change. She yelled, 'Just taking my dress off!' to be sure he wouldn't come back. 'I'll wear my underclothes.' Anil was conscious of how dark it was around her on this slope of the forest, then saw they would be able to swim farther down to a pool full of sunlight.

When she reached the water, he was already swimming, looking up at the trees. She took two steps forward on the sharp stones and dove in with a belly flop. 'Ah, a professional,' she heard him drawl.

The brightness on her skin caused by the river's coldness stayed with her during the last leg of the drive—small bumps of flesh on her forearm, the subliminal hairs upright. They had walked up the slope into the heat and light and she stood by the van drying her hair, beating it gently with her hands. She rolled her wet underclothes into the towel and wore just her dress as they travelled into the mountains.

'At this altitude you get headaches,' Sarath said. 'There's one good hotel in Bandarawela but we'll stop and set up a work space at a rest house instead, what do you say? That way we can keep our equipment and findings with us.'

'That monk you told me about. Who killed him?'

Sarath went on as if he hadn't heard her. 'And we'll want to be near the site. . . . There was a rumour that Nārada's murder was organized by his own novice, that it was not a political killing as most thought at first. Those days you didn't know who was killing who.'

Anil said, 'But you do now, don't you?'

'Now we all have blood on our clothes.'

They walked with the owner through the rest house and Sarath selected three rooms.

'The third room is full of mildew, but we'll take the bed out and get the walls painted tonight. Turn it into an office and lab. This okay?' She nodded and he turned back to the manager with instructions.

In 1911, prehistoric remains were discovered in the Banda-rawela region and hundreds of caves and rock shelters began to be explored. Remains of cranial and dental fragments were found, as old as any in India.

It was here, within a government-protected archaeological pre-serve, that skeletons had once again been found, outside one of the Bandarawela caves.

During their first few days there, Sarath and Anil recorded and removed ancient debris—freshwater and arboreal gastropods, bone fragments of birds and mammals, even fish bones from dis-tant eras of the sea. The region felt timeless. They found charred epicarps of wild breadfruit that still grew in the region, even now, twenty thousand years later.

Three almost complete skeletons had been found. But a few days later, while excavating in the far reaches of a cave, Anil discovered a fourth skeleton, whose bones were still held together by dried ligaments, partially burned. Something not pre-historic.

'*Listen,*' she said (they were in the rest house looking at the body), 'there are trace elements you can find in bones—mercury, lead, arsenic, even gold—that don't belong to them, they seep in from the surrounding soil. Or they can move from the bones into the adjacent soil. These elements are always passing into and out of bones, whether they are in coffins or not. Well, in this skeleton, there are traces of lead all over him. But there is no lead in this cave where we found him, the soil samples show none. Do you see? He must have been buried somewhere else before. Someone took precautions to make sure the skeleton was not discovered. This is no ordinary murder or burial. They buried him, then later moved him to an older gravesite.'

'Burying a body and then moving it is not necessarily a crime.'

'It's a probable crime, no?'

'Not if we find a reason.'

'All right. Look. Use that pen and move it along the bone. That way you can see the twist in the bone clearly. It's not as straight as it should be. There's also transverse cracking, but we'll leave that for now, just more proof.'

'Of what?'

'Twisting happens to bones that get burned when they are "green," that is, flesh-covered. An old body whose flesh withered away with time and then was burned later on—that's the pattern with most of the Bandarawela skeletons. This one was barely dead, Sarath, when they tried to burn him. Or worse, they tried to burn him alive.'

She had to wait a long time for him to say something. In the freshly painted room at the rest house, the four cafeteria tables each held a skeleton. They had labelled the bodies TINKER, TAILOR, SOLDIER, SAILOR. The one she was talking about was Sailor. They faced each other across the table.

'Can you imagine how many bodies must be buried all over the island?' he finally asked. He was not denying anything she had said.

'This is a murder victim, Sarath.'

'A murder . . . Do you mean any murder . . . or do you mean a political murder?'

'It was found within a sacred historical site. A site constantly under government or police supervision.'

'Right.'

'And this is a recent skeleton,' she said firmly. 'It was buried no more than four to six years ago. What's it doing here?'

'There are thousands of twentieth-century bodies, Anil. Can you imagine how many murders—'

'But we can prove this, don't you see? This is an opportunity, it's traceable. We found him in a place that only a government official could get into.'

He was tapping his pen on the wooden arm of the chair as she talked.

'We can do palynology tests to identify the type of pollen that fused to the bone, on those parts of him that were not burned. Only the arms and some ribs were burned. Do you have a copy of Wodehouse's *Pollen Grains*?'

'In my office,' he said quietly. 'We need to test for soil extracts.'

'Can you find a forensic geologist?'

'No,' he said. 'No one else.'

They had been whispering in the dark for almost half an hour since she had walked from the skeleton at the fourth table and given Sarath's shoulder a little tug, saying, 'I have to show you something.' 'What?' *'This thing. Listen. . . .'*

They covered Sailor and taped the plastic. 'Let's lock up,' he said. 'I promised to take you to that temple. In an hour it's the best time to see it. We'll catch the dusk drummer.'

Anil didn't like the abrupt switch to something aesthetic. 'You think it's safe?'

'What do you want to do? Take it wherever you go? Don't worry about anything. These will be fine here.'

'It's . . .'

'Leave it.'

She thought she'd say it right out. At once. 'I don't really know, you see, which side you are on—if I can trust you.'

He began to speak, stopped, then spoke slowly. 'What would I do?'

'You could make him disappear.'

He moved out of his stillness and walked to the wall and turned on three lights. 'Why, Anil?'

'You have a relative in the government, don't you?'

'I do have one, yes. I hardly ever see him. Perhaps he can help us.'

'Perhaps. Why did you turn on the light?'

'I need to find my pen. What—did you think it was a signal to someone?'

'I don't know where you stand. I know . . . I know you feel the purpose of truth is more complicated, that it's sometimes more dangerous here if you tell the truth.'

'Everyone's scared, Anil. It's a national disease.'

'There are so many bodies in the ground now, that's what you said . . . murdered, anonymous. I mean, people don't even know if they are two hundred years old or two weeks old, they've all been through fire. Some people let their ghosts die, some don't. Sarath, we can do something. . . .'

'You're six hours away from Colombo and you're whispering—think about that.'

'I don't want to go to the temple now.'

'That's fine. You don't have to. I'll go. I'll see you in the morning.'

'Yes.'

'I'll turn out the lights,' he said.

We are often criminals in the eyes of the earth, not only for having committed crimes, but because we know that crimes have been
committed.' Words about a man buried forever in a prison. *El
Hombre de la Máscara de Hierro*. *The Man in the Iron Mask*. Anil
needed to comfort herself with old friends, sentences from books,
voices she could trust. *'This is the dead-room,' said Enjolras*. Who
was Enjolras? Someone in *Les Misérables*. A book so much a
favourite, so thick with human nature she wished it to accompany her into the afterlife. She was working with a man who was
efficient in his privacy, who would never unknot himself for anyone. A paranoid is someone with all the facts, the joke went.
Maybe this was the only truth here. In this rest house near Bandarawela with four skeletons. *You're six hours away from
Colombo and you're whispering—think about that.*

In her years abroad, during her European and North American
education, Anil had courted foreignness, was at ease whether on
the Bakerloo line or the highways around Santa Fe. She felt completed abroad. (Even now her brain held the area codes of Denver
and Portland.) And she had come to expect clearly marked roads
to the source of most mysteries. Information could always be
clarified and acted upon. But here, on this island, she realized she
was moving with only one arm of language among uncertain
laws and a fear that was everywhere. There was less to hold on
to with that one arm. Truth bounced between gossip and
vengeance. Rumour slipped into every car and barbershop.

Sarath's daily path as a professional archaeologist in this world, she guessed, involved commissions and the favours of ministers, involved waiting politely for hours in their office lobbies. Information was made public with diversions and subtexts—as if the truth would not be of interest when given directly, without waltzing backwards.

She loosened the swaddling plastic that covered Sailor. In her work Anil turned bodies into representatives of race and age and place, though for her the tenderest of all discoveries was the finding, some years earlier, of the tracks at Laetoli—almost-four-million-year-old footsteps of a pig, a hyena, a rhinoceros and a bird, this strange ensemble identified by a twentieth-century tracker. Four unrelated creatures that had walked hurriedly over a wet layer of volcanic ash. To get away from what? Historically more significant were other tracks in the vicinity, of a hominid assumed to be approximately five feet tall (one could tell by the pivoting heel impressions). But it was that quartet of animals walking from Laetoli four million years ago that she liked to think about.

The most precisely recorded moments of history lay adjacent to the extreme actions of nature or civilization. She knew that. Pompeii. Laetoli. Hiroshima. Vesuvius (whose fumes had asphyxiated poor Pliny while he recorded its 'tumultuous behaviour'). Tectonic slips and brutal human violence provided random time-capsules of unhistorical lives. A dog in Pompeii. A gardener's shadow in Hiroshima. But in the midst of such events, she realized, there could never be any logic to the human violence without the distance of time. For now it would be reported, filed in Geneva, but no one could ever give meaning to it. She used to believe that meaning allowed a person a door to escape grief and fear. But she saw that those who were slammed and stained by violence lost the power of language and logic. It was the way to abandon emotion, a last protection for the self. They held on to just the coloured and patterned sarong a missing relative last slept in, which in normal times would have become a household rag but now was sacred.

In a fearful nation, public sorrow was stamped down by the climate of uncertainty. If a father protested a son's death, it was feared another family member would be killed. If people you knew disappeared, there was a chance they might stay alive if you did not cause trouble. This was the scarring psychosis in the country. Death, loss, was 'unfinished,' so you could not walk through it. There had been years of night visitations, kidnappings or murders in broad daylight. The only chance was that the creatures who fought would consume themselves. All that was left of law was a belief in an eventual revenge towards those who had power.

And who was this skeleton? In this room, among these four, she was hiding among the unhistorical dead. *To fetch a dead body: what a curious task! To cut down the corpse of an unknown hanged man and then bear the body of the animal on one's back . . . something dead, something buried, something already rotting away?* Who was he? This representative of all those lost voices. To give him a name would name the rest.

Anil bolted the door and went looking for the owner of the rest house. She requested a light dinner, then ordered a shandy and walked out onto the front verandah. There were no other guests, and the rest-house owner followed her.

'Mr. Sarath—he always comes here?' she asked.

'Sometimes, madame, when he comes to Bandarawela. You live in Colombo?'

'In North America, mostly. I used to live here.'

'I have a son in Europe—he wishes to be an actor.'

'I see. That's good.'

She stepped off the polished floor of the porch into the garden. It was the politest departure from her host she could make. She didn't feel like hesitant small-talk this evening. But once she reached the red darkness of the flamboyant tree she turned.

'Did Mr. Sarath ever come here with his wife?'

'Yes, madame.'

'What was she like?'

'She's very nice, madame.'

A nod for proof, then a slight tilt of his head, a J stroke, to suggest possible hesitance in his own judgement.

'*Is?*'

'Yes. Madame?'

'Even though she is dead.'

'No, madame. I asked Mr. Sarath this afternoon and he said she is well. Not dead. He said she said to give me her wishes.'

'I must have been mistaken.'

'Yes, madame.'

'She comes with him on his trips?'

'Sometimes she comes. She does radio programmes. Sometimes his cousin comes. He's a minister in the government.'

'Do you know his name?'

'No, madame. I think he came only once. Is prawn curry all right?'

'Yes. Thank you.'

To avoid further conversation, during her meal she pretended to be looking over her notes. She thought about Sarath's marriage. It was difficult to imagine him as a married man. She was already used to him in the role of a widower, with a silent presence around him. Well, she thought, night falls and you need company. A person will walk through a hundred doors to carry out the whims of the dead, not realizing he is burying himself away from the others.

After dinner she returned to the room where the skeletons were. She didn't want to sleep yet. She didn't want to think about the minister who had come with Sarath to Bandarawela. The dim lights didn't give her enough voltage to read by so she found an oil lamp and lit it. Earlier, she had come across the rest house's one-shelf library. Agatha Christie. P. G. Wodehouse. Enid Blyton. John Masters. The usual suspects in any Asian library. She had read most of them as a child or as a teenager. Instead she leafed through her own copy of Bridges's *World Soils*. Anil knew Bridges like the back of her hand, but she was processing the text now towards her present situation, and as she read she sensed she was leaving the others, the four skeletons, in the darkness.

She was in the chair, her head down towards her thighs, fast asleep, when Sarath woke her.

. . .

He touched her shoulder, then pulled the earphones off her hair and put them on his head, pressing the start button to hear cello suites that sewed everything together as he walked around the room.

A swallow, as if she were coming up for air.

'You didn't lock the door.'

'No. Is everything okay?'

'Everything's here. I arranged for a breakfast. It's already late.'

'I'm up.'

'There's a shower out back.'

'I don't feel good. I'm coming down with something.'

'If we have to we can break the journey back to Colombo.'

She went out carrying her Dr. Bronner's, with which she travelled all over the world. The anthropologist's soap! She was still half asleep in the shower. Her toes nestled against a piece of rough granite, cold water gushing down onto her hair.

She washed her face, rubbing the peppermint soap on her closed eyelids, then rinsing it off. When she looked over the plantain leaves at shoulder level into the distance she could see the blue mountains beyond, the out-of-focus world, beautiful.

But by noon she was encased in a terrible headache.

*

She was feverish in the back seat of the van, and Sarath decided to stop halfway back to Colombo. Whatever sickness she had was like an animal in her, leading her from sudden shivers to sweat.

Then, sometime past midnight, she was in a room that was on

the edge of the sea. She had never liked the south coast around Yala, not as a child, not now. The trees appeared to have been grown only for the purpose of shade. Even the moon seemed like a compound light.

At dinner she had been delirious, almost in tears. Sarath appeared to be a hundred miles away across the table. One of them was shouting unnecessarily. She was hungry but couldn't chew, not even her favourite prawn curry. She just kept spooning the soft lukewarm dhal into her mouth, then drinking lime juice. In the afternoon she had woken to a thumping noise. She managed to climb out of bed and looked down the open-air passageway and saw monkeys disappearing around the far corner of the hall. She believed what she saw. She took capsules every four hours to keep away headaches. This was sunstroke or dengue fever or malaria. When they got back to Colombo she would have tests done. 'It's the sun,' Sarath murmured. 'I'll buy you a bigger hat. I'll buy you a bigger hat. I'll buy you a bigger hat.' He was always whispering. She kept saying, *What? What?* Could hardly bother to say it. Were there monkeys? Monkeys were stealing towels and swimming trunks off the laundry lines during the afternoons while everyone slept. She prayed the hotel wouldn't turn off the generator. She couldn't face the thought of no fan or shower to cool her down. All that worked was the telephone. She was expecting a call in the night.

When dinner was over she took the carafe of lime juice and ice to her room and fell asleep immediately. She woke at eleven and took more pills to blanket the headache she knew would return soon. Clothes wet from perspiration. To perspire. To aspire. Discuss. The fan was hardly moving, air didn't even reach her arms. Where was Sailor? She hadn't thought about him. She rolled over in the dark and dialed Sarath's room number. 'Where is he?'

'Who?'

'Sailor.'

'He's safe. In the van. Remember?'

'No, I— Is that safe?'

'It was your idea.'

She hung up, making certain the phone was cradled properly, and lay there in the dark. Wanting air. When she opened the curtains she saw light spraying off the compound pole. There were people on the dark sand preparing boats. If she turned on the lamp she would look like a fish in an aquarium to them.

She left her room. She needed a book to keep her awake till the phone call came. In the alcove she stared at the shelves for a while, grabbed two books and scurried back to her room. *In Search of Gandhi,* by Richard Attenborough, and a life of Frank Sinatra. She drew the curtains, turned on the light and peeled off her damp clothes. In the shower she put her hair under the cold water and leaned against a corner of the stall, just letting the coolness lull her. She needed someone, Leaf perhaps, to sing along with her. One of those dialogue songs they were always singing together in Arizona . . .

She dragged herself out and sat at the foot of the bed, wet. She was hot but couldn't open the curtains. It would have meant putting on clothes. She began reading. When she got bored she switched to the other book, and was soon carrying a larger and larger cast of characters in her head. The light was bad. She remembered Sarath had told her the one essential thing he always took on any trip out of Colombo was a sixty-watt bulb. She crawled across the bed and called him. 'Can I use your lightbulb? It's a rotten light here.'

'I'll bring it.'

They taped down sheets from the Sunday Observer so the pages covered the floor. You have the felt pen? Yes. She began removing her clothes, her back to him, then lay down next to the skeleton of Sailor. She was wearing just her red knickers, silk ones she usually put on with irony. She hadn't imagined them for public consumption. She looked up at the ceiling, her hands on her breasts. Her body felt good against the hard floor, the coolness of the polished concrete through the newspaper, the same firmness she had felt as a child sleeping on mats.

He was using the felt marker to trace her shape. You will have to put your arms down for a moment. She could feel the pen move around her hands and alongside her waist, then down her legs, both sides, so he linked the blue lines at the base of her heels.

She rose out of the outline, turned back and saw he had drawn outlines of the four skeletons as well.

There was a knocking and she roused herself. She hadn't moved. All evening she kept discovering herself stilled, unable to think. Even reading she'd gotten entangled sleepily in the arms of paragraphs that wouldn't let her go. Something about the phrasing of Ava Gardner's complaint about Sinatra held her. Wrapped in a sheet she opened the door. Sarath passed her the bulb and disappeared from sight. He had been in a shirt and sarong. She was going to ask him to . . . She pulled the table to the centre of the room, switched the light off. She used the sheet to unscrew the hot bulb. She feared wild electricity somewhere in the wire. She could hear the noise of the waves outside. With effort she lifted her head and screwed the bulb Sarath had brought into the socket. Everything was suddenly heavy and slowed down.

She lay flat on the bed, cold once more, shivering, a moan in her mouth. She rummaged through her bag and found two small bottles of scotch she had taken from the plane. Sarath had taken off her clothes and traced her outline. Had he done that?

The telephone rang. It was America. A woman's voice.

'Hello? Hello? Leaf? God it's you! You got my message.'

'You've picked up an accent already.'

'No, I— Is this a legal call?'

'Your voice is all up and down.'

'Yes?'

'Are you okay, Anil?'

'I'm sick. It's very late. No, no. It's fine. I've been waiting for you. It's just I'm sick and it makes me feel even further away from everybody. Leaf? Are you well?'

'Yes.'

'Tell me. How well?'

There was silence. 'I'm not remembering. I'm forgetting your face.'

Anil could hardly breathe. She turned from the phone to wipe her cheek on the pillow. 'Are you there? Leaf?' She heard the noise of great distances on the line between them. 'Is your sister with you?'

'My sister?' Leaf said.

'Leaf, listen, remember—who killed Cherry Valance?'

Crackle and silence as she held the phone tight to her ear.

In the next room Sarath had his eyes open, unable to escape the sound of Anil's weeping.

*

Sarath reached his hand across the breakfast plates and held Anil's wrist. His thumb on her pulse. 'We'll get to Colombo this afternoon. We can work on the skeleton in the ship lab.'

'And keep the skeleton with us, whatever happens,' she said.

'We keep all four. A unit. A disguise. We claim they're all ancient. Your fever is down.'

She pulled her hand away. 'I'll remove a chip from Sailor's heel—to have a private ID.'

'If we take more pollen and earth samples, we can find out where he was buried first. Then do the study on the boat.'

'There's a woman who has been working on pupae around here,' Anil said. 'I read an article. I'm sure she was from Colombo. It was a very good junior thesis.'

He looked at her quizzically. 'Don't know. Try the young faculty when you're at the hospital.'

They sat facing each other in silence.

'I said to my girlfriend Leaf before I came here, *Perhaps I'll meet the man who is going to ruin me.* Can I trust you?'

'You have to trust me.'

They were at the Mutwal docks in Colombo by early evening. She helped him carry the four skeletons into the lab on board the *Oronsay*.

'Take tomorrow off,' he said. 'I have to find more equipment, so I'll need a day.'

Anil remained on the ship after he left, wanting to work for a while. She walked down the stairs and entered the lab, picked up the metal pole they kept by the door and began banging on the walls. Scurrying. Eventually the darkness was silent. She struck a match and walked with it held out in front of her. She pulled down the lever of the generator and soon there was a shaky hum and electricity emerged slowly into the room.

She sat there watching him. The fever was starting to leave and she was feeling lighter. She began to examine the skeleton again under sulphur light, summarizing the facts of his death so far, the permanent truths, same for Colombo as for Troy. One forearm broken. Partial burning. Vertebrae damage in the neck. The possibility of a small bullet wound in the skull. Entrance and exit.

She could read Sailor's last actions by knowing the wounds on bone. He puts his arms up over his face to protect himself from the blow. He is shot with a rifle, the bullet going through his arm, then into the neck. While he's on the ground, they come up and kill him.

Coup de grace. The smallest, cheapest bullet. A .22's path that her ballpoint pen could slide through. Then they attempt to set fire to him and begin to dig his grave in this burning light.

Anil entered Kynsey Road Hospital and passed the sign by the chief medical officer's door.

Let conversations cease.
Let laughter flee.
This is the place where Death
Delights to help the living.

It was printed in Latin, Sinhala and English. Once in the laboratory, where she worked now and then in order to use better equipment, she could relax, alone in the large room. God, she loved a lab. The stools always had a slight rake so you sat in a lean. There would always be that earnest tilt forward. On the perimeter, along the walls, were the bottles that held beet-coloured liquids. She could walk around the table watching a body from the corner of her eye, then sit on the stool and time would be forgotten. No hunger or thirst or desire for a friend or lover's company. Just an awareness of someone in the distance hammering a floor, banging through ancient concrete with a mallet as if to reach the truth.

She stood against the table and it nestled into her hipbones. She slid her fingers along the dark wood to feel for any grain of sand, any chip or crumb or stickiness. In her solitude. Her arms dark as the table, no jewellery except the bangle that would click as she lay her wrist down gently. No other sound as Anil thought through the silence in front of her.

These buildings were her home. In the five or six houses of her adult life, her rule and habit was always to live below her means. She had never bought a house and kept her rented apartments sparse. Though in her present rooms in Colombo there was a small pool cut into the floor for floating flowers. It was a luxury to her. Something to confuse a thief in the dark. At night, returning from work, Anil would slip out of her sandals and stand in the shallow water, her toes among the white petals, her arms folded as she undressed the day, removing layers of events and incidents so they would no longer be within her. She would stand there for a while, then walk wet-footed to bed.

She knew herself to be, and was known to others as, a determined creature. Her name had not always been Anil. She had been given two entirely inappropriate names and very early began to desire 'Anil,' which was her brother's unused second name. She had tried to buy it from him when she was twelve years old, offering to support him in all family arguments. He would not commit himself to the trade though he knew she wanted the name more than anything else.

Her campaign had caused anger and frustration within the household. She stopped responding when called by either of her given names, even at school. In the end her parents relented, but then they had to persuade her irritable brother to forfeit his second name. He, at fourteen, claimed he might need it someday. Two names gave him more authority, and a second name suggested perhaps an alternative side to his nature. Also there was his grandfather. Neither of the children had in fact known the grandfather whose name it had been. The parents threw their hands up and finally the siblings worked out a trade between them. She gave her brother one hundred saved rupees, a pen set he had been eyeing for some time, a tin of fifty Gold Leaf cigarettes she had found, and a sexual favour he had demanded in the last hours of the impasse.

After that she allowed no other first names on her passports or school reports or application forms. Later when she recalled her childhood, it was the hunger of not having that name and the joy of getting it that she remembered most. Everything about the name pleased her, its slim, stripped-down quality, its feminine air, even though it was considered a male name. Twenty years later she felt the same about it. She'd hunted down the desired name like a specific lover she had seen and wanted, tempted by nothing else along the way.

Anil recalled the nineteenth-century air of the city she had left behind. The prawn sellers holding out their wares to passing traffic on Duplication Road, the houses in Colombo Seven painted that meticulous flat white. This was where the old money and the politically powerful lived. 'Heaven . . . Colombo Seven . . .' her father would sing, to the tune of 'Cheek to Cheek,' as he let Anil thread his cuff links into his shirtsleeves while he dressed for dinner. There was always this whispering pact between them. And she knew that no matter what time he returned home from dances or other engagements or emergency operations, he would drive her to her dawn swimming practice the next morning, through the empty streets towards the Otters Club. On the drive home they would pause at a stall for a bowl of milk and sugar hoppers, each wrapped in a shiny page from an English magazine.

Even during the monsoon months, at six in the morning she would run from the car through heavy rain and dive into the pocked water and swim her heart out for an hour. Just ten girls and the coach, the noise of the rain clattering on the tin roofs of cars, on the hard water and the taut rubber bathing caps as the swimmers sloshed, turned and emerged again, while a handful of parents read the *Daily News*. All real effort and energy when she was a kid seemed to have happened by seven-thirty in the morning. She kept that habit in the West, studying for two or three hours before going off to classes at medical school. In some ways her later obsessive tunneling toward discovery was similar to that underwater world, where she swam within the rhythm of intense activity, as if peering through time.

So in spite of Sarath's suggestion the day before that she sleep in, Anil had breakfasted and was already on her way to Kynsey Road Hospital by six in the morning. The eternal prawn sellers were there on the side of the road, holding out last night's catch. The smell of hemp idled in the air from ropes lit outside cigarette stalls. She had always veered towards this smell as a child, loitered beside it. Suddenly, and she didn't know why, she recalled the schoolgirls of Ladies' College on a balcony looking down at the boys from St. Thomas's, cads all of them, singing as many verses as they could of 'The Good Ship Venus' before the matron chased them off the grounds.

> *It was on the Good Ship Venus—*
> *By Christ, you should have seen us.*
> *The figurehead was a whore in bed*
> *Astride a rampant penis.*

The girls, normally as secure in their school as women within the bounds of courtly love, had thus been startled at the age of twelve and thirteen by this strange choreography, but had no desire to stop listening. It was not until Anil was twenty and in England that she heard the song again. And there—at a post–rugby match party—it seemed a more natural context, in tune with the male braying around her. But the trick of the boys of St. Thomas's had been to hold up sheet music, and at first the song had sounded like a carol, with trills and descants and preverbal humming, and in this way they had fooled the matron, who was not really listening to anything but the tone. It was only the girls of the fourth and fifth forms who heard every word.

> *The captain's name was Mugger,*
> *A dirty-minded bugger.*
> *He wasn't fit to shovel shit*
> *From one deck to another.*

Anil was fond of that verse, and its neatly packed rhyme slid back into her mind at odd moments. She loved songs of anger and judgement. So at six a.m., walking towards the hospital, she tried to recall the other verses to 'The Good Ship Venus,' singing the first out loud. The rest she was less certain about, and played them on her lips, a faux tuba. 'One of the greats,' she muttered to herself. 'One of the crucial ones.'

The trainee in Colombo who had written about pupae research turned out to be working in one of the offices off the postmortem lab. It had taken Anil some time to remember the name, but she now found Chitra Abeysekera typing an application form, the paper limp from the humidity of the room. She was standing as she typed, wearing a sari, with what seemed a portable office beside her—two large cardboard boxes and one metal case. They contained research notes, lab specimens, petri dishes and test tubes. The metal case held growing bugs.

The woman looked up at her.

'Am I disturbing . . . ?' Anil looked down at the four lines the woman had just typed. 'Why don't you take a break and let me type it for you?'

'You're the woman from Geneva, right?' The face was disbelieving.

'Yes.'

Chitra looked at her hands and they both laughed. Her skin was covered with cuts and bites. They could probably slip easily into a beehive and come out with plunder.

'Just tell me what to say.'

Anil sidled up and, as Chitra spoke, did a quick edit, adding adjectives, improving her request for funds. Chitra's blunt description of her project would not have gone far. Anil gave it the necessary drama and turned Chitra's list of abilities into a more suggestive curriculum vitae. When they finished she asked if Chitra would like to get something to eat.

'Not the hospital cafeteria,' Chitra said helpfully. 'The cook moonlights in the postmortem labs. You know what I'd like? Chinese air-conditioned. Let's go to Flower Drum.'

There were three businessmen eating at the restaurant, but otherwise it was empty.

'Thank you for the application help,' Chitra said.

'It's a good project. It'll be important. Can you do all that here? Do you have facilities?'

'I have to do it here . . . the pupae . . . the larvae. The tests have to be done in this temperature. And I don't like England. I'll go to India sometime.'

'If you need help, contact me. God, I'd forgotten what cool air feels like. I might just move in here. I want to talk to you about your research.'

'Later, later. Tell me what you like about the West.'

'Oh—what do I like? Most of all I think I like that I can do things on my own terms. Nothing is anonymous here, is it. I miss my privacy.'

Chitra looked totally uninterested in this Western virtue.

'I have to be back by one-thirty,' she said, and ordered chow mein and a Coke.

The cardboard box with test tubes was open and Chitra was prodding a larva under the microscope. 'This is two weeks old.' She tweezered it out and placed it in a tray holding a piece of human liver, which Anil assumed must have been obtained illegally.

'It's necessary,' Chitra said, aware of Anil's gaze, trying to be casual about it. 'A little got removed before someone was buried, a small favour. There is an important difference in the speed of growth when insects feed on this as opposed to organs from an animal.' She dropped the rest of the liver into a picnic cooler, pulled out her charts and spread them over the central table. 'So tell me how I can help you. . . .'

'I've got a skeleton, partially burned. Can one still pick up information about pupae from it?'

Chitra covered her mouth and burped, as she had been doing continually since the meal. 'It helps if it is in situ.'

'That's the problem. I've got earth from the location where we found it, but we think it was moved. We don't know the first location. I've got earth only from the last site.'

'I could look at the bone. Some insects are attracted to bone, not flesh.' Chitra smiled at her. 'So there might be pupae remains from the first location. We could reduce the site possibilities by knowing the type of insect. It's strange, it's just those first couple of months when bone attracts some creatures.'

'Unusual.'

'Mmm,' Chitra said, as if eating chocolate. 'Some butterflies also go to bone for moisture. . . .'

'Can I show you some of the bone?'

'I go up-country tomorrow for a few days.'

'Then later tonight? Is that all right?'

'Mmm.' Chitra sounded unconcerned, preoccupied with a clue, a timing on one of her charts. She turned from Anil to an array of insects, then selected one of the right plumpness and age with her forceps.

That night within the ship's hold Sarath poured plastic that had been dissolved in acetone into a shallow dish, and brought out the camel-hair brush he would use on the bones. A diffuse light, the hum of the generator around him.

He moved to the lab table where a skeleton lay, picked up the alligator-clip lamp—the one source of focussed bright light here—and walked with it and the long cord, still lit, to a cupboard at the far end of the deep room. He opened it, poured himself three-quarters of a tumbler of arrack from a bottle and walked back to the skeleton.

The four skeletons from Bandarawela, revealed now to the air, would soon begin to weaken.

He loosened a new tungsten-carbide needle from its plastic container and attached it to a hand pick and began cleaning the bones of the first skeleton, drilling free the fragments of dirt. Then he turned on a slim hose and let it hover over each bone, air nestling into the evidence of the trauma as if he were blowing cool breath from a pursed mouth onto a child's burn. He dipped the camel-hair brush into the dish and began painting a layer of protective plastic over the bones, moving down the spine and ribs. After that he carried the alligator-clip lamp to the second table and started on the second skeleton. Then the third. When he came to Sailor's table he turned the heel bone sideways to find the centimetre-deep chip Anil had furrowed out of the calcaneus.

Sarath stretched and walked out of the light into the darkness, his hands out feeling for the arrack bottle, which he brought back with him to Sailor under the cone of light. It was about two in the morning. When he'd coated all four skeletons, he made notes on each of them and photographed three from anterior and lateral views.

He drank as he worked. The smell of the plastic was now strong in the room. There was no opening for fresh air. He unlocked the doors noisily and climbed up with the bottle of arrack onto the deck. Colombo was dark with curfew. It would be a beautiful hour to walk or cycle through it. The fraught quietness of the roadblocks, the old trees a panoply along Solomon Dias Mawatha. But in the harbour around him there was activity, the light from a tug rolling in the water, the white beams from tractors moving crates on the quay. Three or four a.m. He would lock up and sleep on the ship for the rest of the night.

The hold was still full of the smell of plastic. He pulled out a tied bundle of beedis from a drawer and lit one, then inhaled its rich mortal thirty-two rumours of taste. Picked up the clip lamp and walked over to Sailor. He still had to photograph him. Okay, do it now, he said to himself, and took two shots, anterior and lateral. He stood there as the Polaroids developed, waving them in the air. When Sailor's image was fully revealed he put the pictures in a brown envelope, sealed and addressed it, and dropped it into his coat pocket.

The three other skeletons had no skulls. But Sailor had a skull. Sarath put the half-smoked beedi on the metal sink and leaned forward. With a scalpel he cut apart the ligaments that attached the skull to the neck vertebrae, and separated it. He brought the skull to his desk. The burning hadn't reached the head, so the frontal, orbital and lacrimal plates were smooth, the knit marks on the skull tight. Sarath wrapped it in plastic and placed it in a large shopping bag that said 'Kundanmal's.' He returned and photographed Sailor without the skull, twice, lateral and anterior.

He was aware now more than anything that he and Anil needed help.

The Grove of Ascetics

The epigraphist Palipana was for a number of years at the centre of a nationalistic group that eventually wrestled archaeological authority in Sri Lanka away from the Europeans. He had made his name translating Pali scripts and recording and translating the rock graffiti of Sigiriya.

The main force of a pragmatic Sinhala movement, Palipana wrote lucidly, basing his work on exhaustive research, deeply knowledgeable about the context of the ancient cultures. While the West saw Asian history as a faint horizon where Europe joined the East, Palipana saw his country in fathoms and colour, and Europe simply as a landmass on the end of the peninsula of Asia.

The 1970s had witnessed the beginning of a series of international conferences. Academics flew into Delhi, Colombo and Hong Kong for six days, told their best anecdotes, took the pulse of the ex-colony, and returned to London and Boston. It was finally realized that while European culture was old, Asian culture was older. Palipana, by now the most respected of the Sri Lankan group, went to one such gathering and never went to another. He was a spare man, unable to abide formality and ceremonial toasts.

The three years Sarath spent as a student of Palipana's were the most difficult of his academic life. All archaeological data proposed by a student had to be confirmed. Every rock cuneiform or carving had to be drawn and redrawn onto the pages of journals, in sand, on blackboards, until it was a part of dreams. Sarath had thought of Palipana during the first two years as someone mean with praise and mean (rather than spare) in the way he lived. He seemed incapable of handing out compliments, would never buy anyone a drink or a meal. His brother, Nārada, who had no car and was always cadging rides, at first appeared similar, but was generous with time and friendship, generous with his laughter. Palipana always seemed to be saving himself for the language of history. He was vain and excessive only in how he insisted on having his work published a certain way, demanding two-colour diagrams on good paper that would survive weather and fauna. And it was only when a book was completed that his terrierlike focus would shift away from a project, so he could go empty-handed into another era or another region of the country.

History was ever-present around him. The stone remnants of royal bathing pools and water gardens, the buried cities, the nationalistic fervour he rode and used gave him and those who worked with him, including Sarath, limitless subjects to record and interpret. It appeared he could divine a thesis at any sacred forest.

Palipana had not entered the field of archaeology until he was middle-aged. And he had risen in the career not as a result of family contacts but simply because he knew the languages and the techniques of research better than those above him. He was not an easily liked man, he had lost charm somewhere in his youth. He would discover among his students over the years only four dedicated protégés. Sarath was one of them. By the time Palipana was in his sixties, however, he had fought with each of them. Not one of the four had forgiven him for their humiliations at his hands. But his students continued to believe two things— no, *three*: that he was the best archaeological theorist in the country, that he was nearly always right, and that even with his fame and success he continued to live a life-style more minimal than any of them. Perhaps this was the result of being the brother of a monk. Palipana's wardrobe was, apparently, reduced to two identical outfits. And as he grew older he linked himself less and less with the secular world, save for his continuing vanity regarding publication. Sarath had not seen him for several years.

During these years Palipana had been turned gracelessly out of the establishment. This began with his publication of a series of interpretations of rock graffiti that stunned archaeologists and historians. He had discovered and translated a linguistic subtext that explained the political tides and royal eddies of the island in the sixth century. The work was applauded in journals abroad and at home, until one of Palipana's protégés voiced the opinion that there was no real evidence for the existence of these texts. They were a fiction. A group of historians was unable to locate the runes Palipana had written about. No one could find the sentences he had quoted and translated from dying warriors, or any of the fragments from the social manifestos handed down by kings, or even the erotic verses in Pali supposedly by lovers and confidants of the court mentioned by name but never quoted in the *Cūlavaṃsa*.

The detailed verses Palipana had published seemed at first to have ended arguments and debates by historians; they were confirmed by his reputation as the strictest of historians, who had always relied on meticulous research. Now it seemed to others he had choreographed the arc of his career in order to attempt this one trick on the world. Though perhaps it was more than a trick, less of a falsehood in his own mind; perhaps for him it was not a false step but the step to another reality, the last stage of a long, truthful dance.

But no one admired this strange act. Not his academic followers. Not even protégés like Sarath, who had been consistently challenged by his mentor during his academic years for crimes of laxness and inaccuracy. The gesture, 'Palipana's gesture,' was seen as a betrayal of the principles on which he had built his reputation. A forgery by a master always meant much more than mischief, it meant scorn. Only when seen at its most innocent could it be regarded as an autobiographical or perhaps chemical breakdown.

The graffiti at the great rock fortress of Sigiriya were located below an overhang at the first quarter-mile mark of ascent. Looking older than the more famous paintings of goddesslike women on the Mirror Wall, they had been cut into an ancient wall from the sixth century onwards. The faded moth-coloured writings had always been a magnet and a mystery for historians—they were enigmatic statements—and Palipana himself had studied them and worried over them for fifteen years of his life. As a historian and a scientist he approached every problem with many hands. He was more likely to work beside a stonemason or listen to a *dhobi* woman washing clothes at a newly discovered rock pool than with a professor from the University of Peradeniya. He approached runes not with a historical text but with the pragmatic awareness of locally inherited skills. His eyes recognized how a fault line in a rock wall might have insisted on the composure of a painted shoulder.

Having studied languages and text until he was forty, he spent the next thirty years in the field—the historical version already within him. So that approaching a site Palipana knew what would be there—whether a distinct pattern of free-standing pillars in a clearing or a familiar icon drawn on a cave wall high above. It was a strange self-knowledge for someone who had always been humble in his assumptions.

He spread his fingers over every discovered rune. He traced each letter on the Stone Book at Polonnaruwa, a boulder carved into a rectangle four feet high, thirty feet long, the first book of the country, laid his bare arms and the side of his face against this plinth that collected the heat of the day. For most of the year it was dark and warm and only during the monsoons would the letters be filled with water, creating small, perfectly cut harbours, as at Carthage. A giant book in the scrub grass of the Sacred Quadrangle of Polonnaruwa, chiselled with letters, bordered by a frieze of ducks. Ducks for eternity, he whispered to himself, smiling in the noon heat, having pieced together what he had picked up in an ancient text. A secret. His greatest joys were such discoveries, as when he found the one dancing Ganesh, possibly the island's first carved Ganesh, in the midst of humans in a frieze at Mihintale.

He drew parallels and links between the techniques of stonemasons he met with in Matara and the work he had done during the years of translating texts and in the field. And he began to see as truth things that could only be guessed at. In no way did this feel to him like forgery or falsification.

Archaeology lives under the same rules as the Napoleonic Code. The point was not that he would ever be proved wrong in his theories, but that he could not prove he was right. Still, the patterns that emerged for Palipana had begun to coalesce. They linked hands. They allowed walking across water, they allowed a leap from treetop to treetop. The water filled a cut alphabet and linked this shore and that. And so the unprovable truth emerged.

However much he himself had stripped worldly goods and social habits from his life, even more was taken from him in reaction to his unprovable theories. There was no longer any respect accorded to his career. But he refused to give up what he claimed to have discovered, and made no attempt to defend himself. Instead he retreated physically. Years earlier, on a trip with his brother, he had found the remaining structures of a forest monastery, twenty miles from Anuradhapura. So now, with his few belongings, he moved there. The rumour was that he was surviving in the remnants of a 'leaf hall,' with little that was permanent around him. This was in keeping with the sixth-century sect of monks who lived under such strict principles that they rejected any religious decoration. They would adorn only one slab with carvings, then use it as a urinal stone. This was what they thought of graven images.

He was in his seventies, his eyesight worrying him. He still wrote in cursive script, racing the truth out of himself. He was thin as a broom, wore the same cotton trousers bought along the Galle Road, the same two plum-coloured shirts, spectacles. He still had his dry, wise laugh that seemed, to those who knew them both, the only biological connection he had with his brother.

He lived in the forest grove with his books and writing tablets. But for him, now, all history was filled with sunlight, every hollow was filled with rain. Though as he worked he was conscious that the paper itself that held these histories was aging fast. It was insect-bitten, sun-faded, wind-scattered. And there was his old, thin body. Palipana too now was governed only by the elements.

*

Sarath drove with Anil north beyond Kandy, into the dry zone, searching for Palipana. There was no way the teacher could be told they were coming, and Sarath had no idea how they would be greeted—whether they would be spurned or grudgingly acknowledged. By the time they reached Anuradhapura they were in the heat of the day. They drove on and within an hour were at the entrance to the forest. They left the car and walked for twenty minutes along a path that snaked between large boulders, then opened unexpectedly into a clearing. There were abandoned stone-and-wood structures strewn in front of them—the dry remnants of a water garden, slabs of rock. There was a girl sifting rice, and Sarath went towards her and spoke with her.

The girl boiled water for tea over a twig fire and the three of them sat on a bench and drank it. The girl still had said nothing. Anil assumed Palipana was asleep in the darkness of a hut, and a while later an old man came out of one of the structures in a sarong and shirt. He went around to the side, pulled up a bucket from a well and washed his face and arms. When he returned he said, 'I heard you talking, Sarath.' Anil and Sarath both stood, but Palipana made no further gesture towards them. He just stood there. Sarath bent down and touched the old man's feet, then led him to the bench.

'This is Anil Tissera. . . . We're working together, analyzing some skeletons that were found near Bandarawela.'

'Yes.'

'How do you do, sir?'

'A most beautiful voice.'

And Anil suddenly realized he was blind.

He reached out and held her forearm, touching the skin, feeling the muscle underneath; she sensed he was interpreting her shape and size from this fragment of her body.

'Tell me about them—how ancient?' He let go of her.

Anil looked quickly at Sarath, who gestured to the forest around them. Who was the old man going to tell?

Palipana's head kept tilting, as if trying to catch whatever was passing in the air around him.

'Ah—a secret against the government. Or perhaps a government secret. We are in the Grove of Ascetics. We are safe here. And I am the safest secret-holder. Besides, it makes no difference to me whose secret it is. You already know that, don't you, Sarath? Otherwise you would not have come all this way for help. Is that not correct?'

'We need to think something through, perhaps to find someone. A specialist.'

'As you can tell, I am unable to see anymore, but bring what you have over to me. What is it?'

Sarath went to his bag beside the twig fire, removed the plastic wrapping, and walked over and put the skull in Palipana's lap.

Anil watched the old man as he sat in front of them, calm and still. It was about five in the evening and without the harsh sunlight the rock outcrops around them were now pale and soft. She became aware of the quieter sounds around them.

'Bell and other archaeologists thought this place the location of a secular summer palace when he came upon it in the nineteenth century. But the *Cūlavaṃsa* describes the establishment of forest-dwelling fraternities—by monks who opposed rituals and luxuries.'

Palipana gestured to his left without moving his head. Of the five structures in the clearing, he was living in the simplest one, built against a rock outcrop, with a contemporary leaf roof.

'They were not really poor, but they lived sparsely—you know the distinction between the gross material world and the "subtle" material world, don't you? Well, they embraced the latter. Sarath has no doubt told you about the elaborate urinal stones. He always enjoyed that detail.'

Palipana pursed his lips. There was a tinge of dry humour to his expression and she supposed it was the closest he came to a smile.

'We are safe here, but of course history teaches. During the reign of Udaya the Third, some monks fled the court to escape his wrath. And they came into the Grove of Ascetics. The king and the Uparaja followed them and cut their heads off. Also recorded in the *Cūlavaṃsa* is the population's reaction to this. They became rebellious, "like the ocean stirred by a storm." You see, the king had violated a sanctuary. There were huge protests all over the kingdom, all because of some monks. All because of a couple of heads . . .'

Palipana fell silent. Anil watched his fingers, beautiful and thin, moving over the outlines of the skull Sarath had given him, his long fingernails at the supraorbital ridge, within the orbital cavities, then cupping the shape as if warming his palms on the skull, as if it were a stone from some old fire. He was testing the jaw's angle, the blunt ridge of its teeth. She imagined he could hear the one bird in the forest distance. She imagined he could hear Sarath's sandals pacing, the scrape of his match, the sound of the fire roasting the tobacco leaf as Sarath smoked his beedi a few yards away. She was sure he could hear all that, the light wind, the other fragments of noise that passed by his thin face, that glassy brown boniness of his own skull. And all the while the blunt eyes looked out, piercing whatever caught them. His face was immaculately shaved. Had he done that, or was it the girl?

'Tell me what you think—*you*.' He turned his head in Anil's direction.

'Well . . . We're not in full agreement. But we both know the skeleton this skull comes from is contemporary. It was found in a cache of nineteenth-century bones.'

'But the pedicle on the back of the neck was recently broken,' the old man said.

'He—'

'I did that,' Sarath said. 'Two days ago.'

'Without my permission,' she said.

'Sarath always does what he does for a reason, he is not a random man. He travels in mid-river, always.'

'A visionary decision while drunk, we are calling it for now,' she said as calmly as she could.

Sarath looked between them, at ease with this wit.

'Tell me more. You.' He turned his head towards her again.

'My name is Anil.'

'Yes.'

She saw Sarath shaking his head and grinning. She ignored Palipana's question and gazed into the darkness of the structure he lived in.

They were not surrounded by verdant landscape. Ascetics always chose outcrops of living rock and cleared the topsoil away. There was just the roof of thatch and palm. His leaf hall. Old pissed-off ascetics.

Still, it was calm here. Cicadas noisy and invisible. Sarath had told her that the first time he visited a forest monastery he had not wanted to leave. He had guessed that his teacher in exile would select one of the leaf halls that ringed Anuradhapura, a traditional home for monks. And Palipana had said once how he wished to be buried in this region.

Anil walked past the old man and stood by the well, looking down into it. 'Where is she going?' she heard Palipana say, no real annoyance in his voice. The girl came out of the house with some passion fruit juice and cut guava. Anil drank from a glass quickly. Then she turned to him.

'It's likely he was buried twice. What's important is that the second time it was in a restricted area—accessible only to the police or the army or some high-level government officials. Someone at Sarath's level, for example. No one else has access to such places. So this doesn't seem a crime by an average citizen. I know that murders are sometimes committed during a war for personal reasons, but I don't think a murderer would have the luxury of burying a victim twice. The skeleton this head is part of was found by us in a cave in Bandarawela. We need to discover if we're talking about a murder committed by the government.'

'Yes.'

'The trace elements on Sailor's bones do not—'

'Who is Sailor?'

'*Sailor* is a name we have given the skeleton. The trace elements of soil in his bones do not match the soil where we found him. We don't necessarily agree about the exact bone age, but we are certain he was buried somewhere else first. That is, he was killed and then buried. Then he was dug up, moved to a new location and buried again. Not only do the trace elements of soil not match, but we suspect the pollen that adhered to him before he was buried comes from a totally different region.'

'Wodehouse's *Pollen Grains* . . .'

'Yes, we used that. Sarath has located the pollen to two possible places, one up near Kegalle and another in the Ratnapura area.'

'Ah, an insurgent area.'

'Yes. Where many villagers disappeared during the crisis.'

Palipana stood and held out the skull for one of them to take. 'It's cooler now, we can have supper. Can you stay the night?'

'Yes,' Anil said.

'I will help Lakma cook, we cook the meals together—while you both rest, perhaps.'

'I'd like a well bath,' she told him. 'We've been on the road since five this morning. Is that all right?'

Palipana nodded.

Sarath went into the darkness of the leaf hall and lay down on a floor mat. He seemed exhausted from the long drive. Anil returned to the car and pulled two sarongs out of her bag, then walked back to the clearing. She undressed by the well, unstrapped her watch and got into the *diya reddha* cloth, and dropped the bucket into the depths. There was a hollow smash far below her. The bucket sank and filled. She jerked the rope so the bucket flew up, and caught the rope near the handle. Now she poured the cold water over herself and its glow entered her in a rush, refreshing her. Once more she dropped the bucket into the well and jerked it up and poured it over her hair and shoulders so the water billowed within the thin cloth onto her belly and legs. She understood how wells could become sacred. They combined sparse necessity and luxury. She would give away every earring she owned for an hour by a well. She repeated the mantra of gestures again and again. When she had finished she unwrapped the wet cloth and stood naked in the wind and the last of the sunlight, then put on the dry sarong. She bent over and beat the water off her hair.

Sometime later she woke and sat up on the bench. She heard splashing and turned to see Palipana at the well, the girl pouring water over his naked body. He stood facing Anil, his arms straight down. He was thin, like some lost animal, some *idea*. Lakma kept pouring water over him, and they were both gesturing and laughing now.

*A*t five-fifteen in the morning those who had woken in the dark had already walked a mile, left the streets and come down into the fields. They had blown out the one lantern among them and now moved confidently in the darkness, their bare feet in the mud and wet grass. Ananda Udugama was used to the dark paths. He knew they would soon come upon the scattering of sheds, the mounds of fresh earth, and the water pump and the three-foot-diameter hole in the ground that was the pit head.

With the dark-green light of morning around them the men appeared to float over the open landscape. They could hear and almost see the birds that shot out of the fields with life in their mouths. They began stripping off their vests. They were all gem-pit workers. Soon they would be under the earth, on their knees digging into walls, feeling for any hardness of stone or root or gem. They would move in the underground warrens, sloshing barefoot in mud and water, combing their fingers into the wet clay, the damp walls. Each shift was six hours long. Some entered the earth in darkness and emerged in light, some returned to dusk.

Now the men and women stood by the pump. The men doubled their sarongs and retied them at the waist, hung their vests on the beams of the shed. Ananda took a mouthful of petrol and sprayed it onto the carburetor. When he pulled the cord, the motor jumped to life, thudding against the earth. Water began pouring out of a hose. They heard another motor start up half a mile away. In the next ten minutes the dawn landscape became visible, but by then Ananda and three others had disappeared down a ladder into the earth.

Before the men went down, seven lit candles were lowered in a basket through the three-foot-diameter hole, forty feet below into the darkness by rope. The candles gave light as well as a warning in case the air was unsafe. At the base of the pit, where the candles rested, were three tunnels that disappeared into deeper darkness where the men would go.

Alone now on the surface the women began arranging the silt baskets and within fifteen minutes they heard the whistles and started pulling baskets of mud from below. By the time there was full light in the fields the entire flat region of Ratnapura district was sputtering into life as pumps drained water from the pits and the women used it to flush mud free from what had been sent up in the search for anything of value.

The men in the earth worked in a half-crouch, damp with sweat and tunnel water. If someone cut an arm or a thigh with a digging blade the blood looked black in the tunnel light. When candles smoked out because of the ever-present moisture, the men would lie there in the water, while the digger closest to the entrance would drag himself through darkness and send the candles up to the dry daylight of the pit head to be lit and returned.

At noon Ananda's shift was over. He and the men with him climbed the ladder and paused ten feet below the surface to accustom themselves to the glare, then continued and stepped out onto the fields. Helped by the women, they moved to the mound where they could be hosed off, beginning with hair and shoulders, the water jetting onto their almost naked bodies.

They dressed and began their walk home. By three in the afternoon, in the village where he lived with his sister and brother-in-

law, Ananda was drunk. He would roll off the pallet he had been put on, would move in his familiar half-crouch out the door and piss in the yard, unable to stand or even look up to be aware who might be watching him.

In the leaf hall, shade-filled and muted in colour, the only bright object Anil was conscious of was Sarath's wristwatch. There were two rolled mats and a small table where Palipana still wrote, in spite of blindness, in large billowing script that was half language, half pageantry—the borders between them blurred. This was where he sat most mornings while his thoughts circled and then were caught in the dark room.

The girl placed a cloth on the floor, and they sat around it and leaned towards their food, eating with their fingers. Sarath remembered how Palipana used to travel around the country with his students, how he would eat in silence, listening to them, and suddenly expose his opinions in a twenty-minute monologue. So Sarath had eaten *his* first meals in silence, never putting forward a theory. He was learning the rules and methods of argument the way a boy watching a sport from the sidelines learns timing and skills with his still body. If the students ever assumed something, their teacher would turn on them. They had trusted him because of his severity, because he was incorruptible.

You, Palipana would say, pointing. Never using anyone's name, as if that were immaterial to the discussion or search. Just, *When was this rock cut? The missing letter? The name of the artificer who drew that arm?*

They would travel on side roads, stay at third-rate rest houses, drag chiselled slabs from brush into sunlight, and at night draw

maps of courtyards and palace sites based on the detritus of pillars and archways they had seen during the day.

'I removed the head for a reason.'

Palipana's hand kept moving towards the bowl.

'Have some brinjals, this is my pride. . . .'

Sarath knew that Palipana's interruptions at moments like this
meant he was eager. It was a little taunt. The reality of life versus
a concept.

'I photographed the skeleton with and without the head for a
record. Meanwhile we'll continue analyzing the skeleton—its soil
traces, palymology. The brinjals are very good. . . . Sir, you and I
work on ancient rocks, fossils, rebuild dried-up water gardens,
concern ourselves with why an army moved into the dry zone. We
can identify an architect by his habit of building winter and summer palaces. But Anil lives in contemporary times. She uses contemporary methods. She can cut a cross-section of bone with a
fine saw and determine the skeleton's exact age at death that way.'

'How is that?'

Sarath said nothing in order that Anil would answer. She used
her food-free hand to emphasize her method. 'You put the cross-
section of bone under a microscope. It's got to be one-tenth of a
millimetre—so you can see the blood-carrying canals. As people
get older, the canals, channels really, are broken up, fragmented,
more numerous. If we can get hold of such a machine, we can
guess any age this way.'

'Guess,' he muttered.

'Five-percent margin of error. I'd guess that the person whose
skull you inspected was twenty-eight years old.'

'How certain . . .'

'More certain than what you could know feeling the skull and
the brow ridges and measuring the jaw.'

'How wonderful.' He turned his head to her. 'What a wonder you are.'

She flushed with embarrassment.

'I suppose you can tell how old a geezer like me is too, with a piece of bone.'

'You're seventy-six.'

'How?' Palipana was disarmed. 'My skin? Nails?'

'I checked the Sinhala encyclopaedia before we left Colombo.'

'Ah. Yes, yes. You're lucky you got hold of an old edition. I'm erased from the new one.'

'Then we will have to build a statue of you,' Sarath said, a bit too gracefully.

There was an awkward silence.

'I've lived around graven images all my life. I don't believe in them.'

'Temples have secular heroes too.'

'So you removed the head. . . .'

'We don't know yet the year he was murdered. Ten years ago? Five years ago? More recently? We don't have the equipment to discover that. And given the circumstances of where he was buried, we can't ask for such assistance.'

Palipana was silent, sitting with his head down, his arms crossed. Sarath continued. 'You have reconstructed eras simply by looking at runes. You've used artists to re-create scenes from just paint fragments. So. We have a skull. We need someone to re-create what he might have looked like. One way to discover *when* he was twenty-eight is to have someone identify him.'

No one moved. Even Sarath was looking down now. He went on. 'But we don't have a specialist or knowledge of how to do it. That's why I brought the skull here. For you to tell us where to go, what to do. It is something we have to do quietly.'

'Yes. Of course.'

Palipana stood, so they all did, and walked out of the leaf hall into the night. They were treating his sudden movements the way they would have given a dog rein. The four of them walked to the *pokuna* and stood by the dark water. Anil kept thinking of Palipana's sightlessness in this landscape of dark green and deep gray. The stone steps and rock nestled into the inclines of earth just as the fragments of brick and wood nestled against rock. These bones of an old settlement. It felt to Anil as if her pulse had fallen asleep, that she was moving like the slowest animal in the world through grass. She was picking up intricacies of what was around them. Palipana's mind was probably crowded with such things, in his potent sightlessness. I will not want to leave this place, she thought, remembering that Sarath had said the same thing to her.

'Do you know the tradition of Nētra Mangala?' He was asking them in a murmur, as if thinking aloud. Palipana raised his right hand and pointed it to his own face. He seemed to be talking to her more than to Sarath or the girl.

'*Nētra* means "eye." It is a ritual of the eyes. A special artist is needed to paint eyes on a holy figure. It is always the last thing done. It is what gives the image life. Like a fuse. The eyes are a fuse. It has to happen before a statue or a painting in a *vihara* can become a holy thing. Knox mentions it, and later on Coomaraswamy. You've read him?'

'Yes, but I don't remember.'

'Coomaraswamy points out that before eyes are painted there is just a lump of metal or stone. But after this act, "*it is thenceforward a God.*" Of course there are special ways to paint the eye. Sometimes the king will do it, but it is better when done by a professional artificer, the craftsman. Now of course we have no kings. And Nētra Mangala is better without kings.'

. . .

Anil and Sarath and Palipana and the girl had reached and now sat within the square wooden structure of an *ambalama,* an oil lamp at the centre of it. The old man had gestured towards it and said they could talk there perhaps, even sleep within it this night. It was a structure of wood, with no walls and a high ceiling. Travellers or pilgrims used its shade and coolness during the day. At night it was simply a skeletal wooden form open to the dark, its few beams creating an idea of order. A structure built on rock. A home of wood and boulders.

It was almost dark, and they could smell the air that came towards them over the water of the *pokuna,* could hear the rustling of unseen creatures. Each evening Palipana and the girl walked from their forest clearing to sleep in the *ambalama.* He could relieve himself off the edge of the platform without having to wake the girl to lead him somewhere. He would lie there conscious of the noises from the surrounding ocean of trees. Farther away were the wars of terror, the gunmen in love with the sound of their shells, where the main purpose of war had become war.

The girl was to his left, Sarath to his right, the woman across from him. He knew the woman was now standing up, either looking towards him or beyond, towards the water. He had also heard the splash. Some water creature on this calm night. There was a turkey vulture coming out of the trees. Between him and the woman—on the rock, beside the ochre lamp—was the skull they had brought with them.

'There was one man who painted eyes. He was the best I knew. But he stopped.'

'Painting eyes?'

He heard the fresh curiosity in her voice.

'There is a ceremony to prepare the artificer during the night before he paints. You realize, he is brought in only to paint the eyes on the Buddha image. The eyes must be painted in the morning, at five. The hour the Buddha attained enlightenment. The ceremonies therefore begin the night before, with recitations and decorations in the temples.

'Without the eyes there is not just blindness, there is nothing. There is no existence. The artificer brings to life sight and truth and presence. Later he will be honoured with gifts. Lands or oxen. He enters the temple doors. He is dressed like a prince, with jewellery, a sword at his waist, lace over his head. He moves forward accompanied by a second man, who carries brushes, black paint and a metal mirror.

'He climbs a ladder in front of the statue. The man with him climbs too. This has taken place for centuries, you realize, there are records of this since the ninth century. The painter dips a brush into the paint and turns his back to the statue, so it looks as if he is about to be enfolded in the great arms. The paint is wet on the brush. The other man, facing him, holds up the mirror, and the artificer puts the brush over his shoulder and paints in the eyes without looking directly at the face. He uses just the reflection to guide him—so only the mirror receives the direct image of the glance being created. No human eye can meet the Buddha's during the process of creation. Around him the mantras continue. *May thou become possessed of the fruits of deeds.... May there be an increase on earth and length of days.... Hail, eyes!*

'His work can take an hour or less than a minute, depending on the essential state of the artist. He never looks at the eyes directly. He can only see the gaze in the mirror.'

Anil was standing on the wood ledge that she would later sleep on, thinking of Cullis. Where he might be. No doubt in the arms of his busy marriage. She would avoid thinking of him there. He had not allowed her much room in that world, and her view of him had always been a partially blindfolded one.

'Why don't you let go, Cullis? Let's stop. Why carry on? After two years I still feel like your afternoon date.'

She was beside him on the bed. Not touching him. Just needing to look into his eyes, to talk. He reached out and clutched her hair with his left hand.

'Whatever happens, don't let go of me,' he said.

'Why not?' She pulled her head back but he would not release her.

'Let go!'

He held on to her.

She knew where it was. She reached back and her fingers grabbed it, and she swung the small knife he had been cutting an avocado with earlier in a sure arc and stabbed it into the arm holding her. There was an escape of breath from him. *Ahhh*. All emphasis on the *h*'s. She could almost see the letters coming out of him in the darkness, and the stem of the weapon in his arm muscle.

She looked at his face, his grey eyes (they were always bluer in daylight), and saw the softness he had accepted into his looks during his forties disappear, suddenly go. The face taut, his emotion open. He was weighing everything, this physical betrayal. Her right hand was still curled around the knife, not quite touching it, grazing it.

They looked at each other, neither of them giving in. She wouldn't step back from her fury. When she pulled back this time he released her wet dark hair out of his fingers. She rolled away and picked up the telephone. Carrying it into the light of the bathroom she dialed a taxi. She turned to him. 'Remember this is what I did to you in Borrego Springs. You can make a story out of it.'

Anil dressed in the bathroom, put on makeup, and returned to the bedroom. She switched on all the lights so nothing, no piece of clothing, would escape her while she repacked her bag. Then she switched the lights off and sat and waited. He was on the twin bed, not moving. She heard the taxi draw up and sound its horn.

When she walked to the cab she could feel that her hair was still damp. The car took off under the Una Palma Motel sign. Their romance had been a long intimacy that had existed mostly in secrecy, the good-bye was quick and fatal, though in the taxi to the bus station she put a hand to her breast and felt her heart thumping, as if blurting out the truth.

She had one arm up, holding on to the rafter above her head. She herself felt like a whip that could leap out and catch something in its long finger. Palipana faced the woman who had come with Sarath. *Hail, eyes!* He said it again. Sarath was conscious of her pale arm in the light of the oil lamp as he listened to Palipana. 'When he is finished, the painter of eyes is blindfolded and led out of the temple. The king would endow all those responsible with goods and land. All this is recorded. He defined boundaries for new villages—high and low lands, jungles and ponds. He directed the artificer to be allowed thirty *amunu* of seed-paddy, thirty pieces of iron, ten buffaloes from the fold and ten she-buffaloes with calves.' Palipana's conversation always seemed to include remembered phrases from historical texts.

'She-buffaloes with calves,' Anil said quietly to herself. 'Seed-paddy . . . You were rewarded for the right things.' But he heard her.

'Well, kings also caused trouble in those days,' he said. 'Even then there was nothing to believe in with certainty. They still didn't know what truth was. We have never had the truth. Not even with your work on bones.'

'We use the bone to search for it. "The truth shall set you free." I believe that.'

'Most of the time in our world, truth is just opinion.'

There was a crackle of thunder far away, as if earth and trees were being torn and moved. The wooden *ambalama* felt like a raft or four-poster bed drifting in the black clearing. Perhaps they were not nestled on rock but unmoored, on a river. She was lying on the lip of the structure, on one of the sleeping platforms. She had woken and could hear Palipana turning every few minutes as if it was difficult for him to find the precise location and posture for sleep.

Anil turned back into her own privacy, to Cullis. She felt there was this physical line to him wherever he was on the planet, beyond ocean or storm, some frail telephone cord that one had to tug clear of branches or rocks deep in the sea. And did he hold the image of her stride from that room in Borrego? They had both hoped for a seven-bangled night. She'd decided when she left him that she would call later to make sure he had not given in to sleep, but the fury was still taut in her and she did not.

Sarath struck a match against the rock beside the *ambalama*. So it was not a river down there. Light flickered up and she smelled the smoke of his beedi. An insect chirped like the sound of a watch being wound, one of the inhabitants in this forest of ascetics. 'There has always been slaughter in passion,' she heard Palipana say.

In the dark he continued speaking: 'Even if you are a monk, like my brother, passion or slaughter will meet you someday. For you cannot survive as a monk if society does not exist. You renounce society, but to do so you must first be a part of it, learn your decision from it. This is the paradox of retreat. My brother entered temple life. He escaped the world and the world came after him. He was seventy when he was killed by someone, perhaps someone from the time when he was breaking free—for that is the difficult stage, when you leave the world. I am the last of my siblings. For my sister too is dead. This girl is her daughter.'

A few years before, the girl Lakma had seen her parents killed. A week after their murder, the twelve-year-old child was taken to a government ward run by nuns, north of Colombo, that looked after children whose parents had been killed in the civil war. The shock of the murder of the girl's parents, however, had touched everything within her, driving both her verbal and her motor ability into infancy. This was combined with an adult sullenness of spirit. She wanted nothing more to invade her.

She lay hidden there for over a month, silent, non-reacting, physically forced from her room to do exercises in sunlight. The nightmares continued for Lakma, who was unable to deal with the possible danger around her. A child who knew the falseness of the supposed religious security around her, with its clean dormitories and well-made beds. When Palipana, her only remaining relative, came to visit her he saw she was immune to any help in this place. Any sudden sound was danger to her. She would finger through every meal looking for insects or glass, would not sleep in the safety of her bed but hidden underneath it. It was the time of Palipana's own crisis in his career, and his eyes were in the last stages of glaucoma. He had bundled her up and travelled by train up to Anuradhapura, the girl terrified during the whole journey, then brought her in a cart to the forest monastery, the leaf hall and *ambalama,* in the Grove of Ascetics. They slipped this way out of the world, not noticed by anyone—an old man, a twelve-year-old girl who was scared of the evidence of anything human, even of this person who had brought her into the dry zone.

He wished more than anything to deliver her from the inflicted isolation. Whatever skills she learned from her parents had been abandoned too deep within her. Palipana, the country's great epigraphist, began to educate her on two levels—gave her the mnemonic skills of alphabet and phrasing, and conversed with her at the furthest edge of his knowledge and beliefs. All this occurred as his own vision darkened and he began to move slowly, with exaggerated gestures. (It was later, when he trusted the dark and the girl more, that his movement became minimal.)

He supposed he had always trusted her, in spite of her fury and rejection of the world. He weaved into her presence his conversations about wars and medieval *sloka*s and Pali texts and language, and he spoke of how history faded too, as much as battle did, and how it could exist only with remembrance—for even the *sloka*s on papyrus and bound *ola* leaves would be eaten by moths and silverfish, dissolved by rainstorms—how only stone and rock could hold one person's loss and another's beauty forever.

She took journeys with him—a two-day walk to a chapter house in Mihintale, climbing the 132 steps, clinging to this blind man with her fear when he insisted they go once by bus to Polonnaruwa so he could be in the presence of the Stone Book, his hands upon the ducks—that were for eternity—for the last time. They rode in bullock carts and he would sniff the air or hear the hum within the gum trees and know where he was, would know there was a half-buried temple nearby, and his lean body would be off the cart and she would follow him. 'We are, and I was, formed by history,' he would say. 'But the three places I love escaped it. Arankale. Kaludiya Pokuna. Ritigala.'

So they journeyed south as far as Ritigala, getting rides in slow bullock carts, where she felt safer, and climbed the holy mountain for hours up through the hot forest alongside the noise of cicadas. They came upon the footpath that curved uphill in a giant S. They broke a small branch as the two of them entered the forest and dedicated that as an offering, and took nothing else from there.

Every historical pillar he came to in a field he stood beside and embraced as if it were a person he had known in the past. Most of his life he had found history in stones and carvings. In the last few years he had found the hidden histories, intentionally lost, that altered the perspective and knowledge of earlier times. It was how one hid or wrote the truth when it was necessary to lie.

He had deciphered the shallowly incised lines during lightning, had written them down during rain and thunder. A portable sulphur lamp or a thorn brushfire by the overhang of cave. The dialogue between old and hidden lines, the back-and-forth between what was official and unofficial during solitary field trips, when he spoke to no one for weeks, so that these became his only conversations—an epigraphist studying the specific style of a chiselcut from the fourth century, then coming across an illegal story, one banned by kings and state and priests, in the interlinear texts. These verses contained the darker proof.

Lakma watched him and listened, never speaking, a silent amanuensis for his whispered histories. He blended fragments of stories so they became a landscape. It did not matter if she could not distinguish between his versions and the truth. She was safe, finally, with him, this man who was her mother's elder brother. They slept on mats in the leaf hall in the afternoon, within the frames of the *ambalama* at night. As his vision left him he gave more and more of his life to her. The last days of his sight he spent simply gazing at her.

With his blindness she gained the authority he had been unable to give her. She rearranged the paths of the day. What she did in proximity to him was now a part of the invisible world. Her new semi-nakedness in a way represented her state of mind. She wore a sarong as a man would. Palipana would not see this, or her left hand on her pubis tugging the new hair or playing with it while he talked to her. The only governor to her manner was to do with his safety and comfort. She would bound over to him if he was walking towards a root. Every morning she wet his face with water she had boiled over a fire, and then shaved him. They were early risers and early sleepers, aligned to the sun and moon. She was with him this way for two years before the appearance of Sarath and Anil. With their arrival the girl stepped back, although by then they were invading what was her home more than Palipana's. It was *her* pattern of the day that was broken. If Anil witnessed politeness or kindness in the old man, it was only in his hand gestures and murmurs to Lakma, just loud enough to be heard a step away, so Anil and Sarath were excluded from most of their conversation. In the late afternoon the girl sat between his legs, and his hands were in her long hair searching for lice with those thin fingers and combing it while the girl rubbed his feet. When he walked she steered him away from any obstacle in his path with a slight tug of the sleeve.

*

The girl would slip into the forest, nocturnal, still as bark, when Palipana died.

She would dress his nakedness with thambili leaves that were part of the decoration for death, sew his last notebooks into his clothes. She had already prepared a pyre for him on the edge of the *pokuna,* whose sound he loved—and now its flames shivered in the water of the lake. She had already cut one of his phrases into the rock, one of the first things he had said to her, which she had held on to like a raft in her years of fear. She had chiselled it where the horizon of water was, so that, depending on tide and pull of the moon, the words in the rock would submerge or hang above their reflection or be revealed in both elements. Now she stood waist-deep in the water, cutting the Sinhala letters into the dark stone the way he had described the methods of artisans to her. He had once shown her such runes, finding them even in his blindness, and their marginalia of ducks, for eternity. So she carved the outline of ducks on either side of his sentence. In the tank at Kaludiya Pokuna the yard-long sentence still appears and disappears. It has already become an old legend. But the girl who stood waist-deep and cut it into rock in the last week of Palipana's dying life and carried him into the water beside it and placed his hand against it in the slop of the water was not old. He nodded, remembering the words. And now he would remain by the water and each morning the girl undressed and climbed down against the wall of submerged rock and banged and chiselled, so that in the last days of his life he was accompanied by the great generous noise of her work as if she were speaking out loud. Just the sentence. Not his name or the years of his living, just a gentle sentence once clutched by her, the imprint of it now carried by water around the lake.

He had handed Lakma his old, weathered spectacles, and in the end, after she had sewn his notebooks into his clothing, she would take only this talisman of these glasses with her when she went into the forest.

*

But that night, with the two strangers on the *ambalama,* the girl could sense the restlessness of Anil, as clear to her as Sarath's beedi brightening now and then in the dark. Palipana sat up and Lakma knew he would speak, as if there had been no half-hour pause.

'The man I mentioned, the artist, there was tragedy in his life. Now he works in the gem pits, goes down into them four or five days a week. An arrack drinker, I've heard. It is not safe to be with him underground. Maybe he's still there. He was the craftsman who painted eyes—as his father and grandfather did. An inherited talent, though I think he was the best of the three. I think he's the one you should find. You will have to pay him.'

Anil said, 'Pay him for what?'

'To rebuild the head,' Sarath murmured in the darkness.

They set out for Colombo the next day, although neither of them wished to leave the spell of the old man and his forest site. They waited for the cool of sundown and left when Palipana and the girl walked towards the *ambalama* to sleep. An hour south of Matale, the car took a corner and Sarath saw the lights of a truck coming towards them. He braked hard and the car shuddered and skidded on the macadam. Then he saw it was not moving; the truck was parked on the road facing them, its headlights on.

He released the brake and they drifted slowly forward. She had been asleep and now she put her head out the window. There was a man lying on the road in front of the truck. Spread-eagled on his back. The truck was immense above him, the glare of its lights shot beams ahead, but the man was below them in darkness. He was shirtless, his bare feet pointed up saucily, his arms out. Their fear was followed by the humour of it all. Everything was quiet around them as their car crept past. Not even a dog barking. No cicadas. The motor of the truck turned off.

'Is he the driver?' She whispered it, not wanting to break the silence.

'This is how they sometimes sleep, take a short rest. Simply stop in the wrong lane, leave the lights on, and stretch out on the road for half an hour or so. Or he could just be drunk.'

They drove on, Anil now fully awake, leaning with her back to the door so she could face Sarath as he spoke, hardly audible in the wind rushing into the windows. As an archaeologist he always travelled on night roads, more since his wife died, he said. There would be two trips every week—up to Puttalam or to the south coast. He accompanied teams of students puttering along the bunds of prawn farms for ancient village sites or he went to oversee the restoration of a stone bridge in Anuradhapura.

They were just south of Ambepussa and would reach the out-skirts of Colombo in an hour. 'When I was young, my father took bets with us—how many drunks we'd see sleeping by trucks, how many dogs we'd pass. A bonus if we saw a dog with a sleeping man. Or sometimes it would be a group of three or four dogs in the moon shadow of a stilled night truck. He'd bet with us to keep himself awake as he drove. He loved to bet.'

After a long pause Sarath continued. 'All his life he gambled. We didn't realize this when we were children. He had an ordered business life, he was a respected lawyer. We were a stable family. But he loved gambling, and our fortunes went up and down.'

'All you want when you're a kid is certainty.'

'Yes.'

'When you met your wife, you were sure, were you . . . that you were both . . . ?'

'I knew I loved her. But I was never certain of us, as a pair.'

'Sarath, can you stop the car, please.' She heard the slight hol-low thump as his right foot slipped away from the accelerator. The car began to slow, not stopping. She was silent, staring ahead into the dark. He veered onto the shoulder and they sat in the dark purring vehicle.

'You realize there were no dogs back there, by the truck.'

'Yes. I thought that as soon as I spoke. There was something wrong.'

'Perhaps it was a village of no dogs. . . . We have to go back.' She took her eyes off the road and looked at him, and the car jerked loose into a half-circle and drove north again.

. . .

They reached the truck in twenty minutes. The man by the truck was alive but couldn't move. He was almost unconscious. Someone had hammered a bridge nail into his left palm and another into his right, crucifying him to the tarmac. He was the driver of the truck and as Sarath and Anil approached him a terrified look appeared on his face. As if they were coming back to kill him or torture him further.

She held the man's face between her hands while Sarath prized the nails from the tarmac, freeing his hands.

'You have to leave the nails in for now,' she said. 'Don't remove them.'

Sarath explained to the man that she was a doctor. They got a blanket out of the trunk and wrapped him in it and carried him to the back seat. There was nothing to drink besides an inch or two of cordial, which he quickly swallowed.

They were going south again. Every time she turned to see how the man was, his eyes were wide open looking at them. She told Sarath they needed saline solution. She saw a faint light ahead and put her hand on Sarath's arm to get him to stop. The car pulled over quietly and he shut off the motor.

'What village is this?'

'Galapitigama. The village of beautiful women,' he said, like a refrain. She looked at him. 'Supposedly. McAlpine said so.'

She climbed out and walked to the door of a house behind which she could see light. She smelled tobacco. Sarath was beside her.

'We want salt. Hot water. If not hot, then cold will have to do. A small bowl of it—we need to take the bowl with us.'

When the door opened they saw a room busy at knee level. There were seven men around the perimeter, rolling cigarettes, weighing batches of them on scales, packaging them with thin string. Illegal night work. They wore only cotton sarongs in the hot, closed room, which was windowless. Three lamps on the floor where the piles of beedis were stacked up. Everything had a brownness, an orangeness, from the contained weaving flame of the lights. All of the men were in checkered blue-green sarongs.

The bare-chested man who opened the door stared past them to the car, nervous at their possible authority. Sarath explained that they needed a pot of hot water and salt, then as an afterthought asked for some beedis, if they would be willing to sell them. At which the man laughed.

One of the other men went out through the far door while she and Sarath stood on the threshold, then he returned with salt in one hand and a small bowl in the other. Anil enclosed his wrist with her fingers and turned it so the salt clouded into the water.

This time she got into the back seat beside the truck driver. Sarath said something to him over his shoulder and the man tentatively gave her his left hand. Under the faint roof light Anil soaked a handkerchief in the saline solution and squeezed it onto his palm, the bridge nail still in it. Then the other hand, then back again to the first.

Sarath started the engine.

There were forests on either side of the empty road. The motor's hum filled the quietness, a thread in this silent world, just her and Sarath and the wounded man. Now and then a village, now and then an unmanned roadblock where they had to slow down and twist through the eye of a needle. As they passed a streetlamp Anil saw that what she was squeezing into his palms was now bloody water. Still she didn't stop, because the movement kept him calm and awake, kept him from drifting into shock. The mutual gestures—her pull, his giving—were becoming hypnotic to both.

'What's your name?'

'Gunesena.'

'Do you live near here?'

The man rolled his head slightly, a tactful yes and no, and Anil smiled. In an hour they were within the outskirts of Colombo, and later drove into the compound of Emergency Services.

A Brother

In the operating rooms of the base hospitals in the North Central Province there were always four books in evidence: Hammon's *Analysis of 2,187 Consecutive Penetrating Wounds of the Brain in Vietnam; Gunshot Wounds* by Swan and Swan; C. W. Hughes's *Arterial Repair During the Korean War;* and *Annals of Surgery.* Doctors in the midst of an operation would have an orderly turn pages so they could skim the text while continuing surgery. After two weeks of fifteen-hour days they no longer needed assistance from books and moved with ease alongside wounds and suture techniques. But the medical texts remained, for future doctors in training.

In the doctors' common room in a North Central Province hospital someone had left a copy of *Elective Affinities* among the other, more porous paperbacks. It remained there throughout the war, unread save by someone who might pick it up while waiting, consider its back-cover description, then replace it respectfully on the table with the others. These—a more popular gang that included Erle Stanley Gardner, Rosemary Rogers, James Hilton and Walter Tevis—were consumed in two or three hours, swallowed like sandwiches on the run. Anything to direct your thoughts away from a war.

The buildings that made up the hospital had been erected at the turn of the century. It had been managed in a lackadaisical way before the exaggeration of war. In the grass courtyard, signs from a more innocent time would last throughout the waves of violence. Half-dead soldiers who wished for sun and fresh air rested there and ate morphine tablets beside a BETEL CHEWING IS PROHIBITED sign.

The victims of 'intentional violence' had started appearing in March 1984. They were nearly all male, in their twenties, damaged by mines, grenades, mortar shells. The doctors on duty put down *The Queen's Gambit* or *The Tea Planter's Bride* and began arresting the haemorrhages. They removed metal and stone from lungs, sutured lacerated chests. In one of the hospital texts that the young doctor Gamini read was a sentence he became excessively fond of: *In diagnosing a vascular injury, a high index of suspicion is necessary.*

During the first two years of the war more than three hundred casualties were brought in as a result of explosions. Then the weapons improved and the war in the north-central province got worse. The guerrillas had international weaponry smuggled into the country by arms dealers, and they also had homemade bombs.

The doctors saved the lives first, then the limbs. There were mostly grenade injuries. An antipersonnel mine the size of an inkwell would destroy most of a person's feet. Wherever there was a base hospital in the country, new villages sprang up nearby. There was a need for rehabilitation programmes, and the making of what came to be known as the 'Jaipur Limb.' In Europe a new artificial foot cost 2,500 pounds. Here the Jaipur Limb was made for 30 pounds—cheaper because Asian victims could walk without a shoe.

The hospital would run out of painkillers during the first week of any offensive. You were without self in those times, lost among the screaming. You held on to any kind of order—the smell of Savlon antiseptic that was used to wash floors and walls, the 'children's injection room' with its nursery murals. The older purpose of a hospital continued alongside the war. When Gamini finished surgery in the middle of the night, he walked through the compound into the east buildings, where the sick children were. The mothers were always there. Sitting on stools, they rested their upper torso and head on their child's bed and slept holding the small hands. There were not too many fathers around then. He watched the children, who were unaware of their parents' arms. Fifty yards away in Emergency he had heard grown men scream for their mothers as they were dying. *'Wait for me!' 'I know you are here!'* This was when he stopped believing in man's rule on earth. He turned away from every person who stood up for a war. Or the principle of one's land, or pride of ownership, or even personal rights. All of those motives ended up somehow in the arms of careless power. One was no worse and no better than the enemy. He believed only in the mothers sleeping against their children, the great sexuality of spirit in them, the sexuality of care, so the children would be confident and safe during the night.

Ten beds skirted the edge of the room, and in the centre was a nurse's desk. Gamini loved the order of these closed wards. If he had a few free hours he avoided the doctors' dormitory and came here to lie on one of the empty beds, so that even if he could not sleep he was surrounded by something he would find nowhere else in the country. He wanted a mother's arm to hold him firm on the bed, to lie across his rib cage, to bring a cool washcloth to his face. He would turn to watch a child with jaundice bathed in the pale-blue light as if within a diorama. A blue light that was warm rather than clear, with a specific frequency. *'Pass me a gentian. Give me a torch.'* Gamini wished to be bathed in it. The nurse looked at her watch and walked from her desk to wake him. But he was not asleep. He drank a cup of tea with her and then left the pediatric ward, which had its own woes. He reached out and touched the small Buddha in the niche of the wall as he passed it.

Crossing the open grass lot, Gamini returned to the war rooms, where there seemed little difference between pre-operative and post-operative patients. The only reasonable constant was that there would be more bodies tomorrow—post-stabbings, post–land mines. Orthopaedic trauma, punctured lungs, spinal cord injuries . . .

A few years earlier a story had gone around about a Colombo doctor—Linus Corea—a neurosurgeon in the private sector. He came from three generations of doctors, the family name was as established as the most permanent banks in the country. Linus Corea was in his late forties when the war broke out. Like most doctors he thought it was madness and unlike most he stayed in private practice; the Prime Minister was one of his clients, as was the leader of the opposition. He had his head massages at Gabriel's at eight a.m. and saw his patients from nine till two, then golfed with a bodyguard at his side. He dined out, got home before curfew and slept in an air-conditioned room. He had been married for ten years and had two sons. He was a well-liked man; he was polite with everyone because it was the easiest way not to have trouble, to be invisible to those who did not matter to him. This small courtesy created a bubble he rode within. His gestures and politeness disguised an essential lack of interest or, if not that, a lack of time for others on the street. He liked photography. He printed his own pictures in the evening.

In 1987, while he was putting on a golf green, his bodyguard was shot dead and Dr. Linus Corea was kidnapped. They came out of the woods slowly, unconcerned about being seen by him. It meant it did not matter to them and that frightened him more than anything. He had been alone with the bodyguard. He stood beside the prone body and was surrounded by the men who had shot him from a distance of forty yards precisely through the correct point in the head. No thrashing around.

They spoke to him calmly in a made-up language, which again increased his anxiety. They hit him once and broke a rib to warn him to behave, and then they walked back to their car and drove away with him. For months no one knew where he had got to. The police, the Prime Minister, the head of the Communist Party were called in, and all were outraged. There was no communication from kidnappers wanting payment. It was the Colombo mystery of 1987, and offers of rewards were made throughout the press, none of which was answered.

Eight months after Linus Corea's disappearance, his wife was alone in the house with their two children when a man came to the door and handed her a letter from her husband. The man stepped inside. The note was simple. It said: *If you wish to see me again, come with the children. If you do not wish to, I will understand.*

She moved to the phone, and the man produced a gun. She stood there. To her left was a pool where some flowers floated in shallow water. All her valuables were upstairs. She stood there, the children busy in their rooms. It had not been a joyous marriage. Comfortable but not happy. Affections on the thin scale of things. But the letter, while it held his terseness, had a quality she would never have expected. It gave her a choice. It was laconically stated but it was there, graciously, with no strings. Later she thought that if it had not been for that she would not have gone. She muttered to the man. He spoke back to her in an invented language that she did not understand. Some of the news reports at the time of her husband's disappearance had spoken of UFO kidnappings, and this strangely came to her mind now, there in her front hall.

'We'll come with you,' she said again, out loud, and this time the man came towards her and gave her another letter.

This one was just as abrupt and said: *Please bring these books.* A list followed, eight titles. He told her where they could be found in his office. She told her sons to get a few extra clothes and shoes, but she packed nothing for herself. She carried only the books, and once they were outside the man directed them to an already humming car.

Linus Corea made his way to the tent in the dark and lay down on the cot. It was nine at night, and if they came they would be there in about five hours. He had told the men when it was most likely for her to be home alone. He needed to sleep. He had been working in the triage tent for close to six hours, so even with the brief nap after lunch he was exhausted.

He had been at the camp of the insurgents ever since they had picked him up in Colombo. They had got him a little after two in the afternoon and by seven he was in the southern hills. No one had spoken to him in the car, just the idiot language, a joke of theirs. What good it did he wasn't sure. When he reached the camp they explained in Sinhala what they wanted him to do, which was to work as a doctor for them. Nothing more. It was not an intense conversation, he wasn't threatened. They told him he could see his family in a few months. They said he could sleep now but in the morning he would have to work. A few hours later they woke him and said there was an emergency, and led him into the triage tent with a lantern and hung it on a hook above a half-dead body and asked him to operate on the skull in lamplight. The man was too far gone, still they asked him to operate. He himself was uncomfortable with his broken rib and whenever he leaned forward pain tore through him. Half an hour later the man died and they carried the lantern to another bed, where someone else who had been shot had been waiting in silence. He had to remove the leg above the knee, but the man lived. Linus Corea went back to sleep at two-thirty. At six a.m. they woke him again to begin work.

After a few days he asked them to get some smocks for him, some rubber gloves, some morphine. He gave them a list of things he needed, and that night they attacked a hospital near Gurutulawa and got the medical essentials and kidnapped a nurse for him. She too, strangely, did not complain about her fate, just as he hadn't. Privately he was irritated, and tired of a world that necessitated this, but the device of courtesy that had been false in his other life continued. He thanked people for nothing much and he didn't ask for anything unless it was badly needed. He became accustomed to this lack of need, was rather proud of it. If he wanted something—syringes, bandages, a book—he would write out a list and give it to them. Maybe a week later, maybe six weeks, he'd get them. The first hospital attack was the only one they planned just for him.

He did not know how long they would keep him so he began to teach the nurse everything he could about surgery. Rosalyn was about forty, very smart under her seeming complacency. He had her operating alongside him when they were overrun with wounded.

After the first month he admitted to himself that he didn't miss his children or wife anymore, even that much of Colombo. Not that he was happy here, but being busy he was preoccupied.

There was no energy in him to be angry or insulted. Six till noon. Two hours off for lunch and sleep. Then he worked six more hours. If there was a crisis he worked longer. The nurse was always beside him. She wore one of the smocks that he had requested and was very proud of it, washing it out every evening so it would be clean in the morning.

It was just another day but to him it was his birthday. And he thought about that on his walk to the tent. He was fifty-one. The first birthday in the mountains. At noon the jeep swept by and he and the nurse were bundled in. They drove for some time and then he was blindfolded. Soon after, they pulled him from the vehicle. He gave up then. A lot of wind in his face. With his probing feet he sensed he was on a ledge. A cliff? He was pushed and he was flying in mid-air, falling, but before there was fear he hit water. Mountain cold. He was all right. He pulled off the blindfold and heard a cheer. The nurse, in her clothes, dove off the rock into the water beside him. The men dove in after that. They somehow knew about his birthday. From then on, a swim became a part of the day's schedule, if there was time. He always thought of it before he fell asleep. It heightened his excitement about the oncoming day. The swim.

He was asleep when his family arrived. The nurse tried to wake him, but he was dead to the world. She suggested that the wife come into her tent with the two boys so he could sleep undisturbed, he had to be up in a few hours to work. At what? the wife said. He's a doctor, the nurse said.

It was just as well. The drive had been arduous and she and the children were tired themselves. This was not the time to greet and talk. When they woke the next morning it was ten, and her husband had already been working for four hours. Had walked into their tent carrying his mug of tea, looked at them, and then had gone to work with the nurse. The nurse had told him she was surprised his wife was that young, and the doctor had laughed. In

Colombo he would have reddened or become angry. He was aware this nurse could say anything to him.

So when his wife and children woke they were ignored. The nurse was gone, the soldiers they saw went their own way. The mother insisted they stay together, and they went searching around the compound like lost tourists till they found the nurse washing bandages outside a dirty tent.

Rosalyn came up to him and said something he did not catch and she repeated it, that his wife and children were by the tent entrance. He looked up, then asked her if she could take over, and she nodded. He walked away from the close focus of the tent work, passed people lying on the ground, towards his wife and the children. The nurse could see him almost bouncing with pleasure. When he came closer his wife saw the blood on his smock and she hesitated. 'It doesn't matter,' he said, lifting her into an embrace. She touched his beard, which he had forgotten he had grown. There were no mirrors and he hadn't seen it.

'You met Rosalyn?'

'Yes. She helped us last night. You of course wouldn't wake up.'

'Mmm.' Linus Corea laughed. 'They keep me going.' He paused, then said, 'It's my life.'

*

Whenever a bomb went off in a public place, Gamini stood at the entrance of the hospital, the funnel of the triage, and categorized the incoming victims, quickly assessing the state of each person—sending them to Intensive Care or to the operating theatre. This time there were women too, because it had been a street bomb. All survivors in the outer circle of the explosion came in within the hour. The doctors didn't use names. Tags were put on the right wrist, or on a right foot if there was no arm. Red for Neuro, green for Orthopaedic, yellow for Surgery. No profession or race. He liked it this way. Names were recorded later if the survivors could speak, in case they died. Ten cc's of sample blood were taken from each of the patients and attached to their mattresses, along with disposable needles that would be reused if they were needed.

The triage separated the dying from those who needed immediate surgery and those who could wait; the dying were given morphine tablets so time would not be spent on them. Distinguishing the others was more difficult. Street bombs, usually containing nails or ball bearings, could cut open an abdomen fifty yards from the explosion. Shock waves travelled past someone and the suction could rupture the stomach. 'Something happened to my stomach,' a woman would say, fearing she had been cut open by bomb metal, while in fact her stomach had flipped over from the force of passing air.

Everyone was emotionally shattered by a public bomb. Months later survivors would come into the ward saying they feared they might still die. For those on the periphery, the shrapnel and fragments that flew through their bodies, magically not touching any vital organs, were harmless because the heat of the explosion would sterilize the shrapnel. But what did harm was the emotional shock. And there was deafness or semi-deafness, depending on which way one's head was turned on the street that day. Few could afford to have an eardrum reconstructed.

In these times of crisis junior staff members did the work of orthopaedic surgeons. Roads to larger medical centres were often closed because of mines, and helicopters were unable to travel in darkness. So all versions of trauma, all versions of burns, surrounded the trainees. There were only four neurosurgeons in the country: two brain surgeons in Colombo, one in Kandy and one in the private sector—but he had been kidnapped a few years earlier.

Meanwhile, far away in the south, there were other interruptions. Insurgents entered the Ward Place Hospital in Colombo and killed a doctor and two of his assistants. They had come looking for one patient. 'Where is so and so?' they had asked. 'I don't know.' There was bedlam. After finding the patient, they pulled out long knives and cut him to pieces. Then they threatened the nurses and demanded they not come to work anymore. The next day the nurses returned, not in uniforms but in frocks and slippers. There were gunmen on the roof of the hospital. There were informers everywhere. But the Ward Place Hospital remained open.

There was little of that kind of politics in the base hospitals. Gamini and his assistants, Kasan and Monica, managed a quick nap in the doctors' lounge when they could. Half the time curfews kept them from going home. Gamini wasn't able to sleep, in any case. He hadn't come down yet from the pills he had recently started taking, the adrenaline still in him though his brain and motor senses were exhausted, so he would walk outside into the night under the trees. There would be a few people smoking, relatives of the wounded. He had no wish for contact, there was just his blood racing. He came back inside and picked up a paperback and stared at a page as if it were a scene on another planet. Finally he would go again to the children's ward to find a bed where he was a stranger and felt safer. A few mothers would look up with suspicion, concerned to protect their children from this unknown man, like hens, before recognizing him as the doctor who had come to the area two years before, who could never sleep, who climbed now onto a sheetless mattress and lay on his back, still, until his head fell to the left watching the blue light.

When he was asleep the desk nurse unlaced his shoes and removed them. He snored loudly, and sometimes it woke the children.

He was thirty-four years old then. Things would get worse. By the time he was thirty-six, he was working in Accident Services Hospital in Colombo. 'Gunshot Services,' they called it. But he remembered the pediatric wards in the North Central Province, the blue light above that jaundiced child which somehow also comforted him, its specific frequency of 470 to 490 nanometres that all night kept breaking down the yellow pigment. He remembered the books, the four essential medical texts and the stories he never finished reading though he kept them in his hands for hours as he sat in the cane chair trying to rest, trying to come down to some kind of human order, but instead only darkness came down on him in the room, his eyes peering at the pages while his brain stared past them to the truth of their times.

It was one a.m. when Sarath and Anil arrived in the centre of Colombo, having driven through the city's empty grey streets. As they got to Emergency Services, she said, 'Is it okay? Us moving him like this?'

'It's okay. We're taking him to my brother. With luck he'll be somewhere there in Emergency.'

'You have a brother here?'

Sarath parked and was still for a moment. 'God, I'm exhausted.'

'Do you want to stay here and sleep? I can take him in.'

'It's okay. I'd better talk to my brother anyway. If he's there.'

Gunesena was asleep and they woke him and walked him between them into the building. Sarath spoke to someone at the desk and the three of them sat down to wait, Gunesena's hands on his lap like a boxer's. There was a daylight sense of work going on around Admissions, though everyone moved in slow motion and quietly. A man in a striped shirt came towards them and chatted with Sarath.

'This is Anil.'

The man in the striped shirt nodded at her.

'My brother, Gamini.'

'Right,' she said, flatly.

'He's my younger brother—he's our doctor.'

There had been no touching between him and Sarath, not a handshake.

'Come—' Gamini helped Gunesena to his feet and they all followed him into a small room. Gamini unstoppered a bottle and began swabbing the man's palms. She noticed he wasn't wearing gloves, not even a lab coat. It looked as if he had just come from an interrupted card game. He injected the anaesthetic into the man's hands.

'I didn't know he had a brother,' she said, breaking the silence.

'Oh, we don't see much of each other. I don't speak of him either, you know. We go our own way.'

'He knew you were here, though, and what shift you were on.'

'I suppose so.'

They were both intentionally excluding Sarath from their conversation.

'How long have you been working with him?' Gamini now asked.

She said, 'Three weeks.'

'Your hands—they are steady,' Sarath said. 'Have you recovered?'

'Yes.' Gamini turned to Anil. 'I'm the family secret.'

He pulled the bridge nails from Gunesena's anaesthetized hands. Then he washed them with Betalima, a crimson sudsing fluid that he squirted out of a plastic bottle. He dressed the wounds and talked quietly to his patient. He was very gentle, which for some reason surprised her. He pulled open a drawer, got another disposable needle and gave him a tetanus shot. 'You owe the hospital two needles,' he murmured to Sarath. 'There's a shop on the corner. You should get them while I sign out.' He led Sarath and Anil out of the room, leaving the patient behind.

'There are no beds left here tonight. Not for this level of injury. See, even crucifixion isn't a major assault nowadays. . . . If you can't take him home I'll find someone to watch him while he sleeps out in Admissions—I'll okay it, I mean.'

'He can come with us,' Sarath said. 'If he wants I'll get him a job as a driver.'

'You better replace those needles. I'm going off duty soon. Do you want to eat? Along the Galle Face?' He was talking again to Anil.

'It's two in the morning!' Sarath said.

She spoke up. 'Yes. Sure.'

He nodded at her.

Gamini pulled open the passenger-side door and got in beside his brother, which left Anil in the back seat with Gunesena. Well, she'd have a better view of both of them.

The streets were empty save for a silent patrol of military moving under the arch of trees along Solomon Dias Mawatha. They were stopped at a roadblock and asked for their passes. A half-mile beyond that they came to a food stall and Gamini got out and bought them all something to eat. On the road the younger brother looked thin as his shadow, feral.

They left Gunesena sleeping in the car and walked onto Galle Face Green and sat near the breakwater by the darkness of the sea. While Gamini unwrapped his spoils, Anil lit a cigarette. She was not hungry, but Gamini would in the next hour consume several packets of *lamprais,* a startling amount for someone she considered slight and bony. She noticed him palm a pill and swill it down with Orange Crush.

'We get a lot like this one. . . .'

'Nails in hands?' She realized she sounded horrified.

'Nowadays we get everything. It's almost a relief to find a common builder's nail as a weapon. Screws, bolts—they pack their bombs with everything to make sure you get gangrene from explosions.'

He unwrapped the leaf of another *lamprais* and ate with his fingers. '. . . Thank God it's not a full moon. *Poya* days are the worst. Everyone thinks they can see. They go out and step on something. Are you the team working on the new skeletons?'

'How do you know about that?' She was suddenly tense.

'It's the wrong time for unburials. They don't want results. They're fighting a war on two sides now, the government. They don't need more criticism.'

'I understand that,' Sarath said.

'But does she?' Gamini paused. 'Just be careful. Nobody's perfect. Nobody's right. And too many people know about your investigation. There is always someone paying attention.'

There was a short silence. Then Sarath asked his brother what else he was doing.

'Just sleep and work,' Gamini yawned. 'Nothing else. My marriage disappeared. All that ceremony—and then it evaporated in a couple of months. I was too intense then. I'm probably another example of trauma, you see. That happens when there is no other life. What the fuck do my marriage and your damn research mean. And those armchair rebels living abroad with their ideas of justice—nothing against their principles, but I wish they were here. They should come and visit me in surgery.'

He leaned forward to take one of Anil's cigarettes. She lit it and he nodded.

'I mean, I know everything about blast weaponry. Mortars, Claymore mines, antipersonnel mines which contain gelignite and trinitrotoluen. And I'm the doctor! That last one results in amputations below the knee. They lose consciousness and the blood pressure falls. You do a tomography of the brain and brain stem, and it shows haemorrhages and edema. We use dexamethasone and mechanical ventilation for this—it means we have to open the skull up. Mostly it's hideous mutilation, and we just keep arresting the haemorrhages. . . . They come in all the time. You find mud, grass, metal, the remnants of a leg and boot all blasted up into the thigh and genitals when the bomb they stepped on went off. So if you plan to walk in mined areas, it's better to wear tennis shoes. Safer than combat boots. Anyway, these guys who are setting off the bombs are who the Western press calls freedom fighters. . . . And you want to investigate the *government*?'

'There are innocent Tamils in the south being killed too,' Sarath said. 'Terrible killings. You should read the reports.'

'I get the reports.' Gamini laid his head back. It was resting against her thigh but he seemed unaware of this. 'We're all fucked, aren't we. We don't know what to do about it. We just throw ourselves into it. Just no more high horses, please. This is a war on foot.'

'Some of the reports . . .' she said. 'There are letters from parents who have lost children. Not something you can put aside, or get over in a hurry.'

She touched his shoulder. He brought his hand up for a moment and then his head slipped away and soon she saw he had fallen asleep. His skull, his uncombed hair, the weight of his tiredness on her lap. *Sleep come free me.* The words of a song in her head, she could not find the tune that went with it. *Sleep come free me. . . .* She would remember later that Sarath was looking out into the black shift of the sea.

*A*mygdala.

The name had sounded Sri Lankan when Anil first heard it. Studying at Guy's Hospital in London, having cut tissue away to reveal a small knot of fibres made up of nerve cells. Near the stem of the brain. The professor standing beside her gave her the word for it. *Amygdala*.

'What does it mean?'

'Nothing. It's a location. It's the dark aspect of the brain.'

'I don't—'

'A place to house fearful memories.'

'Just fear?'

'We're not too certain of that. Anger too, we think, but it specializes in fear. It is pure emotion. We can't clarify it further.'

'Why not?'

'Well—is it an inherited thing? Are we speaking of ancestral fear? Fears from childhood? Fear of what might happen in old age? Or fear if we commit a crime? It could just be projecting fantasies of fear in the body.'

'As in dreams.'

'As in dreams,' he agreed. 'Though sometimes dreams are not the result of fantasy but old habits we don't know we have.'

'So it's something created and made by us, by our own histories, is that right? A knot in this person is different from a knot in another, even if they are from the same family. Because we each have a different past.'

He paused before speaking again, surprised at the degree of her interest. 'I don't think we know yet how similar the knots are, or if there are essential patterns. I've always liked those nineteenth-century novels where brothers and sisters in different cities could feel the same pains, have the same fears. . . . But I digress. We don't know, Anil.'

'It sounds Sri Lankan, the name.'

'Well, check its derivation. It doesn't sound scientific.'

'No. Some bad god.'

She remembers the almond knot. During autopsies her secret habit of detour is to look for the amygdala, this nerve bundle which houses fear—so it governs everything. How we behave and make decisions, how we seek out safe marriages, how we build houses that we make secure.

Driving with Sarath once. He asked, '*Is your tape recorder off?*' 'Yes.' 'There are at least two unauthorized places of detention in Colombo. One of the locations is off Havelock Road in Kollupi-tiya. Some of those picked up are there for a month, but the torture itself doesn't last that long. Most can be broken within an hour. Most of us can be broken by just the possibility of what might happen.'

'Is your tape recorder off?' he had said. 'Yes, it's off.' And only then had he talked.

'*I wanted to find one law to cover all of living. I found fear. . . .*'

Anil's name—the one she'd bought from her brother at the age of thirteen—had another stage to go through before it settled. By the time Anil was sixteen, she was taut and furious within the family. Her parents brought her to an astrologer in Wellawatta in an attempt to mollify these aspects of her nature. The man wrote down her birth hour and date, subtracted and fractioned them, considered her neighbouring stars and, not realizing the involved commerce behind it, said the problem resided in her name. Her tempestuousness could be harnessed with a name change. Unknown to him was the deal that had involved Gold Leaf cigarettes and rupees. He spoke with a voice that approached serenity and wisdom in the small cubicle, behind whose curtain other families waited in the hall hoping to overhear gossip and family history. What they heard were loud insistent refusals from the girl. The astrologer-soothsayer had eventually compromised his solution down to a simple appendage—the addition of an *e*, so she would be *Anile*. It would make her and her name more feminine, the *e* would allow the fury to curve away. But she refused even this.

Looking back, she could see her argumentativeness was only a phase. There is often a point in a person's life where there is bodily anarchy: young boys whose hormones are going mad, young girls bouncing like a shuttlecock in the family politics between a father and a mother. Girls and their dad, girls and their mum. It was a minefield in one's teens, and it was only when the relationship between her parents broke down completely that she calmed and sailed, or essentially swam, through the next four years.

The family wars continued to reside in her, and hadn't left her when she went abroad to study medicine. In the forensic labs she made it a point to distinguish female and male traits as clearly as possible. She witnessed how women were much more easily discombobulated by the personal slights of a lover or husband; but they were better at dealing with calamity in professional work than men. They were geared to giving birth, protecting children, steering them through crisis. Men needed to pause and dress themselves in coldness in order to deal with a savaged body. In all her training in Europe and America she saw that again and again. Women doctors were more confident in chaos and accident, calmer in dealing with the fresh corpse of an old woman, a young beautiful man, small children. The times Anil would slip into woe were when she saw a dead child in clothes. A dead three-year-old with the clothes her parents had dressed her in.

We are full of anarchy. We take our clothes off because we shouldn't take our clothes off. And we behave worse in other countries. In Sri Lanka one is surrounded by family order, most people know every meeting you have during the day, there is nothing anonymous. But if I meet a Sri Lankan elsewhere in the world and we have a free afternoon, it doesn't necessarily happen, but each of us knows all hell could break loose. What is that quality in us? Do you think? That makes us cause our own rain and smoke?'

Anil is talking to Sarath, who in his path from youth to manhood, she suspects, remained held within parental principles. He, she is sure, obeyed while not necessarily believing the rules. He would not have known the realities of sexual freedom available to him, though his head might have loafed through anarchy. He, she suspects, is a shy man, in that sense of lacking the confidence to approach and proposition. In any case, she knows they both come from a society that has involved hazardous intrigues of love and marriage and an equally anarchic system of planetary influence. Sarath told her about the *henahuru* in his family during a rest-house meal. . . .

To be born under a certain star made people unsuitable as marriage partners. A woman born with Mars in the Seventh House was '*malefic.*' Whoever she married would die. Meaning, in the minds of Sri Lankans, she would in essence be responsible for his death, she would kill him.

Sarath's father, for instance, had two brothers. The older brother married a woman their family had known for years. He was dead within two years of a harsh fever, during which she nursed him day and night. There had been one child. The woman's grief and retreat from the world at this death were terrible. The second brother was called upon by the family to bring her back into the world, for the sake of the boy. He brought the child gifts, insisted on taking mother and son on his vacations up-country, and eventually he and the woman, the former wife of his brother, fell in love. In many ways it was a greater and more subtle love than had existed in the first marriage. The intention of passion and sharing had not been there at the start. The woman had been brought back into the world. There was gratefulness towards the younger and good-looking brother. So when, during a car ride, the fragment of desire emerged with her first laughter in a year, it must have seemed a betrayal of his former motive, which was simply generous concern for his brother's widow. They married, he cared for his brother's child. They had a daughter, and within a year and a half he too fell ill and died in the arms of his wife.

It turned out, of course, that the woman was *malefic*. The only one she could have married safely was a man with the same star pattern. Thus any man born under such a star was sought after by such women. Men who were *malefic* also had to marry a woman with the same star, but it was believed that women in this state were considerably more dangerous than men. When a *malefic* man married a non*malefic* woman, she did not necessarily die. But if a woman did, the man would always die. She was *henahuru,* literally 'a pain in the neck.' Though more dangerous.

Ironically, Sarath, the son of the third brother, born some years later and having no connection with the wife of the first two brothers, was born with Mars in the Seventh House. 'My father married the woman he fell in love with,' Sarath says. 'He did not even consult her stars. I was born. My brother was born. I heard the story years later. I saw it as just an old wives' tale, random celestial positioning. Such beliefs seem a medieval comfort. I could say, for instance, that during the years I studied abroad I had Jupiter in my head and it helped me pass my exams. And when I returned, Venus replaced it and I fell in love. Venus is sometimes not good, it can make you frivolous in judgement. But these are not beliefs I hold.'

'Neither do I,' she says. 'We do it to ourselves.'

Anil had come out of her first class at Guy's Hospital in London with just one sentence in her exercise book: *The bone of choice would be the femur.*

She loved the way the lecturer had stated it, offhand, but with the air of a pompatus. As if this piece of information were the first rule needed before they could progress to greater principles. Forensic studies began with that one thighbone.

What surprised Anil as the teacher delineated the curriculum and the field of study was the quietness of the English classroom. In Colombo there was always a racket. Birds, lorries, fighting dogs, a kindergarten's lessons of rote, street salesmen—all their sounds entered through open windows. There was no chance of an ivory tower existing in the tropics. Anil wrote Dr. Endicott's sentence down and a few minutes later underlined it with her ballpoint in the hushed quiet. For the rest of the hour she just listened and watched the lecturer's mannerisms.

It was while studying at Guy's that Anil found herself in the smoke of one bad marriage. She was in her early twenties and was to hide this episode from everyone she met later in life. Even now she wouldn't replay it and consider the level of damage. She saw it more as some contemporary fable of warning.

He too was from Sri Lanka, and in retrospect she could see that she had begun loving him because of her loneliness. She could cook a curry with him. She could refer to a specific barber in Bambalapitiya, could whisper her desire for jaggery or jakfruit and be understood. That made a difference in the new, too brittle country. Perhaps she herself was too tense with uncertainty and shyness. She had expected to feel alien in England only for a few weeks. Uncles who had made the same journey a generation earlier had spoken romantically of their time abroad. They suggested that the right remark or gesture would open all doors. Her father's friend Dr. P. R. C. Peterson had told the story of being sent to school in England as an eleven-year-old. On the first day he was called a 'native' by a classmate. He stood up at once and announced to the teacher, 'I'm sorry to say this, sir, but Roxborough doesn't know who I am. He called me a "native." That's the wrong thing to do. *He* is the native and I'm the visitor to the country.'

But acceptance was harder than that. Having been a mild celebrity in Colombo because of her swimming, Anil was shy without the presence of her talent, and found it difficult to enter conversations. Later, when she developed her gift for forensic work, she knew one of the advantages was that her skill signalled her existence—like a neutral herald.

In her first month in London she'd been constantly confused by the geography around her. (What she kept noticing about Guy's Hospital was the number of doors!) She missed two classes in her first week, unable to find the lecture room. So for a while she began arriving early each morning and waited on the front steps for Dr. Endicott, following him through the swing doors, stairways, grey-and-pink corridors, to the unmarked classroom. (She once followed him and startled him and others in the men's bathroom.)

She seemed timid even to herself. She felt lost and emotional. She murmured to herself the way one of her spinster aunts did. She didn't eat much for a week and saved enough money to phone Colombo. Her father was out and her mother was unable to come to the phone. It was about one in the morning and she had woken her *ayah*, Lalitha. They talked for a few minutes, until they were both weeping, it felt, at the far ends of the world. A month later she fell within the spell of her future, and soon-to-be, and eventually ex-, husband.

It seemed to her he had turned up from Sri Lanka in bangles and on stilts. He too was a medical student. He was not shy. Within days of their meeting he focussed his wits entirely on Anil—a many-armed seducer and note writer and flower bringer and telephone-message leaver (he had quickly charmed her landlady). His organized passion surrounded her. She had the sense that he had never been lonely or alone before meeting her. He had panache in the way he could entice and choreograph the other medical students. He was funny. He had cigarettes. She saw how he mythologized their rugby positions and included such things in the fabric of their conversations until they were familiar touchstones—a trick that never left any of them at a loss for words. A team, a gang, that was in fact only two weeks deep. They each had an epithet. Lawrence who had thrown up once on the Underground, the siblings Sandra and Percy Lewis whose family scandals were acknowledged and forgiven, Jackman of the wide brows.

He and Anil were married quickly. She briefly suspected that for him it was another excuse for a party that would bond them all. He was a fervent lover, even with his public life to choreograph. He certainly opened up the geography of the bedroom, insisting on lovemaking in their nonsoundproof living room, on the wobbly sink in the shared bathroom down the hall, on the boundary line quite near the long-stop during a county cricket match. These private acts in an almost public sphere echoed his social nature. There seemed to be no difference for him between privacy and friendship with acquaintances. Later she would read that this was the central quality of a monster. Still, there was considerable pleasure on both their parts during this early period. Though she realized it was going to be crucial for her to come back to earth, to continue her academic studies.

When her father-in-law visited England he swept them up and took them out to dinner. The son was for once quiet, and the father attempted to persuade them to return to Colombo and have his grandchildren. He kept referring to himself as a philanthropist, which appeared to give him a belief that he was always on higher moral ground. As the dinner progressed she felt that every trick in the Colombo Seven social book was being used against her. He objected to her having a full-time career, keeping her own name, was annoyed at her talking back. When she described classroom autopsies during the trifle, the father had been outraged. 'Is there nothing you won't do?' And she had replied, 'I won't go to crap games with barons and earls.'

The next day the father lunched alone with his son, then flew back to Colombo.

At home the two of them fought now over everything. She was suspicious of his insights and understanding. He appeared to spend all his spare energy on empathy. When she wept, he would weep. She never trusted weepers after that. (Later, in the American Southwest, she would avoid those television shows with weeping cowboys and weeping priests.) During this time of claustrophobia and marital warfare, sex was the only mutual constant. She insisted on it as much as he. She assumed it gave the relationship some normality. Days of battle and fuck.

The disintegration of the relationship was so certain on her part that she would never replay any of their days together. She had been fooled by energy and charm; he had wept and burrowed under her intelligence until she felt she had none left. Venus, as Sarath would say, had been in her head, when it should have been the time of Jupiter.

She would return from the lab in the evenings and be met by his jealousy. At first this presented itself as sexual jealousy, then she saw it was an attempt to limit her research and studies. It was the first handcuff of marriage, and it almost buried her in their small flat in Ladbroke Grove. After she escaped him she would never say his name out loud. If she saw his handwriting on a letter she never opened it, fear and claustrophobia rising within her. In fact, the only reference to the era of her marriage she allowed into her life was Van Morrison's 'Slim Slow Slider' with its mention of Ladbroke Grove. Only the song survived. And only because it referred to separation.

> *Saw you early this morning*
> *With your brand-new boy and your Cadillac . . .*

She would sing along hoping that he did not also join in with his sentimental heart, wherever he was.

> *You've gone for something,*
> *And I know you won't be back.*

Otherwise the whole marriage and divorce, the hello and good-bye, she treated as something illicit that deeply embarrassed her. She left him as soon as their term at Guy's Hospital was over, so he could not locate her. She had plotted her departure for the end of term to avoid the harassment he was fully capable of; he was one of those men with time on his hands. *Cease and desist!* she had scrawled formally on his last little whining billet-doux before mailing it back to him.

She emerged with no partner. Cloudless at last. She was unable to bear the free months before she could begin classes again, before she could draw her studies close to her, more intimately and seriously than she had imagined possible. When she did return she fell in love with working at night, and sometimes she couldn't bear to leave the lab, just rested her happily tired dark head on the table. There was no curfew or compromise with a lover anymore. She got home at midnight, was up at eight, every casebook and experiment and investigation alive in her head and reachable.

Eventually she heard he'd returned to Colombo. And with his departure there was no longer any need to remember favourite barbers and restaurants along the Galle Road. Her last conversation in Sinhala was the distressed chat she'd had with Lalitha that ended with her crying about missing egg *rulang* and curd with jaggery. She no longer spoke Sinhala to anyone. She turned fully to the place she found herself in, focussing on anatomical pathology and other branches of forensics, practically memorizing Spitz and Fisher. Later she won a scholarship to study in the United States, and in Oklahoma became caught up in the application of the forensic sciences to human rights. Two years later, in Arizona, she was studying the physical and chemical changes that occurred in bones not only during life but also after death and burial.

She was now alongside the language of science. The femur was the bone of choice.

Anil stood in the Archaeological Offices in Colombo. She moved down the hall from map to map. Each one depicted an aspect of the island: climate, soil, plantation, humidity, historical ruins, birds, insect life. Traits of the country like those of a complex friend. Sarath was late. When he arrived they would load up the jeep.

'. . . Don't know much en-tomology,' she sang, looking at the map of mines—a black scattering of them like filaments. She glanced at herself reflected vaguely in the map's glass. She was in jeans, sandals and a loose silk shirt.

If she were working in America she would probably be listening to a Walkman while sawing off slim rings of bone with the microtone. This was an old tradition among the people she'd worked with in Oklahoma. Toxicologists and histologists always insisted on rock and roll. You stepped in through the airtight door and some heavy metal would be bumping and thrashing through the speakers, while Vernon Jenkins, who was thirty-six years old and weighed ninety pounds, studied lung tissue mounted on a slide. Around him it could have been civil war at the Fillmore. Next door was the Guard Shack, where people entered to identify dead relatives and friends, unaware of the music because of the airtight room, unaware of the shorthand descriptions circulating over the transistor headset intercoms: '*Bring up the Lady in the Lake.*' '*Bring up the by-herselfer.*'

She loved their rituals. The people in the lab would traipse into the greenroom at lunchtime with their thermoses and sandwiches and watch *The Price Is Right,* all of them in awe at this other civilization, as if only they—working in a building where the dead outnumbered the living—were in a normal world.

It was in Oklahoma, within a month of her arrival, that they established the Fuck Yorick School of Forensics. This was not just a principle of necessary levity but the name of their bowling team. Wherever she worked, first in Oklahoma, then in Arizona, her cohorts ended the evenings with beer in one hand, a cheese taco in the other, cheering or insulting teams and scuffing along the edges of the bowling alleys in their shoes from the planet Andromeda. She had loved the Southwest, missed being one of the boys, and was now light-years beyond the character she had been in London. They would go through a heavy day's work load, then drive to the wild suburban bars and clubs on the outskirts of Tulsa or Norman, with Sam Cooke in their hearts. In the greenroom a list was tacked up of every bowling alley in Oklahoma with a liquor license. They ignored job offers that came from dry counties. They snuffed out death with music and craziness. The warnings of *carpe diem* were on gurneys in the hall. They heard the rhetoric of death over the intercom; 'vaporization' or 'microfragmentation' meant the customer in question had been blown to bits. They couldn't miss death, it was in every texture and cell around them. No one changed the radio dial in a morgue without a glove on.

Meanwhile, bright tungsten bulbs gave the labs a clear optic light, the music in Toxicology was perfect for sit-ups and stretches when you found your neck and back had become tense from close-focus work. And around her was a quick good-old-boy debate and an explanation of a dead body in a car.

'When'd they report her missing?'

'She's been gone, lo, these five or six years.'

'She drove into the lake, Clyde. She already had to stop the car once to open a gate. She'd been drinking. Her husband said she just took the dog and left.'

'No dog in the car?'

'No dog in the car. I wouldn't have missed a Chihuahua, though it was full of mud. Her bones had demineralized. Car lights were on. Skip the photo, Rafael.'

'So—when she opened the gate she let the dog free. She already had a plan. It's a by-herselfer. When the car started filling up, she lost it and climbed into the back seat. That's where she was found. Right?'

'She should have knocked off her husband. . . .'

'He could have been a saint.'

Anil would always love the clatter and verbal fling of pathologists.

She had arrived in Colombo directly from working in sparse high-tech desert towns of the American Southwest. Although her last location, Borrego Springs, hadn't seemed, at the start, enough of a real desert to satisfy her. Too many cappuccino bars and clothing shops on the main street. But after a week she was comfortable in what was really a narrow strip of civilization, a few mid-twentieth-century luxuries surrounded by the starkness of the desert. The beauty of the place was subtle. In the southwestern deserts you needed to look twice at emptiness, you needed to take your time, the air like ether, where things grew only with difficulty. On the island of her childhood she could spit on the ground and a bush would leap up.

The first time Anil had gone into the desert, her guide had a water-mist bottle attached to his belt. He gestured her over, sprayed the thin leaves of a plant and pulled her head down towards it. She inhaled the smell of creosote. The plant spilled this toxic quality when it rained, to keep away anything that tried to grow too near it—and so reserved the small area around it for its own water supply.

She learned about agave, which had at least seven uses, among them its thorn as a needle, its fibres as thread. She saw cheese bushes, dyeweed, dead-man's-fingers (a succulent you could eat only during one month of the year), smoke trees with their rare system of roots (an exact underground reflection of their size and shape above ground), and ocotillo, which dropped its leaves to preserve moisture. And plants whose colours seemed washed out and those that doubled their rich colours in twilight. She spent as little time as possible in the small house she shared on H Street. She was usually within the flat-roofed paleontology lab by seven-thirty with a coffee and a croissant. In the evenings she jeeped into the desert with her co-workers. There had been zebras here three million years before. Camels. All the usual browsers and grazers. She walked above the bones of these great defunct creatures, on atolls left from ocean days seven million years earlier. There was a slight flirtation as she brushed the hand of someone passing binoculars to her to search out a sparrow hawk.

Once again she discovered the passion for bowling among forensic anthropologists. Perhaps too much care during the day picking up fragments with tweezers or using whisper brushes made them want to hurl things around with six-drink abandon. There was no alley in Borrego Springs, so each night they'd clamber into a museum van and drive out of the valley into nearby hill towns. They brought their own 'hammers'—specially weighted balls for competition bowling. All through these nights, in spite of the active jukebox in the Quonset hut, she kept singing a woeful song: *Better days in jail, with your back turned towards the wall. . . .* Though there was no sadness in her during this time. It was as if she was expecting the sadness of that song to reach her eventually, almost knowing there would be a conflict with Cullis when he arrived.

Lovers who read stories or look at paintings about love do so supposedly for clarity. But the more confusing and anarchic the story, the more those caught in love will believe it. There are only a few great and trustworthy love drawings. And in these works is an aspect that continues to remain unordered and private, no matter how famous they become. They bring no sanity, give just a blue tormented light.

The writer Martha Gellhorn had said, 'The best relationship is with someone who lives five blocks away with a great sense of humour and who is preoccupied with his work.' Well, that was her lover Cullis, though make it five states, make it five thousand miles. Make him married.

It seemed they loved each other most when they were apart. They were too careful when together, when the extremes of possible joy remained dangerous. She had been content in Borrego Springs with just their phone conversations. Women love distance, he'd said to her once.

What happened in Borrego Springs took place during their first night together. She needed to be at work early the next day: something unexpected had come up. A beautiful new tusk, but she didn't tell him that. He had arrived a few hours earlier, having flown a thousand miles. His sullenness and annoyance at the change of weekend plans forced an old fury out of her. They had been singing their fucking arias of romance with limits for too long.

She rose from the bed in Borrego and took a shower sitting on the edge of the bath, facing the rain of it. Her tight, furious wrists. Steam filled the room. A week before Cullis's arrival she had booked a room for him, for them, at the Una Palma Motel. He was to come in on the eight-o'clock bus from the airport on a Friday night to coincide with her three-day weekend. Then they had unearthed the tusk.

Meeting him at the bus depot she gave him a carefully selected sprig of desert lavender, which he broke trying to insert into his buttonhole.

*

A good archaeologist can read a bucket of soil as if it were a complex historical novel. If a bone had been grazed by any kind of stone, Sarath, she knew, could follow such grains of evidence to their likely origin. As she had taken the few fragments of the damaged section of Sailor's skull and reconstructed it with a glue gun. But in Colombo she couldn't locate half the equipment she and Sarath really needed, equipment they had in excess in America. It would be picks and shovels, strings and stones. She'd gone to Cargill's department store and picked up a couple of shaving brushes and a whisk.

When Sarath finally arrived at the Archaeological Offices, he joined her by the wall maps. It was a few days after their evening on Galle Face Green with his brother. She had tried reaching Sarath the next day, but he seemed to have disappeared, gone to ground. In the meantime a package had come for her from Chitra, so during that first afternoon she consumed the entomologist's badly typed notes, then pulled a road map out of her bag.

Now, on this Sunday morning, Sarath had called at dawn, apologizing not for the hour but for being away, out of touch. He'd asked her to meet him at the offices, 'in an hour,' he said. 'You know how to get there? You go right from your place and fall into Buller's Road.'

She'd hung up, looking at the luxury of the bed, and went off to shower.

'I have samples from the first burial site,' he said, 'taken from the cranial cavities. Probably from a swamp. They buried him temporarily in wet earth. It makes sense. Less digging. They could have put him in a paddy field, then taken him later to the restricted area and hidden him there to disguise the fact that he was contemporary. Anyway, I think the original burial was in this general vicinity'—he pointed—'Ratnapura district. That's southeast from here. We need to check the water tables.'

'Somewhere where there are fireflies,' she said. And he looked at her with a blank face.

'We can be more specific, we can make a smaller radius,' she continued. 'Fireflies. So not a busy settlement. Somewhere more open. Like a riverbank that people do not go to. Chitra, the entomologist I told you about—those marks that looked like freckles, she came to the boat and studied them and made notes. She has hundreds of charts of insect life on the island. She said it was pupae-encagle glue, from the "shout-and-die" cicadas—you find them in forest areas like Ritigala. Here—she drew a map for us of the possible places—they are all further south, which links with your soil results. Somewhere on the outskirts of Sinharaja Forest, maybe.'

'On the north side of it,' he said. 'The soil on the other peripheries wouldn't fit.'

'Okay, then this stretch here.'

Sarath drew a rectangle with a red felt pen on the glass that covered the map. Weddagala to the west, Moragoda to the east. Ratnapura and Sinharaja.

'Somewhere in here is a swamp or small lake, a *pokuna* in the forest,' he said, clarifying.

'Who else is there, I wonder.'

Since the Archaeological Offices were deserted, they took their time collecting whatever maps and books they needed. Sarath was walking in and out of the building, packing the jeep he had borrowed. She had no idea how long they would be away from Colombo, or where they would stay. Another of Sarath's favourite rest houses perhaps. While he looked through various soil charts she grabbed a field manual from the library shelves.

'So we stay where? In Ratnapura?' She said it loud. She liked the echoes in this large building.

'Beyond that. There is a place we can stay, a *walawwa*, an old family estate—we can continue working there. With luck it's still empty. Sailor must have been killed somewhere in that area, perhaps even came from there. We can try to find Palipana's artist on the way. I suggest you break contact with Chitra.'

'And *you've* told no one.'

'I have to meet officials, give them summaries of what we're up to, but for them our investigation is *nothing*. I haven't spoken about this.'

'How can you bear it.'

'You don't understand how bad things were. Whatever the government is possibly doing now, it was worse when there was real chaos. You were not here for that—the law abandoned by everyone, save a few good lawyers. Terror everywhere, from all sides. We wouldn't have survived with your rules of Westminster then. So illegal government forces rose up in retaliation. And we were caught in the middle. It was like being in a room with three suitors, all of whom had blood on their hands. In nearly every house, in nearly every family, there was knowledge of someone's murder or abduction by one side or another. I'll tell you a thing I saw. . . .'

Sarath was speaking in the empty offices, but he looked around.

'I was in the south. . . . It was almost evening, the markets closed. Two men, insurgents I suppose, had caught a man. I don't know what he had done. Maybe he had betrayed them, maybe he had killed someone, or disobeyed an order, or not agreed quickly enough. In those days the justice of death came in at any level. I don't know if he was to be executed, or harassed and lectured at, or in the most unlikely scenario, forgiven. He was wearing a sarong, a white shirt, the long sleeves rolled up. His shirt hung outside the sarong. He had no shoes on. And he was blindfolded. They propped him up, made him sit awkwardly on the crossbar of a bicycle. One of the captors sat on the saddle, the one with the rifle stood by his side. When I saw them they were about to leave. The man could see nothing that was going on around him or where he would be going.

'When they took off, the blindfolded man had to somehow hang on. One hand on the handlebars, but the other he had to put around the neck of his captor. It was this necessary intimacy that was disturbing. They wobbled off, the man with the rifle following on another bike.

'It would have been easier if they had all walked. But this felt in an odd way ceremonial. Perhaps a bike was a form of status for them and they wished to use it. Why transport a blindfolded victim on a bicycle? It made all life seem precarious. It made all of them more equal. Like drunk university students. The blindfolded man had to balance his body in tune with his possible killer. They cycled off and at the far end of the street, beyond the market buildings, they turned and disappeared. Of course the reason they did it that way was so none of us would forget it.'

'What did you do?'

'Nothing.'

There are images carved into or painted on rock—a perspective of a village seen from the height of a nearby hill, a single line depicting a woman's back bent over a child—that have altered Sarath's perceptions of his world. Years ago he and Palipana entered unknown rock darknesses, lit a match and saw hints of colour. They went outside and cut branches off a rhododendron, and returned and set them on fire to illuminate the cave, smoke from the green wood acrid and filling the burning light.

These were discoveries made during the worst political times, alongside a thousand dirty little acts of race and politics, gang madness and financial gain. War having come this far like a poison into the bloodstream could not get out.

Those images in caves through the smoke and firelight. The night interrogations, the vans in daylight picking up citizens at random. That man he had seen taken away on a bicycle. Mass disappearances at Suriyakanda, reports of mass graves at Ankumbura, mass graves at Akmeemana. Half the world, it felt, was being buried, the truth hidden by fear, while the past revealed itself in the light of a burning rhododendron bush.

Anil would not understand this old and accepted balance. Sarath knew that for her the journey was in getting to the truth. But what would the truth bring them into? It was a flame against a sleeping lake of petrol. Sarath had seen truth broken into suitable pieces and used by the foreign press alongside irrelevant photographs. A flippant gesture towards Asia that might lead, as a result of this information, to new vengeance and slaughter. There were dangers in handing truth to an unsafe city around you. As an archaeologist Sarath believed in truth as a principle. That is, he would have given his life for the truth if the truth were of any use.

And privately (Sarath would consider and weigh this before sleep), he would, he knew, also give his life for the rock carving from another century of the woman bending over her child. He remembered how they had stood before it in the flickering light, Palipana's arm following the line of the mother's back bowed in affection or grief. An unseen child. All the gestures of motherhood harnessed. A muffled scream in her posture.

The country existed in a rocking, self-burying motion. The disappearance of schoolboys, the death of lawyers by torture, the abduction of bodies from the Hokandara mass grave. Murders in the Muthurajawela marsh.

Ananda

They weaved towards the inland hills.

'We don't have the equipment to do that sort of work here,' she said. 'You know that.'

'If the artist is as good as Palipana says, he'll improvise the tools. Have you ever been involved with this kind of thing?'

'No. Never done reconstruction. I have to say we sort of scorn it. They look like historical cartoons to us. Dioramas, that sort of thing. Are you getting a cast made of the skull?'

'Why?'

'Before you give it to him—whoever this noncertified person is. I'm glad we've decided on a drunk, by the way.'

'You can't get a cast done without waking up all of Colombo. We'll just give him the skull.'

'I wouldn't.'

'And it would take weeks to arrange. This isn't Brussels or America. Only the weapons in this country are state-of-the-art.'

'Well, let's find the guy first and see if he can even hold a paint-brush without shaking.'

They arrived at a scattering of mud-and-wattle huts on the edge of a village. It turned out the man named Ananda Udugama was no longer living with his in-laws but in the next town, at a petrol station. They drove on, and she watched as Sarath got out and walked up and down the one street of the town, asking for him.

When they located him it appeared that he had just woken from an early-evening sleep. Sarath gestured to her and she joined them.

Sarath explained what they wanted him to do, mentioned Palipana, and that he would be paid. The man, who wore thick spectacles, said he would need certain things—erasers, the kind on the end of school pencils, small needles. And he said he needed to see the skeleton. They opened the back of the jeep. The man used their squat flashlight to study the skeleton, running it up and down the ribs, the arcs and curves. Anil felt there was little he could learn from such a viewing.

Sarath persuaded the man to come with them. After a slight shake of the head, he went into the room he was living in and came out with his belongings in a small cardboard box.

Two hours before Ratnapura they were stopped by a roadblock, soldiers moving languidly out of the shadows towards them from both sides of the road. They sat in silence, falsely polite, handing over their identity cards when a hand snaked into the jeep and snapped its fingers. Anil's card seemed to give the soldiers trouble, and one of them opened her door and stood waiting. She was not aware of what was expected of her until Sarath explained under his breath; then she climbed out.

The soldier leaned into the jeep and lifted out her shoulder bag and emptied it noisily on the hood. Everything out there in the sun, a pair of glasses and a pen sliding off onto the tarmac, where he let them remain. When she moved forward to pick them up he put his hand out. In the noon sunlight he slowly handled every object in front of him: unscrewed and sniffed a small bottle of eau de cologne, looked at the postcard with the bird, emptied her wallet, inserted a pencil into a cassette and twisted it silently.

There was nothing of real value in her bag, but the slowness of his actions embarrassed and irritated her. He opened the back of her alarm clock and pulled out the battery, and when he saw the packets of batteries still sealed in plastic, he collected them too, and gave them to another soldier, who carried them to a sand-bagged cave on the side of the road. Leaving the bag and its contents, the soldier walked away and signalled them on, without even looking back. 'Don't do anything,' she heard Sarath say from the darkness of the jeep.

She gathered her things into the bag and got into the passenger seat.

'The batteries are essential for making homemade bombs,' Sarath explained.

'I know that,' she snapped back. 'I know that.'

As they drove away she turned to see Ananda, unconcerned, twirling a pencil.

A *walawwa* in Ekneligoda, the house belonging to a family named Wickramasinghe, who had lived in it for five generations. The last Wickramasinghe, an artist, had lived there during the 1960s. After his death the two-hundred-year-old house was taken over by the Archaeological Society and Historical Board. (There was a distant family member connected with archaeology.) But when the region became unsafe and rife with disappearances, the building was no longer inhabited, and like a well that has gone dry it took on a sense of absence.

Sarath had come to this family estate for the first time as a boy, when his younger brother was expected to die. '*Diphtheria,*' they had said. '*Something white in the mouth,*' the doctors had whispered to his parents. So before Gamini was brought home from the hospital, Sarath, along with his favourite books, was packed into the car and driven to Ekneligoda, out of harm's way. The Wickramasinghes were travelling in Europe, so for two months the thirteen-year-old, looked after by just an *ayah,* ranged into their gardens, drew maps of the mongoose paths in the thickets, created imaginary towns and neighbours. While on Greenpath Road in Colombo the family closed their doors and prepared to look after the dying younger son, ensconced like a small prince and armed with the secret of death he himself did not know about.

In his thirties Sarath would visit the house again whenever field trips brought him into the region, but he had not been back for at least a decade, and now the dishevelled vacuum of the building and grounds depressed him. Still, he knew where the old keys were hidden on the lower strut of the fence, found the same eternal path of the mongoose through the thornbush thicket in the lower garden.

With Anil and Ananda at his side, he opened all the rooms so they could each choose a work space and bedroom, then locked the unwanted rooms once more. They would camp out in the smallest space needed, not sprawl over the property. He walked with Anil through a house that now seemed much smaller to him, and he felt himself to be in two eras. He described the paintings that had been on the walls in an earlier decade, when he had lived there for two months and evolved into a privacy he had perhaps never fully emerged from. Few survive diphtheria, it had been emphasized to him. And he had accepted with certainty the likelihood of his brother's death, that he would soon be the only son.

Now the whisper of Anil's foot was beside him. Then her quiet voice. '*What's that?*' They'd entered a room off the courtyard, where someone had charcoaled two Sinhala words in giant script on the walls. MAKAMKRUKA. And on the wall opposite, MADANARAGA. '*What's that? Are those names?*' 'No.' He reached up so his hand could touch the brown lettering.

'Not names. A *makamkruka* is—it's difficult to describe—a man who is a *makamkruka* is a churner, an agitator. Someone who perhaps sees things more truly by turning everything upside down. He's a devil almost, a *yaksa*. Though a *makamkruka*, strangely, guards the sacred spot in a temple ground. No one knows why this kind of person is honoured with such a responsibility.'

'And?'

'The other is stranger. *Madanaraga* means "with the speed of love," sexual arousal. It's the kind of word you find in ancient romances. Not in the vernacular.'

While Ananda laboured over the head, Anil was to continue work on Sailor's skeleton, trying to discover among other things his 'markers of occupation.' She had been with Sarath for more than three weeks now, and they were 'in the field,' not in contact with Sarath's political networks in the city. No one in Colombo would expect them to be camped in this family estate, close to the area where Sailor had possibly been buried the first time. Perhaps Sailor was locally 'important' or 'identifiable.' Here they would be closer to the source and they would be undisturbed.

The first morning they were there, Ananda Udugama had gone off without a word. Leaving Sarath frustrated and Anil carefully silent. She set up her workbench and temporary lab in a court-yard under a banyan's ragged shade and brought Sailor out with her. Sarath decided to do his own research work in the grand din-ing room. He would occasionally have to return to Colombo for supplies and to report in. There were no telephones, except for his on-again, off-again cell phone, and they felt isolated from the rest of the country.

Ananda had in fact, that first morning, woken early and walked to the nearby village market, bought some fresh toddy and established himself by the public well. He chatted with any-one who sat near him, shared his few cigarettes and watched the village move around him, with its distinct behaviour, its local body postures and facial characteristics. He wanted to discover what the people drank here, whether there was a specific diet that would puff up cheeks more than usual, whether lips would be fuller than in Batticaloa. Also the varieties of hairstyle, the quality of eyesight. Did they walk or cycle. Was coconut oil used in food and hair. He spent a day in the village and then went into the fields and collected mud in three sacks. He could mix the two browns and one black into a variety of shades. Then he bought several bottles of arrack in the village and returned to the *walawwa*.

He would be up at dawn and would park himself in a square of sun and move as it moved, the way a cat would. He may have looked at the skull now and then, but that was all. He would go to the village and return with kite papers in several colours, suet, food dyes and one day two old turntables and a random selection of 78s.

Of all the possible spaces in the large house Ananda had chosen the room the artist had worked in. He knew nothing about the history of the place but liked the light within this room, where the two words MAKAMKRUKA and MADANARAGA were written. The courtyard where Anil worked was just outside. The morning he actually began to work on the skull she heard music coming from his room. A tenor burst into song, sang with energy for a few moments, then slowed before the song ended. Curious, she went in, to see Ananda winding the gramophone. Beside it was another turntable, where he was moulding a clay base, on which the skull rested. His free hand could spin it to the left or right like a potter's wheel. He was already working on the throat. She stepped back and out.

She recognized the technique of face construction. He had marked several pins with red paint to represent the various thicknesses of the flesh over the bone, and then placed a thin layer of plasticine on the skull, thinning or thickening it according to the marks on the pins. Eventually he would press finer layers of rubber eraser onto the clay to build the face. Collaged this way with various household objects it would look like a five-and-dime monster.

For the three days of the week when Sarath was away in Colombo, there was little communication between her and Ananda, the eye-painter turned drunk gem-pit worker turned head-restorer. They shuffled about each other, rattling around the house, basic courtesies having dropped away after the first day. She continued to see this project as Sarath's folly.

In the evenings she carried whatever equipment might be damaged by rain into the granary. By then Ananda would be drinking. It hadn't become serious until he began working on the head. Now he was easily annoyed if his food had been moved around in the kitchen or if he cut himself with the X-acto, as he was always doing. Once, he shouldered his way into the afternoon sunlight and found her taking some bone measurements, and as he passed her his sarong brushed the table. She barked at him, so he turned in a fury and yelled back at her. This was followed by a silent and even subtler fury. He stalked to his room and she half expected the head to come rolling out.

She went looking for him that night, walking out of the house with a lamp. She was relieved he had not shown up for dinner (they cooked their own meals but ate together, silently). By ten-thirty he was still not back, and before she locked up the house—something he usually did—she felt she should make a brief gesture of searching for him, so with the lamp she walked out into the darkness. And he was there on a low wall, passed out, wearing just his sarong. She pulled him to his feet and staggered back with his weight and arms all over her.

Anil wasn't fond of drunks. She found nothing humorous or romantic about them. In the hallway, where she had steered him, he fell to the floor and was soon asleep. There was no way of waking him and getting him to move. She went to her room and returned with her Walkman and a tape. A little vengeance. She put the earphones on his head, switched the Walkman on. Tom Waits singing 'Dig, Dig, Dig' from *Snow White and the Seven Dwarfs* channeled itself into his inner brain, and he rose off the floor terrified. He was hearing, he must have thought, voices of the dead. He reeled, as if unable to escape the sounds within him, and finally ripped off the wires attached to his head.

She sat on the courtyard steps. The release of the moon so it stared down on what had been once the Wickramasinghe home. She buzzed the tape forward to Steve Earle's 'Fearless Heart,' with its intricate swagger. No one but Steve Earle for her in the worst times. There was a thump in her blood, a sexual hip in her movement, when she heard any of his songs of furious loss. So she moved half-dancing into the courtyard, past the skeleton of Sailor. It was a clear night and she could leave him there.

But undressing in her room she thought of him under the claustrophobia of plastic and went out and unpinned the sheets. So the wind and all the night were in Sailor. After the burnings and the burials, he was on a wooden table washed by the moon. She walked back to her room, the glory of the music now gone.

There were nights when Cullis would lie beside her, barely touching her with the tip of his finger. He would move down the bed, kissing her brown hip, her hair, to the cave within her. When they were apart he wrote how he loved the sound of her breath in those moments, the intake and release of it, paced and constant, as if preparing, as if knowing there was to be the long distance ahead. His hands on her thighs, his face wet with the taste of her, her open palm on the back of his neck. Or she sat above him and watched him come into her fast hand movements. The precise and inarticulate sounds of each witnessed by the other.

Ananda drifted in front of her—the emaciated body of a serious drinker, still shirtless. He rubbed his arms and bony chest with his hands, peering around the courtyard unaware that she was in one of its dark corners.

At her worktable he carefully put his hands behind him so as to be sure not to disturb anything, and bent over, looking through those thick spectacles at her calipers, the weight charts, as if he were within the hush of a museum. He bent down further and sniffed at the objects. A mind of science, she thought. Yesterday she had noticed how delicate his fingers were, dyed ochre as the result of his work.

Now Ananda picked up the skeleton and carried it in his arms.

She was in no way appalled by what he was doing. There had been hours when, locked in her investigations and too focussed by hours of intricacy, she too would need to reach forward and lift Sailor into her arms, to remind herself he was like her. Not just evidence, but someone with charms and flaws, part of a family, a member of a village who in the sudden lightning of politics raised his hands at the last minute, so they were broken. Ananda held Sailor and walked slowly with him and placed him back on the table, and it was then he saw Anil. She nodded imperceptibly to show there was no anger in her. Slowly rose and walked over to him. A small yellow leaf floated down and slipped into the skeleton's ribs and pulsed there.

She saw the two moons caught in the mirror of Ananda's glasses. It was a ramshackle pair—the lenses knitted onto the frame with wire and the stems wrapped in old cloth, rag really, so he could wipe or dry his fingers on them. Anil wished she could trade information with him, but she had long forgotten the subtleties of the language they once shared. She would have told him what Sailor's bone measurements meant in terms of posture and size. And he—God knows what insights he had.

In the afternoons when Ananda could go no further with the skull's reconstruction, he took it all apart, breaking up the clay. Strangely. It seemed a waste of time to her. But early the next morning he would know the precise thickness and texture to return to and could re-create the previous day's work in twenty minutes. Then he thought and composed the face a further step. It was as if he needed the warm-up of the past work to rush over so he could move with more confidence into the uncertainty that lay ahead. Thus there was nothing to see if she entered his room when he was not working. After just ten days, the room was more like a nest—rags and padding, mud and clay, colours daubed everywhere, the large letters above him on the wall.

Still, on this night, without words, there seemed to be a pact. The way he had respected the order of her tools, touching nothing, the way he raised Sailor into his arms. She saw the sadness in Ananda's face below what might appear a drunk's easy sentiments. The hollows that seemed gnawed at. Anil put out her hand and touched his forearm, and then left him alone in the courtyard. For the next few days they went back to their mutual silences. It was possible he had been very drunk that night and remembered nothing about it. Two or three times a day he would put on one of the old 78s and stand in his doorway, looking out at whatever was going on in her life in that courtyard.

At six in the morning she dressed, then began walking the mile to the school. A few hundred yards before she climbed the hill, the road narrowed into a bridge, a lagoon on one side, a salt river on the other. This is where Sirissa would start to see the teenagers, some with catapults hanging off their shoulders, some smoking. They would acknowledge her with their eyes but never speak to her, whereas she would always give a greeting. Later, when they saw her on the school grounds, they wouldn't acknowledge her in any way. She would turn after she had gone five yards past them at the bridge, still moving away from them, to catch their curious watching of her. She was not that much older. And they were hungry in their search for a pose, and perhaps only one or two of them would have a knowledge already of women. They were aware of Sirissa's silk-like hair, her litheness as she turned around to look at them, as she kept on walking—a sensual gesture they came to expect.

It was always six-thirty a.m. when she reached the bridge. There would be a few prawn boats, a man up to his neck in the water, whose hands, out of sight, would be straightening the nets that had been dropped by his son from a boat during the night. The man moved in his quietness as she walked past him. From here Sirissa would reach the school in ten minutes, change in a cubicle, soak rags in a bucket, and begin cleaning the blackboards. Then sweep the rooms free of leaves that had slipped in through the grilled windows if there had been wind or a storm in the night. She worked in the empty school grounds until she heard the gradual arrival of the children, the teenagers, the older youths, like a gradual arrival of birds, voices deepening, as if it were a meeting called for in a jungle clearing. She would go among them and wipe clean the blackboards on the edge of the sand courtyard—used by the youngest children, who would sit on the earth in front of the teachers learning their Sinhala, their mathematics, their English: 'The peacock is a beautiful bird. . . . It has a long tail!'

There was a strict stillness during the morning classes. Then, at one in the afternoon, the courtyard filled with noise and bodies again, the school day completed, the students in their white uniforms scattering to three or four villages that fed the school, back into their other life. She ate her lunch at the desk in the math classroom. She opened up the leaf with the food inside, held it in her left hand and wandered beside the blackboard, collecting the food with three fingers and a thumb, not even looking down, but peering at the chalked numbers and symbols to catch and follow the path of the argument. She had been good at theorems in school. Their logic fell clearly in front of her. She could pick an edge and fold it neatly into an isosceles. She would always listen to the teachers as she worked in the flower beds or hallways. Now she washed her hands at the tap and began her walk home, a few teachers still in the hall, a few later cycling past her.

In the evenings during the government curfews she remained indoors, with a lamp and a book in her room. Her husband would be with her in a week. She'd turn a page and find a drawing of her by Ananda on a frail piece of paper he had tucked into the later reaches of the book's plot. Or a line drawing of a wasp she had disliked, its giant eyes. She would have preferred to walk into the streets after dinner, for she loved the closing up of stores. The streets dark, the fall of electric light out of the shops. It was her favourite time, like putting away the senses one by one, this shop of drinks, this cassette store, these vegetables packed away, and the street growing darker and darker as she walked on. And a bicycle riding off with three sacks of potatoes balanced on it into even purer darkness. Into the other life. That existence. For when people leave our company in our time we are never certain of seeing them again, or seeing them unaltered. So Sirissa loved the calm of the night streets that no longer had commerce in them, like a theatre after the performance was over. Vimalarajah's herb shop, or his brother Vimalarajah's silver shop with a shutter halfway down its darkness, the light slowly dwarfed till it revealed just an inch under the metal door, a line of gold varnish, and then the turning off of a switch so that horizon disappeared. The air would breeze around her dress as she imagined herself walking without curfew. The pigeons settled in among the lightbulbs spelling out the name Cargill's. So many things happened during the feathers of night. The frantic running, the terrified, the scared, the pea-brain furious and tired professional men of death punishing another village of dissent.

At five-thirty in the morning, Sirissa wakes and bathes herself at the well behind the house she is living in. She dresses, eats some fruit, and leaves for the school. It is the same twenty-five-minute walk she is familiar with. She knows she will turn lazily after passing the boys on the bridge. There will be the familiar birds, Brahminy kites, perhaps a flycatcher. The road narrows. A hundred yards ahead of her is the bridge. Lagoon on the left. Salt river on the right. This morning there are no fishermen and it is an empty road. She is the first to walk it, being a servant at the school. Six-thirty a.m. Nobody to whirl for, her gesture that shows she knows she is equal to them. She is about ten yards from the bridge when she sees the heads of the two students on stakes, on either side of the bridge, facing each other. Seventeen, eighteen, nineteen years old . . . she doesn't know or care. She sees two more heads on the far side of the bridge and can tell even from here that she recognizes one of them. She would shrink down into herself, go back, but she cannot. She feels something is behind her, whatever is the cause of this. She desires to become nothing at all. Mind capable of nothing. She does not even think of releasing them from this public gesture. Cannot touch anything because everything feels alive, wounded and raw but alive. She begins running forward, past their eyes, her own shut dark until she is past them. Up the hill towards the school. She keeps running forward, and then she sees more.

Anil stood lost in the stricture of no movement, in a precise focus of thought. She had no idea how long she had been there in the courtyard, how long she had been thinking through all the possible trajectories of Sailor, but when she came out of it and moved, her neck felt as if it had an arrow in it.

The central truism in her work was that you could not find a suspect until you found the victim. And in spite of their knowledge that Sailor had probably been killed in this district, in spite of details of age and posture, her theorizing of height and weight, in spite of the "head composition" that she had not much faith in, it seemed unlikely that they would identify him; they still knew nothing about the world Sailor had come from.

And in any case, if they did identify him, if they did discover the details of his murder, what then? He was a victim among thousands. What would this change?

She remembered Clyde Snow, her teacher in Oklahoma, speaking about human rights work in Kurdistan: *One village can speak for many villages. One victim can speak for many victims.* She and Sarath both knew that in all the turbulent history of the island's recent civil wars, in all the token police investigations, not one murder charge had been made during the troubles. But this could be a clear case against the government.

However, without identifying Sailor, they had no victim yet.

Anil had worked with teachers who could take a seven-hundred-year-old skeleton and discover through evidence of physical stress or trauma in those bones what the person's profession had been. Lawrence Angel, her mentor at the Smithsonian, could, from just the curvature of a spine to the right, recognize a stonemason from Pisa, and from thumb fractures among dead Texans tell that they had spent long evenings gripping the saddle on mechanical barroom bulls. Kenneth Kennedy at Cornell University remembered Angel identifying a trumpet player from the scattered remains in a bus crash. And Kennedy himself, studying a first-millennium mummy of Thebes, discovered marked lines on the flexor ligaments of the phalanges and theorized the man was a scribe, the marks attributed to his constantly holding a stylus.

Ramazzini in his treatise on the diseases of tradesmen had begun it all, talking of metal poisoning among painters. Later the Englishman Thackrah spoke of pelvic deformations among weavers who sat for hours at their looms. ('Weaver's bottom,' Kennedy noted, may have led to Bottom the Weaver in *A Midsummer Night's Dream*.) Comparisons were made because of similar anatomical ailments between javelin throwers among Neolithic Saharans of the Niger and modern golf professionals.

These were the markers of occupation. . . .

The night before, Anil had leafed through Kennedy's charts in *Reconstruction of Life from the Skeleton,* one of her constant travelling companions. On Sailor's bones she could find no precise marker of occupational stress. As she stood utterly still in the courtyard, she realized there were *two* possible versions of a life that she could deduce from the skeleton in front of her. And the two aspects of the skeleton did not logically fit together. The first, from her reading of the bones, suggested 'activity' above the height of the shoulder. He had worked with his arms stretched out, reaching up or forward. A man who painted walls perhaps, or chiselled. But it appeared to be a harder activity than painting. And the arm joints showed a symmetrical use, so both arms had been active. His pelvis, trunk and legs also gave the suggestion of agility, something like the swivel of a man on a trampoline. Acrobat? Circus performer? Trapeze, because of the arms? But how many circuses were around in the Southern Province during the emergency? She remembered there had been many roaming ones in her childhood. And she remembered once seeing a children's book on extinct animals where one of the extinct creatures was an *acrobat*.

The other version of him was different. The left leg had been broken badly, in two places. (These wounds were not a part of his murder. She could tell the breaks had occurred about three years before his death.) And the heel bones—the heel bones suggested an alternate profile completely, a man static and sedentary.

Anil looked around the courtyard. Sarath was barely visible, sitting in the darkness of the house, while Ananda squatted comfortably in front of the head on the turntable, a lit beedi in his mouth. She could imagine the squint of his eyes behind his spectacles. She passed him as she walked to the granary cupboards. Then moved back.

'Sarath,' she said quietly, and he came out. He sensed the edge to her voice.

'I— Can you tell Ananda not to move. To stay as he is. That I'm going to have to touch him, okay?'

Sarath's glasses were on his nose. He looked at her.

'Do you understand me?'

'Not really. You want to touch him?'

'Just tell him not to move, okay?'

As soon as Sarath entered his work space, Ananda threw a cloth over the head. There was a brief conversation, then hesitant monosyllabic agreement repeated after each of Sarath's phrases. She walked in slowly and kneeled beside Ananda, but as soon as she touched him he jumped up.

She turned away in frustration.

'Ne, ne!' Sarath tried to explain once more. It took a while for them to arrange Ananda into exactly the same position he had been in.

'Get him to keep it taut, as if he was working.'

Anil took hold of Ananda's ankle in both hands. She pressed her thumbs into the muscle and cartilege, moved them up a few inches above his ankle bone. There was a dry laugh from Ananda. Then down to the heel again. 'Ask him why he works like this.' She was told by Sarath that he was comfortable.

'It's not comfortable,' she said. 'Nothing in the foot is relaxed. There's stress. The ligament is being stretched against the bone. There will be a permanent bruise to it. Ask him.'

'What?'

'Ask him why he works this way.'

'He's a carver. That's how he works.'

'But does he usually squat like this?'

Sarath asked the question and the two men rattled back and forth.

'He said he got used to squatting in the gem mines. The height down there is only about four feet. He was in them for a couple of years.'

'Thank you. Please, will you thank him. . . .'

She was excited.

'Sailor worked in a mine too. Come here, look at the strictures on the ankle bones of the skeleton—this is what Ananda has under his flesh. I *know* this. This was my professor's area of specialty. See this sediment on the bone, the buildup. I think Sailor worked in one of the mines. We need to get a chart of the mines in this area.'

'Are you talking about gem mines?'

'It could be anything. Also, this is just one aspect of his life, the rest is very different. He must have done something more active before he broke his leg. So we have a story about him, you see. A man who was active, an acrobat almost, then he was injured and had to work in a mine. What other mines do they have around here?'

There followed two days of storms when they had to stay indoors. As soon as the bad weather ended, Anil borrowed Sarath's cell phone, found an umbrella and went into a light rain. She clambered down a slope away from the trees and stalked across to the far edge of the paddy field, to where Sarath had told her there was the clearest reception.

She needed communication with the outside world. There was too much solitude in her head. Too much Sarath. Too much Ananda.

Dr. Perera at Kynsey Road Hospital answered the phone. It took a while for him to remember who she was, and he was startled to be told that she was speaking to him from a paddy field. What did she want?

She had wanted to talk to him about her father, knew she had been skirting the memory of him since her arrival on the island. She apologized for not calling and meeting him before she left Colombo. But on the phone Perera seemed muted and wary.

'You sound sick, sir. You should take a lot of liquids. A viral flu comes like that.'

She would not tell him where she was—Sarath had warned her

of that—and when he asked for the second time she pretended she could not hear, said, 'Hello . . . hello? Are you there, sir?' and hung up.

*

Anil moves in silence, the energy held back. Her body taut as an arm, the music brutal and loud in her head, while she waits for the rhythm to angle off so she can open her arms and leap. Which she does now, throwing her head back, her hair a black plume, back almost to the level of her waist. Throws her arms too, to hold the ground in her back flip, her loose skirt having no time to discover gravity and drop before she is on her feet again.

It is wondrous music to dance alongside—she has danced to it with others on occasions of joy and gregariousness, carousing through a party with, it seemed, all her energy on her skin, but this now is not a dance, does not contain even a remnant of the courtesy or sharing that is part of a dance. She is waking every muscle in herself, blindfolding every rule she lives by, giving every mental skill she has to the movement of her body. Only this will lift her backward into the air and pivot her hip to send her feet over her.

A scarf tied tight around her head holds the earphones to her. She needs music to push her into extremities and grace. She wants grace, and it happens here only on these mornings or after a late-afternoon downpour—when the air is light and cool, when there is also the danger of skidding on the wet leaves. It feels as if she could eject herself out of her body like an arrow.

Sarath sees her from the dining room window. He watches a person he has never seen. A girl insane, a druid in moonlight, a thief in oil. This is not the Anil he knows. Just as she, in this state, is invisible to herself, though it is the state she longs for. Not a moth in a man's club. Not the carrier and weigher of bones—she needs that side of herself too, just as she likes herself as a lover. But now it is herself dancing to a furious love song that can drum out loss, 'Coming In from the Cold,' dancing the rhetoric of a lover's parting with all of herself. She thinks she is most sane about love when she chooses damning gestures against him, against herself, against them together, against eros the bitter-sweet, consumed and then spat out in the last stages of their love story. Her weeping comes easy. It is for her in this state no more than sweat, no more than a cut foot she earns during the dance, and she will not stop for any of these, just as she would not change herself for a lover's howl or sweet grin, then or anymore.

She stops when she is exhausted and can hardly move. She will crouch and lean there, lie on the stone. A leaf will come down. Its click of applause. The music continues furious like blood moving for a few more minutes in a dead man. She lies under the sound and witnesses her brain coming back, lighting its candle in the dark. And breathes in and breathes out and breathes in and breathes out.

On the weekend, while they were in the front garden of the *walawwa*, Ananda sat down beside them and talked to Sarath in Sinhala.

'He has finished the head,' Sarath said, not even turning towards her but still watching Ananda's face. 'Apparently, he says, it's done. If there are any problems with it I suggest we don't complain, he's badly drunk. Save whatever hesitations. Or he might disappear on us.'

She said nothing and the two men continued speaking, the dusk settling around them within the sound of the frogs. She got up and strolled towards the twangings and croaks. She was lost in the antiphonies until she felt Sarath's hand on her shoulder.

'Come. Let's see it now.'

'Before he passes out? Yes, yes. *No* criticism.'

'Thank you.'

'I humour him. I humour you. When do I get my turn?'

'I don't think you like being humoured.'

'A favour then, sometime.'

In the courtyard a torch of twigs was stuck into the earth. Sailor's head was on a chair. Nothing else, only the two of them and the presence of the head.

The firelight set the face in movement. But what affected her—who felt she knew every physical aspect about Sailor, who had been alongside him now in his posthumous life as they travelled across the country, who had slept in a chair all night while he lay on the table in the Bandarawela rest house, who knew every mark of trauma from his childhood—was that this head was not just how someone possibly looked, it was a specific person. It revealed a distinct personality, as real as the head of Sarath. As if she was finally meeting a person who had been described to her in letters, or someone she had once lifted up as a child who was now an adult.

She sat on the step. Sarath was walking towards the head and then walking backwards, away from it. Then he would turn, as if to catch it unawares. She just watched it point-blank, coming to terms with it. There was a serenity in the face she did not see too often these days. There was no tension. A face comfortable with itself. This was unexpected coming from such a scattered and unreliable presence as Ananda. When she turned she saw that he had gone.

'It's so peaceful.' She spoke first.

'Yes. That's the trouble,' Sarath said.

'There's nothing wrong with that.'

'I know. It's what he wants of the dead.'

'He's younger-looking than I expected. I like the look on him. What do you mean by that? "What he wants of the dead"?'

'We have seen so many heads stuck on poles here, these last few years. It was at its worst a couple of years ago. You'd see them in the early mornings, somebody's night work, before the families heard about them and came and removed them and took them home. Wrapping them in their shirts or just cradling them. Someone's son. These were blows to the heart. There was only one thing worse. That was when a family member simply disappeared and there was no sighting or evidence of his existence or his death. In 1989, forty-six students attending school in Ratnapura district and some of the staff who worked there disappeared. The vehicles that picked them up had no number plates. A yellow Lancer had been seen at the army camp and was recognized during the roundup. This was at the height of the campaign to wipe out insurgent rebels and their sympathizers in the villages. Ananda's wife, Sirissa, disappeared at that time. . . .'

'My God.'

'He told me only recently.'

'I . . . I feel ashamed.'

'It's been three years. He still hasn't found her. He was not always like this. The head he has made is therefore peaceful.'

Anil rose and walked back into the dark rooms. She could no longer look at the face, saw only Ananda's wife in every aspect of it. She sat down in one of the large cane chairs in the dining room and began weeping. She could not face Sarath with this. Her eyes grew accustomed to the darkness, she could see the rectangular shape of a painting and beside it Ananda standing still, looking through the blackness at her.

*W*ho *were you crying for? Ananda and his wife?'*

'Yes,' she said. 'Ananda, Sailor, their lovers. Your brother working himself to death. There's only a mad logic here, no resolving. Your brother said something, he said, "You've got to have a sense of humour about all this—otherwise it makes no sense." You must be in hell if you can seriously say things like that. We've become medieval. I saw your brother once before that night in the hospital with Gunesena. I'd cut myself badly and gone to Emergency Services to get some stitches. Your brother was there in a black coat and he was covered in blood, covered in blood reading a paperback. I'm sure now it was Gamini. I thought he looked familiar when I saw him with you. I thought he was a patient, part of an attempted murder. Your brother's on speed, isn't he?'

'He's been on various things. I don't know now.'

'He's so thin. Someone needs to help him.'

'He embraces it, what he does to himself. He's reached a balance with it.'

'What are you going to do with the head?'

'He might have come from one of these villages. I can see if anyone recognizes it.'

'Sarath, you can't do this. You said . . . these are communities that lost people. They've had to deal with beheaded bodies.'

'What's our purpose here? We're trying to identify him. We have to start somewhere.'

'Please don't do this.'

. . .

He had been standing, listening to them speaking in English in the courtyard. But now he faced her, not knowing that the tears were partly for him. Or that she realized the face was in no way a portrait of Sailor but showed a calm Ananda had known in his wife, a peacefulness he wanted for any victim.

She would have turned on a light but she had noticed Ananda never stepped into electrically lit areas. He worked always with flare torches in his room if it was too overcast. As if electricity had betrayed him once and he would not trust it again. Or maybe he was of that generation of battery lovers unaccustomed to official light. Just batteries or fire or moon.

He moved two steps forward and with his thumb creased away the pain around her eye along with her tears' wetness. It was the softest touch on her face. His left hand lay on her shoulder as tenderly and formally as the nurse's had on Gamini that night in the emergency ward, which was why, perhaps, she recalled that episode to Sarath later. Ananda's hand on her shoulder to quiet her while the other hand came up to her face, kneaded the skin of that imploded tension of weeping as if hers too was a face being sculpted, though she could tell that wasn't in his thoughts. This was a tenderness she was receiving. Then his other hand on her other shoulder, the other thumb under her right eye. Her sobbing had stopped. Then he was not there anymore.

In all of her time with Sarath, she realized, he had hardly touched her. With Sarath she felt simply *adjacent*. Gamini's shaking her hand in the night hospital, his sleeping head on her lap that one night had been more personal. Now Ananda had touched her in a way she could recollect no one ever having touched her, except, perhaps, Lalitha. Or perhaps her mother, somewhere further back in her lost childhood. She slipped into the courtyard and saw Sarath still there facing the image of Sailor. He would already know as she did that no one would recognize the face. It was not a reconstruction of Sailor's face they were looking at.

Once she and Sarath had entered the forest monastery in Arankale and spent a few hours there. A corrugated overhang was nailed into the rock of a cave entrance to keep out sun and rain. Beyond was a curved road of sand to a bathing pool. A monk swept his way along the path for two hours each morning and removed a thousand leaves. By late afternoon another thousand leaves and light twigs had fallen upon it. But at noon its surface was as clear and yellow as a river. To walk this sand path was itself an act of meditation.

The forest was so still that Anil heard no sounds until she thought of listening for them. Then she located the noisemakers in the landscape, as if using a sieve in water, catching the calls of orioles and parrots. 'Those who cannot love make places like this. One needs to be in a stage beyond passion.' It was practically the only thing Sarath had said that day in Arankale. Most of the time he walked and slept in his own thoughts.

They had wandered within the forest, discovering remnants of sites. A dog followed them and she remembered Tibetans believed that monks who hadn't meditated properly became dogs in the next life. They circled back to the clearing, a clearing like a *kamatha*, the threshing circle in a paddy field. On a ledge of stone a small statue of the Buddha rested, a cut plantain leaf protected him from glare and rain. The forest towering over them so they felt they were within a deep green well. The corrugated overhang by the cave rattled and shook whenever the wind came down through the trees.

There was no wish in her to step away from this place.

Kings and those who are powerful desire what weighs them to the ground. Historical honour, measured ownership, their sure truths. But in Arankale, Sarath told her, in the last years of the twelfth century, Asanga the Wise and his followers lived for decades in solitude, the world unaware of them. When they died the monastery and then the forest were stilled of humans. And in those uninhabited years the paths were leaf-filled, there was no song of sweeping. No odour of saffron or margosa came from the baths. Arankale perhaps became more beautiful, Anil thought, and more subtle without humans in the structure they had designed when they were no longer in the currents of love.

Four centuries later monks began living again in the caves above what had once been the temple clearing. It had been a long era of humanlessness, religiouslessness. The knowledge of such a monastery had vanished from people's minds and the site was an abandoned forest sea. What was left of wooden altars was eaten by colonies of insects. Generations of pollen silted the bathing pool and then rough vegetation consumed it, so it was invisible to any passerby who did not know its sudden loose depth, which was a haven for creatures that scurried on the warmth of the cut rock and on unnamed plants in this nocturnal world.

For four hundred years the unheard throat calls of birds. The hum of some medieval bee motoring itself into the air. And in the remnant of the twelfth-century well, under the reflected sky, a twist of something silver in the water.

Sarath said this to her, the night on Galle Face Green:

'Palipana could move within archaeological sites as if they

were his own historical homes from past lives—he was able to guess the existence of a water garden's location, unearth it, reconstruct its banks, fill it with white lotus. He worked for years on the royal parks around Anuradhapura and Kandy. He'd take one imagined step and be in an earlier century. Standing in the Forest of Kings or at one of the rock structures in the western monasteries, he must have found it difficult to distinguish the present age from ancient times. The *season* was identifiable— temperature, rainfall, humidity, the odour of the grass, its burned colours. But that was all. Nothing else gave away an era. . . . So I can understand what he did. It was just the next step for him—to eliminate the borders and categories, to find everything in one landscape, and so discover the story he hadn't seen before.

'Don't forget, he was going blind. In the last years of partial sight, he thought he finally saw the half-perceived interlinear texts. As letters and words began to disappear under his fingers and from his eyesight, he felt something else, the way those who are colour-blind are used to see through camouflage during war, to see the existing structure of the figure. He was living alone.'

There was a laugh from Gamini, who was also listening.

Sarath paused, then continued. 'In his youth Palipana was mostly solitary while he learned Pali and other languages.'

'But he was *very* fond of women,' Gamini said. 'One of those men who have three women on three hills. Of course you're right, he was living alone. . . . You're probably right.'

Gamini, by repeating the phrase, cancelled out his agreement. He lay back on the grass and looked up. A quiet crash of the combers against the breakwater along Galle Face Green. His brother and the woman had become silent as a result of his inter- ruption, so he went on. 'This was a civilized country. We had "halls for the sick" four centuries before Christ. There was a beautiful one in Mihintale. Sarath can take you around its ruins. There were dispensaries, maternity hospitals. By the twelfth century, physicians were being dispersed all over the country to be responsible for far-flung villages, even for ascetic monks who lived in caves. That would have been an interesting trek, dealing with those guys. Anyway, the names of doctors appear on some rock inscriptions. There were villages for the blind. There are recorded details of brain operations in the ancient texts. Ayurvedic hospitals were set up that still exist—I'll take you there and show them to you sometime. Just a short train journey. We were always good with illness and death. We could howl with the best. Now we carry the wounded with no anaesthetic up the stairs because the elevators don't work.'

'I think I met you before.'

'I don't think so. I've never seen you.'

'Do you remember everyone? You have a black coat.'

He laughed. 'We don't have time to remember. Get Sarath to show you Mihintale.'

'Oh, he did, he showed me a joke there. At the top of that flight of steps leading to the hill temple was a sign in Sinhala that must have once said, WARNING: WHEN IT RAINS, THESE STEPS ARE DANGEROUS. Sarath was laughing at it. Someone had altered one Sinhala syllable on the sign, so it now read, WARNING: WHEN IT RAINS, THESE STEPS ARE BEAUTIFUL.'

'This is my serious brother? He's usually the one in our family with historical irony. We are prime examples for him of why cities become ruins. The seven reasons for the fall of Polonnaruwa as a political centre. Twelve reasons why Galle became a major port and survived into the twentieth century. We don't agree much, my brother and I. He thinks my ex-wife was the best thing that happened to me. He probably wished to fuck her. But didn't.'

'Stop it, Gamini.'

'*I* didn't, anyway. Not much. I got diverted. The bodies were coming in by truckloads. She didn't love the smell of scrub lotion on my arms. The fact that I would use medicinal aids during my shifts. So that later I was not fully awake in her company. Not great courtship. I'd get into a bath and pass out. My honeymoon was at a base hospital. The country was falling apart and my wife's family complained about my unavailability. I was supposed to have my shirt ironed and go to a dinner party, hold her hand as we waited for the car. . . . Maybe I would have laughed if I'd seen that sign about the steps. Dangerous . . . beautiful . . . Lucky for you both to be there. He'—Gamini pointed into the dark—'took me there when he was studying with Palipana. I liked Palipana. I liked his strictness. He was right in the heart of our age. No small talk. What did he call himself?'

'An epigraphist,' Sarath said.

'A skill . . . to decipher inscriptions. Wonderful! To study history as if it were a body.'

'Of course your brother does that too.'

'Of *course*. And then Palipana went mad. What do you say, Sarath?'

'Hallucinations, perhaps.'

'He went mad. Those over-interpretations, what we must call lies, over the interlinear stuff.'

'He isn't mad.'

'Okay, then. Same as you and me. But no one in his clique supported him when it was revealed. He was certainly the only great man I met, but he was just never a "sacred" guy for me. You see, in the heart of any faith is a history that teaches us not to trust—'

'Sarath at least went to see him,' Anil interrupted.

'Did he. Did he . . . ?'

'I didn't. Not till this last week.'

'So he's alone.' Gamini said. 'Just his three women on three hills.'

'He lives with his niece. It's his sister's daughter.'

Anil came out of a deep sleep. Some bird-scramble on the roof or a truck in the distance must have woken her. She removed the silent earphones from her hair, groped for her Prince T-shirt and walked into the courtyard. Four a.m. The beacon from her flashlight went straight towards Sailor's skeleton. So he was safe. She flicked the light to the chair and saw the head wasn't there. Sarath must have moved it. What had woken her? Someone with a nightmare? Was it Gamini in his black coat? She'd been dreaming about him. Or perhaps Cullis in the distance. It was about the same hour she had left him wounded in Borrego. Her funny valentine.

The courtyard was a layer lighter.

A wind in the roof tiles, a stronger wind and rustle high in the tall darkness of the trees. She had not brought one picture of him when she packed, was proud of that. She sat down on a step. She thought there had been birdsong and was listening for more of it. Then she heard the gasp and was running to Ananda's door and pushing it open into the dark.

There were sounds she had never heard before. She ran back for the flashlight, yelled to Sarath and came back in. Ananda was lying against a corner, trying with what energy he had left to stab himself in the throat. The blood on the knife and in his fingers and down his arm. His eyes like a deer in her light. The sound coming from God knows where. Not his throat. It couldn't be his throat. Not now.

'How quick were you?' It was Sarath.

'Quick. I was outside. Rip some cloth off the bed.'

She moved towards Ananda. The eyes open, not blinking, and she thought he might already be dead. She waited for eye movement, and after what felt like a long time it came. His hand was still half gestured into the air. 'I need the cloth fast, Sarath.' 'Right.' She tried pulling the knife out of Ananda's grip but couldn't, and let it be. The blood coming off his elbow onto her sarong, she was close enough to smell it, the flashlight held between her thighs, aimed up as she crouched there.

Sarath began to tear the pillowcase and passed her strips of cloth, which she wrapped around Ananda's neck. She put the large flap of skin flat against his neck and bound it tight.

'I need some antiseptic. Do you know where it is?' When he brought it she soaked the cloth in it so it would reach the wound. The windpipe was still intact, but she needed to tighten the bandage so less blood would be lost, even though he was having difficulty breathing already. She leaned forward and pressed the wound with her fingers, the knife in his hand now behind her.

'You need to phone Gamini and get him to send someone.'

'The cell phone's dead. I'll phone from the village. If I can't get someone, I'll drive him to Ratnapura.'

'Light a lamp, will you, for us. Before you go.'

He returned with an oil lamp. It was too bright for them at that hour, and he turned down the wick, because what he could see was terrible.

'He called forth the dead,' she whispered.

'No. He's just one of those who try to kill themselves because they lost people.'

She caught a waver in the eyes in front of her.

. . .

Anil was not conscious of Sarath's leaving. She remained with Ananda in the corner of the room, lamplight holding them together. She should have been the one to go. Sarath could talk and calm him. Or did he need silence? Perhaps. Perhaps the presence of a woman helped.

She slipped in the blood getting up from her crouch, went to the bed and tore more strips off the pillowcase. She felt an amulet under the pillow and took it. When she returned, his eyes were wide open, seemed to be swallowing everything. Oh my God— he wasn't wearing his glasses. He couldn't see. She found them on the floor, he had been wearing them when he began to kill himself.

She rubbed the blood on her hands onto her sarong and placed the spectacles on his face. Suddenly, in spite of his wound, in spite of the knife still in his right hand, still a threat, he seemed to be back with her, among the living. She felt she could speak in any language, he would understand the purpose of any gesture. How far back was their moment of connection, when his hand had been on her shoulder? Just a few hours earlier. She put the amulet in his left hand but he could not or would not hold it. He was drifting back into unconsciousness or sleep.

What was an amulet, what was a *baila,* to him now? Or spectacles, or a bond. All that was for her own peace. She had interrupted his death. She was the obstacle to what he wanted. The blood had already filled the bandage. She rose and hurried through the courtyard, along with the random glance of the flashlight, into the kitchen, to their portable icebox. Opened it, and at the back, wrapped in newspaper, found the emergency epinephrine she always carried. Perhaps it would slow the bleeding, constrict the blood vessels and help his blood pressure. She rolled an ampule between her palms to warm it. On her knees, beside him, she sucked the epinephrine up into the syringe. He was looking at her, it felt, from a great distance, with no interest in what she was doing. She put her left hand on his chest to keep him from moving—she was pushing him back, she realized, as far as he would go, to stay secure, into the room's corner—then stabbed it into the arm. Continuing to hold him with her left hand, she filled the syringe once more, from a second ampule held between her knees, then gave him another injection. When she looked up he was still gazing through her. But when the drug started to influence him, his eyes became endangered. They slipped slowly, as if grasping for a ledge to stay awake on. As if he thought he would die now should he fall back into stillness.

It was ten in the morning and she heard the sounds of the foreman arriving as usual on the property. He was there to weigh the tea that had been picked and collected into sacks by seven workers. Anil always went out to watch the ceremony. She was there for a memory she'd held on to since she was a child. She always had loved the thick odour from the leaves, and as for that green leaf she knew there was nothing greener. She remembered entering tea and rubber factories as if they were kingdoms and imagining which of those kingdoms she wished to be a part of when she became an adult. A husband in tea or a husband in rubber. There was no other choice. And their house flung on top of a solitary hill.

Sarath had not been able to locate his brother and so had driven Ananda to Ratnapura Hospital. He was still not back. She stood by the neighbouring shed where the weigh-scales were, and when the tea pluckers had gone she stepped onto the platform's wobble, bent down and took a few small green leaves.

Before going to bed the previous night, she'd carried a bucket of water into the room and scrubbed the floor on her hands and knees. She had wanted to do it then, while he was still alive. If he died in the night she could not face going in there again. She worked for half an hour. The blood looked black in that light. Later, in the courtyard, she stripped off her T-shirt and sarong and washed them. And only then began to bathe herself—every inch of skin where she could sense the dried blood, every strand of her thin dark hair. She removed her bangle and scrubbed her wrist, then dropped the bangle into the bucket and washed that too. Several more times she jerked the full bucket up out of the well and poured water over herself. She felt manically awake, shivering, she wanted to talk. She left the clothes by the well and walked to her room and tried to disappear into sleep. She could feel the coldness of the well water reaching her in her exhaustion, knew it had entered her bones. She was with Sarath and Ananda, citizened by their friendship—the two of them in the car, the two of them in the hospital while a stranger attempted to save Ananda. Her hands were at her sides, she was barely able to reach for a sheet to cover herself. It was almost morning and light was in the room with her. Only then did she drift off, believing that the good stranger would save Ananda.

She opened her eyes in the afternoon and Sarath was there.

'He will be all right.'

'Oh,' she murmured. She pressed Sarath's hand to the side of her face.

'You saved him. Getting to him so quickly, then the bandage, the epinephrine. The doctor said he didn't know too many who would know to do that in a crisis.'

'It was lucky. I'm allergic to bees, I always carry it. Some people can't breathe after a bee attack. And epinephrine also slows bleeding.'

'You should live here. Not be here just for another job.'

'This isn't just "another job"! I decided to come back. I wanted to come back.'

There is a long stone path from the village road up to the *walawwa*. There is an old wall on the right hidden by foliage. A fork in the driveway after thirty yards. If you are driving you turn left and park, near the tea pluckers' shed. If you are cycling or walking you veer right and approach the house and enter it through a small east door.

It is a classic building, two hundred years old, handed down through five generations. From no viewing point does the house look excessive or pretentious. The site and location, the careful use of distance—how far back you can stand from the building to look at it, the lack of great views of another person's land—make you turn inward rather than dominate the world around you. It has always seemed a hidden, accidentally discovered place, a *grand meaulnes*.

You enter through the gate with its idiosyncratic slope on the top beam and you are in a walled front garden, with sand-coloured packed-down earth. There are two locations of shade here. The shadowed porch and the shadow under the great red tree. Beneath the tree is a low stone bench. Anil spends much of her time here, under the tree bent like an Aeolian harp that throws a hundred variations of shadow textures onto the sandy earth.

How old was the painter in the Wickramasinghe family when he died? How old is Ananda? How old was Anil, standing once in an airport unable to cry out the pain of her frustrated unreturned desire? What were the missing organs in men that made them stroll through life as courteously unfaithful, nonverbal creatures? If two lovers felt they could kill themselves over loss or desire, what of the rest of the planet of strangers? Those who were not in the slightest way in love and who were led and swayed into enemy camps by the ambitious and vainglorious . . .

She was in the garden alongside the moonamal tree and the kohomba tree. The flowers of the moonamal when shed always turned face up to the moon. The kohomba twigs she could break off and strip to clean her teeth, or burn to keep mosquitoes away. This place seemed the garden of a wise prince. But the wise prince had killed himself.

The aesthetics of the *walawwa* never surfaced among the three of them. It had been a location of refuge and fear, in spite of calm, consistent shadows, the modest height of the wall, the trees that flowered at face level. But the house, the sand garden, the trees had entered them. Anil would never get over her time here. Years later she might see an etching or a drawing and understand something about it, not sure why—unless she were told that the *walawwa* she lived in had belonged to the artist's family and that the artist had also lived there for a time. But what was it about the drawing? This simple series of lines of a naked water carrier, say, and the exactly right distance of his figure from the tree whose arced trunk echoed the shape of a harp.

One can die from private woes as easily as from public ones. Here various families had been solitary, might have begun speaking quietly to themselves while a pencil was being sharpened. Or they would listen to a transistor radio, hearing something faint at the farthest radius point of the antenna. When batteries died it was sometimes a week before one of them walked into the village, that sea of electric light! For it was a grand house built in the era of lamps, built when there seemed to be only the possibility of private woe. But it was here the three of them hunted a public story. 'The drama of our time,' the poet Robert Duncan remarked, 'is the coming of all men into one fate.'

The storm comes towards them from the north. The sky black, fresh wind shaking branches and shadows as they sit under their red tree. The only thing unaffected by the storm is Sarath, his eyes searching into the distance as they talk back and forth.

'Come on, let's go in—'

'Stay,' he says. 'We're already wet.'

She sits down on the stone bench facing him, watching the rain break apart his neatly combed head of hair. She feels irresponsible, to be out in a storm like this. She would have done it as a kid. She can hear drumming from the village, barely audible beneath the sound of rain.

'You look like your brother with your hair dishevelled. Actually I like your brother.' She leans forward. 'I'm going in.'

She walks to the porch and climbs the steps out of the mud, shakes her hair loose and wrings it out like a cloth. She glances back. Sarath's head is bent down, his lips moving, as if speaking with someone. She knows there will never be a boat to reach Sarath, to discover what he might be thinking. His wife? A cave fresco? The bounce of the rain in front of him? She dries her arms in the darkness of the dining room, puts her left hand to her mouth so she can lick the rain off the bangle.

In the rain he remembers what he was going to tell her about Ananda. He thought of it on the drive back from the hospital. No. About Sailor. 'Plumbago,' he says, the word filling his head. 'He may have worked in a plumbago mine.'

. . .

That night, long past midnight, Anil could still hear the drumming through the rain. It paced and choreographed everything. She kept waiting for its silence.

Sailor's head, Ananda's version of him, was already in the village, and it was there that an unknown, unwished-for drummer had attached himself to it, begun playing beside it. Anil knew it was unlikely that identification would occur. There had been so many disappearances. She knew it was not the head that would give the skeleton a name but his markers of occupation. So she and Sarath would go now to the villages in the region where there were plumbago-graphite mines.

The drum continued its intricate antiphonal pulse, like steps that led them down a stairway to the sea. The drumming would stop only when there was a name provided for the head. But that night it didn't stop.

The Mouse

When Gamini's wife, Chrishanti, left their marriage, he remained in the house for a week, surrounded by all the things he had never wished for—state-of-the-art kitchen equipment, her zebra-striped table mats. Without her presence the gardener and sweeper and cook loosened away from necessity. He let his driver go. He would walk to Emergency Services. At the end of that first week he left the house and stayed at the hospital, where he knew he could always find a bed; this way he could rise at dawn and soon be in surgery. Now and then his hand slapped his breast pocket for the pen Chrishanti had given him, which he had lost, but he missed little of his past life.

When his brother phoned, concerned, he told him he did not want his concern. He was already taking pills with a protein drink so he could be continuously awake to those dying around him. *In diagnosing a vascular injury, a high index of suspicion is necessary.* If he had not been such a good doctor his behaviour would have been reported. He knew that what he was able to do in the hospital was his only societal value. It was where he met his fate, this offstage battle with the war. He ignored war news. He was told he had begun to smell, and for some reason this distressed him. He hoarded Lifebuoy soap and showered three times a day.

Sarath's wife visited Gamini once in Emergency Services, putting her arm through his as he came off duty. She said that she and Sarath were offering Gamini a place to stay, he had become too much of a vagabond. She was the only person who could say things like that to him. He took her to lunch, ate more than he had eaten in months, and curled her interrogation back onto her specific interests. All through the meal he just looked at her face and arms. He was as gracious as possible, didn't touch her once, the only touch was when her arm had slipped through his as they met. When they separated he didn't embrace her. She would have felt how thin his frame was.

There was no talk about Sarath. Only about her work at the radio station. She knew he had always liked her. He knew he'd always loved her, her busy arms, the strange lack of confidence in one who seemed to him so complete. He had met her the first time at a fancy-dress party in someone's garden outside Colombo. She was in a man's tuxedo, her hair swept back. He began a conversation and danced twice with her, disguised, so she didn't know who he was. This was years earlier, before either of them was married.

Who he was, that night, was her fiancé's brother.

He proposed marriage to her twice during the party. They were on the *cadju* terrace. He had the paint and the tattered clothes of a *yakka* on him, and she half laughed him off, saying she was engaged already. They had been talking seriously about the war and she thought his proposal was a joke, simply a wish for diver-sion. So he talked about how long he had known the gardens they were in, how many times he had come here. You must know my fiancé, she said, he comes here too. But he claimed not to recall the name. They were both hot and she untied her bow tie so it hung loose. 'You too must be hot. All this stuff on you.' 'Yes.' There was a pond with a bamboo fountain spout that tilted over when it filled, and he kneeled by it. 'Don't get paint in the pond, there are fish.' So he unwrapped the turban he was wear-ing, and soaked it and began wiping the colours from his face.

When he got up she saw who he was, her fiancé's brother, and he asked her to marry him again.

Now, years later, after his own marriage had ended, they walked out of the cafeteria and onto the street where her car was. He kept a distance as he said good-bye, not touching her, just that offhand hungry gaze, that offhand wave to the departing vehicle.

Gamini woke in the almost empty ward of the hospital. He showered and dressed, watched intently by the patient next to him. It was still before dawn and the grand staircase was dark. He walked down slowly, not putting his hand on the banister, which hid who knew what in that old wood. He passed Pediatrics, Communicable Diseases, Bone Work, and entered the front courtyard, bought some tea and a potato roti at the street canteen and consumed them there, under a tree full of loud birds. Apart from a few moments like this he was indoors most of the day. He'd come out and sit on a bench. He'd tell one of the interns to wake him after an hour in case he fell asleep. The boundary between sleep and waking was a cotton thread so faintly coloured he often crossed it unawares. When he performed night surgery he would sometimes feel as if he were cutting into flesh surrounded only by night and stars. He would wake from this reverie and be back in the building, recognize it once more fitting itself around him. His duties made him come upon strangers and cut them open without ever knowing their names. He rarely spoke. It seemed he did not approach people unless they had a wound, even if he couldn't see it—the orderly yawning in the hall, the visiting politician Gamini refused to be photographed with.

Nurses read the charts out to him as he scrubbed. They loved working with him; he was strangely popular though unforgiving.

He was brutal in his decisions when he realized he couldn't save the body he was working on. 'Enough,' he would say, and walk out. '*Basta*,' someone who'd been abroad said, and he laughed by the swinging door. It was almost a moment of human conversation. Gamini knew he had never been good company; small talk plunged to its death around him. Now and then a night nurse woke him and asked for help. She would be cautious, but he would wake quickly and then walk with her in just a sarong to hold an intravenous over a struggling child. Then he would slip back to his borrowed bed. 'I owe you a favour,' the nurse would say as he was leaving her. 'You don't owe anyone favours. Wake me anytime you need help.'

Her light on all night.

Sometimes bodies washed in onto the shore, the combers throwing them onto the beaches. On the Matara coast, or at Wellawatta, or by St. Thomas's College in Mount Lavinia where they, Sarath and Gamini, had learned to swim as children. These were the victims of politically motivated murders—victims of torture in the house at Gower Street or a house off the Galle Road—lifted into the air by helicopter, flown a couple of miles out to sea and dropped through the fathoms of air. But only a few of these ever came back as evidence into the arms of the country.

Inland the bodies came down the four main rivers—the Mahaveli Ganga, the Kalu Ganga, the Kelani Ganga, the Bentota Ganga. All of them were eventually brought to Dean Street Hospital. Gamini had chosen not to deal with the dead. He avoided the south-wing corridors, where they brought the torture victims to be identified. Interns listed the wounds and photographed the bodies. Still, once a week, he went over the reports and the photographs of the dead, confirmed what was assumed, pointed out fresh scars caused by acid or sharp metal, and gave his signature. He was running on the energy of pills when he arrived to do this, and spoke quickly into a tape recorder left for him by an Amnesty man; he stood by the windows so he could get more light on the terrible photographs, covering the faces with his left hand, the pulse in his wrist jumping. He read out the number of the file, gave his interpretation and signature. The darkest hour of the week.

He walked away from the week's pile of photographs. The doors opened and a thousand bodies slid in, as if caught in the nets of fishermen, as if they had been mauled. A thousand bodies of sharks and skates in the corridors, some of the dark-skinned fish thrashing . . .

They had begun covering the faces on the photographs. He worked better this way, and there was no danger of his recognizing the dead.

The joke was that he had entered the medical profession because he assumed it would have a nineteenth-century pace. He liked its manner of amateur authority. There was the anecdote about Dr. Spittel carrying a body out of a hospital when lights failed during a night operation in Kandy, placing it on a bench in the parking lot and aiming car headlights onto the patient. A quietly heroic life remembered in a few such stories. That was the satisfaction. He'd be remembered the way a cricketer was who played one classic innings on an afternoon in 1953, his name emerging in a street *baila* for a week or two. Famous in a song.

As a boy, in the months when he fought off the fate of diphtheria, Gamini would lie on a mat during his afternoon sleeps and wish only for the life that his parents had. Whatever career he chose, he wanted it to move with their style and pace. To rise early and work until a late lunch, then sleep and conversation, then drop in at the office once more, briefly. His father's and grandfather's law offices took up one wing of the family's large house on Greenpath Road. He was never allowed into the mysterious warrens during the workday when he was younger, but at five p.m. he would carry a glass filled with amber fluid, push the swing door with his foot and enter. There were squat filing cabinets and small desk fans. He said hullo to his father's dog and then placed the drink on his father's table.

At this moment his body was yanked into the air and swivelled so that he now sat on his father's lap, large dark arms around him. 'Start at the beginning,' he'd say, and Gamini proceeded to tell him about his day's adventures, his day at school, what his mother had said when he came home. He was, in the early years, fully at ease with the family. When he looked back he never remembered anger or nervousness in the house. He recalled his parents gentle with each other. They were always conversing, sharing everything, and in bed he could hear the continuing hum of it like wool between the house and the world. He realized later that every dimension of his father's world existed in the house. Clients came to *him*. There was a tennis court in the back where guests joined the family on weekends.

It was assumed that the two brothers would be part of the family firm. But Sarath left home, deciding not to be a lawyer. And a few years later, Gamini also betrayed those voices in the house and entered medical school.

*

Two months after his wife left him, Gamini collapsed from exhaustion, and the administration ordered a leave. He had nowhere to go, his home abandoned. He realized Emergency Services had become for him, even in its mad state, a cocoon, as his parents' house had been. Everything that was of value to him took place there. He slept in the wards, he bought his meals from the street vendor just outside the hospital. Now he was being asked to step away from the world he had burrowed into, created around himself, this peculiar replica of childhood order.

He walked to Nugegoda, the neighbourhood where his house was, and banged on the locked door. He could smell cooking. A stranger appeared but would not open it. 'Yes?' 'I'm Gamini.' 'So?' 'I live here.' The man walked away and there were voices in the kitchen.

It was a while before Gamini realized they were going to ignore him. He crossed the small garden. The odour of the food was wonderful to him. He had never felt so hungry. He didn't want the house, he wanted a home-cooked meal. He entered through the back door. Glancing around, he was conscious they were looking after the place much better than he had. The man who had ignored him was with two women. He knew none of them. He had thought at first his wife had sent relatives over. 'Can I have some water?'

The man brought him a glass. Gamini heard children farther back in the bungalow and was pleased about that, that all the space was being used. He remembered something and asked if there was any mail. They brought him a stack of it. A letter from his wife, which he put in his pocket. Several cheques from the hospital. He opened them, signed a couple on the back and gave them to one of the women. Two others he kept for himself. The women gestured and he sat down to eat with them. String hoppers, *pol sambol,* chicken curry. Afterwards he strolled with a comfortably full stomach to the bank. He was flush. He phoned Quickshaw's and hired a car and waited in the air-conditioned lobby of Grindlays until it rolled up. Gamini got in next to the driver.

'To Trincomalee. Then to the Nilaveli Beach Hotel.'

'No, no.'

He was expecting this. It was supposedly dangerous with guerrilla forces in the vicinity. 'It will be quite safe, I'm a doctor. They don't touch doctors, we're like prostitutes. Here's a Red Cross sign for the windshield. I'm hiring you for a week. You don't have to like me or be polite. I'm not one of those who needs to be loved. Stop here.'

He got out of the car and climbed into the back seat, he needed to sprawl out. He was asleep by the time the car weaved itself out of Colombo. 'Take the coast road,' he murmured just before sleep. 'Wake me up in Negombo.'

Gamini and the driver walked into the dark, sunless lobby of the old Negombo rest house. A small lamp by the front desk lit up the manager, who sat in front of a poorly painted mural of the sea, and Gamini, remembering something, turned around, looked through the door and saw the same scene in reality. They had a beer and went on. Near Kurunegala he asked the driver to take a side road. A few miles past Kurunegala, Gamini climbed out and asked the driver to meet him at the same place the next morning. It took a while for the driver to understand. Still, he wanted to be here for the night.

His father had brought him to the forest monastery nearby, in Arankale. He had brought him as a child, and every few years Gamini managed to revisit the place. As a war doctor he had come to have little faith, but he always felt a great peace here. With nothing much, just a light shirt and pants, no umbrella for the sunlight, no food, he made his way into the forest. Sometimes when he came here he saw that the place had been kept up; sometimes it had closed down like an eye in the forest.

There was the well. There was the corrugated sheet that made a roof over the porch where old monks slept. He could stay there. He could bathe at the well in the morning. He buttoned the breast pocket of his shirt so his glasses would not fall out and be lost.

. . .

A week later, Gamini stepped from the Nilaveli Beach Hotel compound and walked to the sea. He was very drunk. He had been shambling around in the deserted resort with a cook and a night manager and two women who cleaned the empty bedrooms and screamed whenever the cook attempted to push them into the swimming pool. They were always wrestling in the halls. On the beach he fell asleep, and when he woke there were gunmen around him laughing.

His sarong had half fallen off. He said, as clearly as he could in the two official languages, '*I—am—a—doctor—*' and passed out again. The next time he woke up he was in a hut full of wounded boys. Seventeen years old. Sixteen years old. Some even younger. This was supposed to be his holiday and he said so to one of the gunmen. 'I'm expected at dinner at seven. If I'm not there by seven-thirty they don't serve—'

'Yes, yes. But this—' The man gestured with his arm all the way down the hut to the wounded. 'There's this, no?'

Gamini had been weaning himself off his pills and was in midstream, in his switch to alcohol, so he was not sure of his present level of drunkenness. He'd been sleeping a lot. He'd wake up and find himself in a stranger's garden. It wasn't so much the desire for sleep as the need for it. Inside a dream he'd be carrying bodies in and out of elevators. Elevators always made him claustrophobic, but they were better than the creaking vertigo of the stairs.

When the guerrillas found him curled up on the beach the sea had been at his ankles. They'd come looking for the tourist who was supposed to be a doctor. One of the women by the swimming pool had directed them to the beach.

Gamini walked up and down, looking at the bodies in the hut.

Rags knotted around the wounds, no painkillers, no bandages. He sent a soldier to his hotel room with the key to get sheets they could tear up and to collect the plastic bag with various things that would be useful—aftershave, pills. The gunman returned wearing one of his shirts. Gamini shook the tablets out onto the table and cut them into quarters. There was going to be a problem with communication. He couldn't speak Tamil well enough, they couldn't speak Sinhala. There was just paltry English between Gamini and the leader.

It was late afternoon and he was hungry. He had missed the lunch sitting and the hotel staff was unbending. He asked the leader to send someone over to scare up some food for him. He hoped he was not going to hear gunshots in the distance. He began to work, moving down the line of the wounded.

Most would survive but would lose an arm or be impaired in some way. He had already seen the evidence of so many woundings in his brief ride through Trincomalee. He continued along the makeshift ward carrying a wooden *pakispetti* box, sat beside a boy and dressed his limbs with strips of sheet. Those he would operate on shortly were each given a quarter of one of his precious pills so they would be high when he worked on them. He was startled to see how strong the effect was of even this small section of pill; he'd been swallowing them whole for more than a year. Fifteen minutes after the patient swallowed the pill, three guerrillas held him firmly to the bed and Gamini sutured a gash. The air was so hot he had already taken off his shirt, tied rags around his wrists to stop the sweat from going down to his fingers. He needed to sleep, his eyes flickering, always a signal, and there was still no food. He came close to throwing a small tantrum, lay down beside the bodies and curled himself up into sleep.

He snored loudly. When his wife was leaving him, Gamini accused her of abandoning him because he snored. Now the boys around him were silent so they would not disturb him.

But he woke to someone shouting in pain. He went out and washed his face at the tap. By this time the cook had been brought over on a bicycle, and slowly, in Sinhala, Gamini ordered ten large meals to be shared among them, and made sure the cook put it on his bill. This had an influence. When the feast arrived surgery was stopped. The hotel staff had brought two bottles of beer for him. During the meal he remembered the disappearance of Dr. Linus Corea and wondered whether he himself would ever return to Colombo.

He worked into the night, bending over patients while someone on the other side of their beds held an old Coleman lamp. Some of the boys were delirious when they emerged from the influence of the pills. Who sent a thirteen-year-old to fight, and for what furious cause? For an old leader? For some pale flag? He had to keep reminding himself who these people were. Bombs on crowded streets, in bus stations, paddy fields, schools had been set by people like this. Hundreds of victims had died under Gamini's care. Thousands couldn't walk or use their bowels anymore. Still. He was a doctor. In a week he would be back working in Colombo.

After midnight he walked along the beach with an escort gunman to his hotel. There he noticed right away that the alarm clock he had bought in Kurunegala was missing. He climbed onto and slept on his sheetless bed.

Where did the secret war begin between him and his brother? It had begun with the desire to be the other, even with the impossibility of emulating him. Gamini would always remain in spirit the younger, unable to catch up, nicknamed 'Meeya.' The Mouse. And he loved his lack of responsibility, loved never being at the centre, while perceptive of what went on there. His parents much of the time weren't even aware of him half buried in an armchair, reading a book, ears perked up, listening to their conversations faithful as a dog. Sarath loved history, their father loved law, Gamini burrowed away unknown. The mother who had wished to be a dancer in her youth now choreographed them all. She would remain mysterious to Gamini. The love she showed was a general affection, never specifically for him. He found it difficult to imagine her as his father's lover. She *seemed* daughterless, simply keeping up with the three males in the house—a garrulous husband, an intelligent and bound-to-be-successful older son, and a second-born secretive one. Gamini. The Mouse.

The fact that neither brother wanted to follow his father into the family law firm left the mother defending everyone's position—a foot in each son's camp, a hand on her husband's shoulder. In any case, they scattered. Sarath moved into archaeological studies and Gamini flung himself into medical school, but most of all into the world outside the family. The only way he visited them now was via the rumours of his wildness. If they had never really been too conscious of Gamini at home, his parents now met a legion of unsavory anecdotes about him. It appeared he wanted them to give up on him, and eventually, out of embarrassment, they did.

In fact he had loved that family world. Though later, in conversations with Sarath's wife, she would argue, 'What kind of family would call a child "the Mouse"?' She could picture him in his youth, irrelevant to adult preoccupations, with his big ears, in that big armchair.

Though he didn't mind. Thought it was true for all children. He and his brother had become content with aloneness, the lack of necessity for speaking. 'Well, it drives me mad,' Sarath's wife retaliated. 'It drives me mad about both of you.' In conversations with her Gamini continued to see his childhood as a time of contentment, while she saw him as a soul who had only just survived, never secure in the love around him. 'I was spoiled,' he'd say. 'You're only secure when you are alone doing things on your own. You weren't spoiled, you were ignored.' 'I'm not going through the rest of my life blaming my mother for my lack of kisses.' 'You could.'

He had loved his childhood, he thought to himself. He had loved the dark living rooms during the afternoons, following the path of ants on the balcony, the costumes he put together by taking clothes out of various almirahs and dressing up and singing in front of mirrors. And the grandeur of that chair remained with him. He wanted to go out and buy one just like it, now, an adult's prerogative and whim. When he thought of succour, it was the chair he remembered, not a mother or a father. 'I rest my case,' Sarath's wife said quietly.

And Sarath, for his parents, was the boy who walked the heavens. The three of them laughed and argued during dinner while

Gamini watched their style and manner. By the time he was eleven he was proud of being a good mimic, could imitate the quizzical expressions of concerned dogs, for instance.

Still, he remained invisible, even to himself, seldom looking into mirrors save when dressed in costumes. He had an uncle who used to direct amateur theatrical productions, and once, alone in his house, Gamini had come across some outfits. He tried them on one by one, wound the record player, then danced over sofas, singing invented songs, until interrupted by the return of his aunt. Who had simply exclaimed, 'Aha! So that's what you do. . . .' And he was humiliated and embarrassed beyond measure or imagining. For years afterwards he judged himself vain, and as a result revealed even less of himself to others. He quietened, became barely aware of the subtler gestures within himself. Later he would be vivid only with strangers—in the storm of the last stages of a party or in the chaos of emergency wards. This was the state of grace. It was *here* that people could lose themselves as if in a dance, too intent on skills or desires to be conscious of their power while they chased romance or reacted to some emergency. He could be at the centre and still feel he was invisible. This was when his notoriousness began.

The barrier that separated him from his family during childhood remained in place. He did not want it dislodged, he did not want the universes brought together. He wasn't self-conscious about this. The awareness of it was to come later in a terrible crisis and with clarity. He would be holding his brother and be aware that as far back as childhood he had known that for him the catalyst for the freedom and secrecy he always wanted was this benign brother. Gamini, beside Sarath years later, would say all this out loud to him, shocked at his own unlearned vengeance. When we are young, he thought, the first necessary rule is to stop invasions of ourselves. We know this as children. There is always that murmuring conviction of family, like the sea around an island. So youth hides in the shape of something lean as a spear, or something as antisocial as a bark. And we become therefore more comfortable and intimate with strangers.

The Mouse insisted that for his final years of school he leave Colombo and go to boarding school at Trinity College in Kandy. In this way he was a good distance from his family for much of the year. He loved the slow-rocking train that took him away, up-country. He always loved trains, never bought a car, never learned to drive. In his twenties he luxuriated in the wind against his drunk head when he leaned into the noise and fear of tunnels, deep space around him. He enjoyed talking intimately and with humour to strangers; oh, he knew all this was a sickness—but he did not dislike it, this distance and anonymity.

He was tender, nervous and gregarious. After more than three years up north, working in the peripheral hospitals, he would become more obsessive. His marriage a year later failed almost instantly, and after that he was mostly alone. In surgery he asked for just one assistant. Others could watch and learn at a distance. He was never articulate in explaining what he did and what was going on. Never a good teacher but a good example.

He had been in love with just one woman and she was not the one he married. Later there was another woman, a wife in a field hospital near Polonnaruwa. Eventually he felt himself on a boat of demons and himself to be the only clearheaded and sane person there. He was a perfect participant in the war.

The rooms Sarath and Gamini lived in as children were hidden from the sunlight of Colombo, from traffic noises and dogs, from other children, from the sound of the metal gate clanging into its socket. Gamini remembers the swivel chair he spun in, bringing whirling chaos to the papers and shelves, the forbidden atmosphere of his father's office. All offices, for Gamini, would have the authority of complex secrets. Even as an adult, stepping into such rooms made him feel unworthy and illicit. Banks, law firms, underlined his uncertainty, gave him a sense of being in a headmaster's room, believing that things would never be explained enough for him to understand.

We evolve deviously. Gamini grew up not knowing half the things he thought he was supposed to know—he was to make and discover unusual connections because he had not known the usual routes. He was for most of his life a boy spinning in a chair. And just as things had been kept away from him, he too became a container of secrets.

In the house of his childhood he would press his right eye into a door handle, he would knock gently and if there was no reply slip into his parents' room, a brother's room, an uncle's room, during their afternoon sleep. Then walk barefoot towards the bed and look at the sleepers, look from the window and leave. Not much going on there. Or silently approach a gathering of adults. He was already in the habit of not speaking unless responding to a question.

. . .

He was staying at his aunt's house in Boralesgamuwa, and she and her friends were playing bridge on the long porch that surrounded the house. He came towards them carrying a lit candle, shielding the flame. He placed it on a side table a yard or so to the right of them. No one noticed this. He drifted back into the house. A few minutes later Gamini crawled on his belly with his air rifle through the grass, stalking his way from the bottom of the garden towards the house. He was wearing a small camouflage hat of leaves to disguise his presence even further. He could almost hear the four women bidding, having halfhearted conversations.

He estimated they were twenty yards away. He loaded the air rifle and positioned himself like a sniper, elbows down, legs at angles to give him balance and firmness, and fired. Nothing was hit. He reloaded and settled in to aim again. This time he hit the side table. One of the women looked up, cocking her head, but she could see nothing around her. What he wished to do was shoot out the flame of the candle with the pellet, but the next shot flew low, only a few inches above the red porch floor, and hit an ankle. At that instant, simultaneous with the gasp from Mrs. Coomaraswamy, his aunt looked up and saw him with the air rifle hugged against his cheek and shoulder, aiming right at them.

Gamini felt happiest when he stepped from disorganized youth into the exhilaration of work. On his first medical appointment, travelling to the hospitals in the northeast, it seemed he was finally part of a nineteenth-century journey. He remembered the memoir he had read by old Dr. Peterson, who wrote of such travels, it must have been, sixty years before. His book included etchings—a hackery travelling along canopied roads, bulbuls drinking at a tank—and Gamini recalled one sentence.

> I travelled by train to Matara and the rest of the way on horse and cart, with a bugler going ahead all the way, blowing his bugle to keep the wild animals off the road.

Now, in the middle of civil war, he rode the slow, wheezing bus at almost the same pace, into almost the same landscape. In a small romantic section of his heart he wished for a bugler.

There were just five doctors working in the northeast. Lakdasa was in charge, responsible for assigning them out to the peripherals and the small villages. Skanda was main surgeon, head of triage operations when there was an emergency. There was the Cuban, with them for just one year. C——, the eye doctor, who had joined three months earlier. 'She's got an unreliable diploma,' Lakdasa said to the others after a week, 'but she works hard, and I'm not letting her go.' And the young graduate Gamini in his first posting.

From the base hospital at Polonnaruwa they would travel to peripheral hospitals, where some of them were to live. An anaesthetist turned up one day a week, which was the day surgery was performed. If there were emergency operations on other days, they improvised with chloroform or whatever pills they could find to knock the patient out. And from the base hospital they drove to places Gamini had never heard of and couldn't even locate on a map—Araganwila, Welikande, Palatiyawa, visiting clinics in half-built schoolrooms, met by mothers and infants, malaria and cholera patients.

The doctors who survived that time in the northeast remembered they never worked harder, were never more useful than to those strangers who were healed and who slipped through their hands like grain. Not one of them returned later into the economically sensible careers of private practice. They would learn everything of value here. It was not an abstract or moral quality but a physical skill that empowered them. There were no newspapers or varnished tables or good fans. Now and then a book, now and then the radio with cricket commentary alternating between Sinhala and English. They allowed a transistor radio into the operating room on special occasions or for a crucial few hours in a test match. When the commentator switched to English there had to be an instant translation into Sinhala by Rohan, the anaesthetist. He was the most bilingual of the staff, having had to read the small-type texts that came with tanks of oxygen. (Rohan was a reader, in any case, often travelling down to Colombo by bus to hear a local or visiting South Asian writer read from a new book at the Kelaniya campus.) Patients in the surgical ward often drifted back into consciousness and found themselves within the drama of a cricket match.

.   .   .

They shaved at night beside a candle and slept clean-shaven as princes. Then they woke at five a.m., in the dark. They would lie there for a moment locating themselves, trying to remember the shape of the room. Was there a mosquito net above them or a fan, or just a Lion brand mosquito coil? Were they in Polonnaruwa? They travelled so much, they slept in so many places. There was the stirring outside of koha birds. A *bajaj*. Predawn loudspeakers being turned on so there was just their hum and crackle. The doctors opened their eyes when someone touched them on the shoulder, in silence, as if in enemy territory. And there was the darkness, and the minimal clues as to where they were. Ampara? Manampitiya?

Or they would wake too soon and it was still only three hours past midnight, and they feared they would not go back to sleep again but did so within the sweep of a minute. Not one of them had sleeplessness in those days. They slept like pillars of stone, remaining in the same position they had lowered themselves into in the bed or cot or on the rattan mat, on their backs or facedown, usually on their backs because it allowed them the pleasure for a few seconds of resting, with all their senses alive, certain of coming sleep.

Within minutes of waking they got dressed in the dark and gathered in the corridors, where there was hot tea. Soon they would be driving the forty miles to clinics, the vehicle chiselling with two weak headlamps through the darkness, jungle and an unseen view alongside them, now and then a villager's fire beside the road. They would stop at a food stall. A ten-minute breakfast of fish cutlets in the lesser dark. The noise of utensils being passed. Lakdasa coughing. Still no conversation. Just the intimacy of walking across a road with a cup of tea for someone. These always felt like significant expeditions. They were kings and queens.

Gamini worked in the northeast for more than three years. Lakdasa would remain there, setting up clinics. And the eye doctor with the dubious diploma would also never leave the peripheral hospitals. During the worst crises Gamini had seen her passing out swabs and lotions to trainees even as she operated on an emergency case. What the others envied most about her, apart from her presence as an attractive woman, was the physical evidence of her work. Gamini loved the sight of her ward as everyone in the fifteen-bed room turned towards the door when he walked in, all with the same white patch taped over their dark faces, the same badge of belonging to her.

Somebody once brought a book about Jung into their midst. In the book one of them had found a sentence and underlined it. (There was a habit among them of critical marginalia. An exclamation point beside something not psychologically or clinically valid. If there was any instance in a novel of outrageous or unlikely physical prowess or sexual achievement, Skanda, the surgeon, would write in the margin beside the scene: *This happened to me once* . . . and add with even more irony, *Dambulla, August 1978*. A scene where a man was met in a hotel room by a woman in a negligée and handed a martini received similar comments. When Skanda left to work in the cancer wards in Karapitiya, near Galle, the others knew he would be defacing books there as well, medical texts as well as novels; he was the worst of the marginalia criminals among them.) In any case, it was the anaesthetist who probably brought in the book about Jung. Pictures, essays, commentaries and biography. And someone had underlined *Jung was absolutely right about one thing. We are occupied by gods. The mistake is to identify with the god occupying you.*

Whatever this meant, it seemed a thoughtful warning, and they let the remark seep into them. They all knew it was about the sense of self-worth that, during those days, in that place, had overcome them. They were not working for any cause or political agenda. They had found a place a long way from governments and media and financial ambition. They had originally come to the northeast for a three-month shift and in spite of the lack of equipment, the lack of water, not one luxury except now and then a tin of condensed milk sucked in a car while being surrounded by jungle, they had stayed for two years or three, in some cases longer. It was the best place to be. Once, after performing surgery for almost five hours straight, Skanda said, 'The important thing is to be able to live in a place or a situation where you must use your sixth sense all the time.'

The quotation about Jung and Skanda's remark were what Gamini carried with him. And the sentence about the sixth sense was the gift he gave to Anil a few years later.

Between Heartbeats

It was in the Arizona labs that Anil met and worked with a woman named Leaf. A few years older, Leaf became Anil's closest friend and constant companion. They worked side by side and they talked continually on the phone to each other when one was on assignment elsewhere. Leaf Niedecker—what kind of name is *that,* Anil had demanded to know—introduced Anil to the finer arts of ten-pin bowling, raucous hooting in bars, and high-speed driving in the desert, swerving back and forth in the night. *'Tenga cuidado con los armadillos, señorita.'*

Leaf loved movies and remained in depression about the disappearance of drive-ins and their al fresco quality. 'All our shoes off, all our shirts off, rolling against Chevy leather—there has been nothing like it since.' So two or three times a week Anil would buy a barbequed chicken and arrive at Leaf's rented house. The television had already been carried into the yard and sat baldly beside a yucca tree. They'd rent *The Searchers* or any other John Ford or Fred Zinnemann movie. They watched *The Nun's Story, From Here to Eternity, Five Days One Summer,* sitting in Leaf's lawn chairs, or curled up beside each other in the double hammock, watching the calm, carefully sexual black-and-white walk of Montgomery Clift.

Nights in Leaf's backyard, once upon a time in the West. The heat still in the air at midnight. They would pause the movie, take a break and cool off under the garden hose. In three months they managed to see the complete oeuvres of Angie Dickinson and Warren Oates. 'I'm asthmatic,' Leaf said. 'I need to become a cowboy.'

They shared a joint and disappeared into the intricacies of *Red River,* theorizing on the strangely casual shooting of John Ireland before the final fight between Montgomery Clift and John Wayne. They rewound the video and watched it once more. Wayne swirling around gracefully, hardly interrupting his walk, to shoot a neutral friend who was trying to stop a fight. On their knees in the parched grass by the television screen they looked at the scene frame by frame for any sign of outrage at this unfairness on the victim's face. There seemed to be none. It was a minor act directed towards a minor character that may or may not have ended the man's life, and no one said anything about it during the remaining five minutes of the film. One of those Jacobean happy endings.

'I don't think the bullet killed him.'

'Well, we can't tell where it hit him, Hawks goes off too quickly. The guy just puts his hand up to his stomach and then drops.'

'If he got hit in the liver he's had it. Don't forget, this is Missouri in eighteen-fuck-knows-when.'

'Yeah. What's his name?'

'Who?'

'The guy shot.'

'Valance. Cherry Valance.'

'Cherry? You mean like Jerry, or Cherry, like apple.'

'Cherry Valance, not Apple Valance.'

'And he's Montgomery's friend.'

'Yeah, Montgomery's friend Cherry.'

'Hmm.'

'I don't think it hit him in the liver. Look at the angle of the shot. The trajectory seems to be going up. Popped a rib, I suspect, or glanced off it.'

'. . . Maybe glanced off and killed some woman on the sidewalk?'

'Or Walter Brennan . . .'

'No, some dame on the sidewalk that Howard Hawks was fucking.'

'Women remember. Don't they know that? Those saloon girls are gonna remember Cherry. . . .'

'You know, Leaf, we should do a book. *A Forensic Doctor Looks at the Movies.*'

'The film noir ones are tough. Their clothes are baggy, it's too dark.'

'I'm doing *Spartacus.*'

In Sri Lankan movie theatres, Anil told Leaf, if there was a great scene—usually a musical number or an extravagant fight— the crowd would yell out 'Replay! Replay!' or 'Rewind! Rewind!' till the theatre manager and projectionist were forced to comply. Now, on a smaller scale, the films staggered backwards and forwards, in Leaf's yard, until the actions became clear to them.

The film they worried over most was *Point Blank.* At the start of the movie, Lee Marvin (who once played Liberty Valance, no relation) is shot by a double-crossing friend in the abandoned Alcatraz prison. The friend leaves him for dead and steals his girl and his share of the money. Vengeance results. Anil and Leaf composed a letter to the director of the film, asking if he remembered, all these years later, where on the torso he imagined Lee Marvin was shot so that he could get to his feet, stagger through the prison while the opening credits came up and swim the treacherous waters between the island and San Francisco.

They told the director that it was one of their *favourite* films, they were simply inquiring as forensic specialists. When they looked at the scene closely they saw Lee Marvin's hand leap up to his chest. 'See, he has difficulty on his right side. When he swims later in the bay he uses his left arm.' 'God, it's a great movie. Very little music. Lots of silence.'

Gamini worked in the base hospital at Polonnaruwa during his last year in the northeast. This was where the serious casualties from all over the Eastern Province, Trincomalee to Ampara, were brought. Family murders, outbreaks of typhoid, grenade injuries, attempted assassinations by one side or another. The wards were always in turmoil—outpatients in General Surgery, floor patients in the corridors, technicians arriving from a radio store to fix the electrocardiogram unit.

The only cool place was the blood bank, where the plasma was refrigerated. The only silent place was Rheumatology, where a man slowly and quietly turned a giant wheel to exercise his shoulders and arms, which had been broken in an accident a few months earlier, and where a solitary woman sat with her arthritic hand in a basin of warm wax. But in the corridors, the walls mildewed with dampness, men would be rolling giant cylinders of oxygen noisily off the carts. Oxygen was the essential river, hissed into neonatal wards where incubators sheltered babies. Outside this room of infants, and beyond the shell of the hospital building, was a garrisoned country. The rebel guerrillas controlled all roads after dark, so even the army didn't move at night. In the children's ward Janaka and Suriya circled their patients—one had a heart murmur, another suffered from fits— but if there was bombing or a village attack they too became part of the hospital 'Flying Squad,' and even those in the neonatal ward worked the triage and operating room. They left an intern behind.

The specialists who came north seldom worked only in their specific area of knowledge. They were in Pediatrics one day, but might spend the rest of the week helping to contain an outbreak of cholera in the village settlements. If cholera drugs were not available, they did what doctors in another era had done— dissolved a teaspoon of potassium permanganate in a pint of water and poured it into every well or standing pool. The past was always useful. At one time Gamini tried to keep an infant alive for four days. The girl could hold nothing down, not her mother's milk, not even water, and she was dehydrating. He remembered something and got hold of a pomegranate and fed the child the juice. It stayed down. Something he'd heard about pomegranates in a song his *ayah* had sung . . . It was legendary that every Tamil home on Jaffna peninsula had three trees in the garden. A mango, a murunga, and the pomegranate. Murunga leaves were cooked in crab curries to neutralize poisons, pomegranate leaves were soaked in water for the care of eyes and the fruit eaten to aid digestion. The mango was for pleasure.

Gamini was working with Janaka Fonseka in children's surgery when they began hearing news in the corridors that a village had been attacked. In front of him on the operating table was a small boy, naked except for white shorts. The two doctors had been preparing for the operation all week; neither of them had attempted it before, they had been reading the text of the procedure in Kirklan's *Cardiac Surgery* over and over. They had to cool the boy's body down to twenty-five degrees Celsius by running cold blood into him, reducing his temperature until the heart stopped. Then they would operate. As they began cutting, the wounded started coming into the halls and they were aware of the Flying Squad in action around them.

He and Fonseka stayed with the boy, keeping just one nurse. A heart the size of a guava. They opened the right atrium. This was as close to magic as the two of them got in their days there. They talked frantically back and forth to be certain of what they were doing. They could hear the carts carrying equipment or bodies, they couldn't tell which, racing down the halls. There'd been a massacre, they now heard, a village thirty miles away had been pretty well wiped out. Somebody had to be sent there to see if any were still alive. The child in front of them had a congenital abnormality, a beautiful kid, Gamini kept wanting to see the boy's dark black eyes, which had been full of trust, which had looked up at him as he gave the needle that had put him into uncontrolled sleep.

Fallot's tetralogy. Four things wrong with the heart, so he would live perhaps only into his early teens if they didn't operate now. A beautiful boy. Gamini was not going to leave him alone, betray him in his sleep. He kept Fonseka with him, not letting him go to the others as Fonseka thought he should. 'I have to leave, they keep calling out my name.' 'I know. This is just one boy.' 'Fuck, that's not what I mean.' 'You have to stay.'

The operation took six hours and all that time Gamini stayed with the boy. He let Fonseka go after three hours. The nurse would have to help him reverse the bypass. He knew her as a starting intern, the Tamil wife of one of the staff. She and her husband had come to the peripheral hospital in the last month. Gamini stood by the boy and explained what they had to do. The boy would have to be rewarmed with blood at a higher temperature, and at the key moment the bypass had to be removed. *Fallot's tetralogy.* No one had ever performed the procedure in this country.

So in the fifth hour Gamini and the nurse reversed the process that he and Fonseka had set up. The young nurse watching him for any sign that what she was doing might be wrong. But she was faultless, faultless, calmer, it seemed, than he was. 'This one?' 'Yes. I need you to cut a shallow three-inch line there. No, to the left.' She cut into the boy's body. 'Don't remain a nurse. You'll be a good doctor.' She was smiling under the mask.

As soon as the boy was in Recovery, Gamini left him with her. There was no one else he could trust. He got two beepers and told her to contact him if something seemed wrong. He washed up and then went into the chaos of the triage. There was blood on everyone except him.

It took a few more hours to deal with the crisis. In surgery they wore white rubber boots and all the doors had to be closed. Sometimes if a doctor had heat exhaustion he slipped into the refrigerated blood bank for a few minutes among the plasma and pack cells. Gamini took over in surgery. There was a small Buddha lit with a low-watt bulb in nearly every ward, and there was one in surgery as well.

All the survivors had been brought in by now. The killings had happened at two in the morning in a small village beside the main road to Batticaloa. They had brought him nine-month-old twins, each shot in the palms and one bullet each in their right legs—so it was no accident, a close-range job and intentional, left to die; the mother had been killed. In a couple of weeks those two children were peaceful things, full of light. You thought, What did they do to deserve this, and then, What did they do to survive this? Their wounds, in reality quite minor, stayed with him. It was the formal evil of the act perhaps, he didn't know. Thirty people had been massacred that morning.

Lakdasa drove to the village and did the postmortems, otherwise relatives would not receive compensation. For everyone in the region was poor as grass. In those villages the father of a family of seven earned one hundred rupees a day working in a wood shop. That meant each of them could have a five-rupee meal a day. For that you could buy a toffee. When political entourages came up to the provinces and received tea and lunch, the visit cost forty thousand rupees.

The doctors were coping with injuries from all political sides and there was just one operating table. When a patient was lifted off, blood was soaked up with newspaper, the surface swabbed with Dettol, and the next patient laid down. The real problem was water, and in the larger hospitals, because of frequent power failures, vaccines and other drugs were being thrown away constantly. Doctors needed to scavenge the countryside for equipment—buckets, Rinso soap powder, a washing machine. 'Surgical clamps for us were like gold for a woman.'

Their hospital existed like a medieval village. A chalkboard in the kitchen listed the numbers of loaves of bread and the bushels of rice needed to feed five hundred patients a day. This was before massacre victims were brought in. The doctors pooled money and hired two market scribes as registrars who moved alongside them in the wards listing and recording the patients' names and their ailments. The most frequently seen problems were snakebite, rabies caused by fox or mongoose, kidney failure, encephalitis, diabetes, tuberculosis, and the war.

Night had its own activity. He woke and was attached instantly to the sounds of the world. A dogfight, a man running to fetch something, the pouring of water into a vessel. When Gamini was a boy, nights were terrifying to him, his eyes wide open till he fell asleep, certain that he and his bed had lost their moorings in the darkness. He needed loud clocks beside him. Ideally he would have a dog in the room, or someone—an aunt or an *ayah* who snored. Now, working or sleeping during the night shifts, he was secure with all of the human and animal activity beyond the ward's light. Only bird life, so vocal and territorial during the day, was shut down, though there was one Polonnaruwa rooster that cried out false dawns from three in the morning on. Interns had been trying to kill it.

He walked the stretch of hospital, from wing to wing, open air on either side of him. There was the buzz of electricity close beside the pools of light as you passed them. You were aware of it only at night. You saw a bush and you sensed it growing. Someone came out and poured blood into a gutter and coughed. Everyone had a bad cough in Polonnaruwa.

He was aware of every sound. A shoe or sandal step, the noise of the bedspring when he lifted a patient, the snapping of an ampule. Sleeping in the wards, he could be one limb of a large creature, linked to the others by the thread of noises.

Later, if he was unable to sleep in the district medical officer's building, he would walk back the two hundred yards along the empty curfewed main street to the hospital. The nurse stationed at a night desk would turn and see the look on him and find a bed for him. He would be asleep in seconds.

In the village clinic were twenty mothers and their infants. They filled out clinic records and the pregnant women were checked for diabetes and anemia. The doctors talked to each of the women, studying their forms as they moved forward in the queue. On a makeshift table a nurse wrapped vitamin pills in newspaper and gave them to the mothers. A pressure cooker was being used as a steam sterilizer for glass syringes and needles.

The screams began as soon as the first baby got a needle, and within seconds most of the babies in the small shack that served as a medical outpost were howling. After about five minutes they were silent again; breasts had been pulled out and mothers beamed at their infants and there was solution and victory for all. This one clinic served four hundred families from the area as well as three hundred from an adjoining region. No one from the Ministry of Health had ever come to the border villages.

For all of the doctors, Lakdasa was the great moral force, the rough brother of justice. 'The problem up here is not the Tamil problem, it's the human problem.' He was thirty-seven and his hair was grey. When he drank he revealed an intricate set of confabulations, as if he were steering himself through a well-mapped harbour. 'If I drink more than seventy-two millimetres, my liver plays up. If I drink less, my heart plays up.'

Lakdasa lived mostly on potato rotis. He smoked Gold Leaf cigarettes in his jeep where a fan rotating air was glued to the dashboard. He kept his sarong in the glove compartment and slept wherever he had to—the DMO's office, a sofa in the living room of a friend. There were months when his weight would suddenly drop ten pounds. Obsessed with his blood pressure, he tested it daily, and any session at a clinic ended with his weighing himself on the scales and checking his blood sugar. He noted the bell curves and continued as usual driving through jungles and garrisoned land to meet his patients. It didn't matter what state he was in as long as he knew what state he was in.

On Saturday mornings Gamini and Lakdasa drove back to

Polonnaruwa listening to the cricket. A long day at a clinic. Sometimes along the road, now and then, there were thirty-foot strips of grain being dried on the tarmac, strips laid so narrow a car could pass over them without having the wheels touch the drying grain. A man with a broom stood nearby to signal to passing cars to be aware of it, and to sweep the grain back to the centre if they were not.

In the cafeteria of the base hospital—a half-hour break in his shift—a woman sat down at Gamini's table and drank her tea, ate a biscuit with him. It was about four in the morning and he didn't know her. He just nodded to her, he felt private and too tired to talk.

'I helped you with an operation once, some months ago. The massacre night.' His mind wheeled back a century.

'I thought you got transferred.'

'Yes, I was, then I came back here.'

He hadn't recognized her at all. She'd had a mask on when he spent the crucial long hours with her over the boy. When she was not wearing a mask, in pre-op, he had probably only glanced at her. Their comradeship had been mostly anonymous.

'You're married to someone here, right?' She nodded. There was a scar at her wrist. It was new, he would have noticed that during the surgery.

He looked up quickly at her face. 'It is very good to meet you.'

'Yes. For me too,' she said.

'Where did you go?'

'He'—a cough—'he got stationed in Kurunegala.'

Gamini kept watching her, the way she was selecting the words carefully. Her face was young and lean and dark, her eyes bright as if it were daylight.

'Actually, I have passed you in the wards a lot!'

'I'm sorry.'

'No. I know you didn't recognize me. Why should you.' A pause. She put her hand through her hair and then was very still.

'I've seen that boy.'

'That boy?'

She looked down, smiling to herself now. 'The boy we operated on. I have visited him. They . . . they renamed the boy Gamini. The parents. After you. It was a lot of trouble, red tape, for them to do that.'

'Good. So I have an heir.'

'Yes, you do. . . . I am training now extra hours in the children's ward.' She was about to continue, then stopped.

He nodded, suddenly tired. What he wanted in his life now seemed a huge thing. What he wished for would involve the lives of others, years of effort. Chaos. Unfairness. Lying.

She looked at her tea and drank the last of it.

'It was good to meet with you.'

'Yes.'

Gamini rarely saw himself from the point of view of a stranger. Though most people knew who he was, he felt he was invisible to those around him. The woman therefore slid alongside him and clattered about in the almost empty house of his heart. She became, as she had done that night of the operation, the sole accompanist to what he thought, what he worked on. When later he turned over the hands of a patient, he thought of the scar at her wrist, the way her fingers had slipped through her hair, what he wished to reveal to her. But it was his own heart that could not step into the world.

*

There is a break before the ward visits at six p.m. Gamini pulls down the registrar's log from the shelf. Since the scribes have taken over, the entries are much better—the handwriting immaculate and small, green ink underlining the months and Sundays. He cannot remember the date so he looks for a flurry of entries, as there would have been around the time of the killings. Then goes down the list of interns and nurses.

> *Prethiko*
> *Seela*
> *Raduka*
> *Buddhika*
> *Kaashdya*

He moves his fingers down the ledger to check the assignments, discovers her name.

He walks almost a mile to the event, in his only good jacket. The rest house is serving the usual bad food in the glassed-in dining room that hangs over the water. The children wait with unlit sparklers, in delirium for any kind of ceremony. Cake in one hand, a sparkler in the other. Lakdasa is organizing the fireworks display and is on the raft lining up his catherine wheels and burning schoolrooms. Gamini has caught a glimpse of her in the distance. He hasn't seen her since the cup of tea they shared two weeks earlier.

When she is close to him later, he sees the small red earrings against her darkness. They were her grandmother's, and the shortness of her boyishly cut hair allows him to see them clearly, the red gem on each lobe tiny as a ladybug. 'I bury them when I am not wearing them,' she says. They stroll towards the ruins, away from the rest house. A sign says: PLEASE DO NOT ENTER AND PUT YOUR FEET AGAINST THE IMAGE AND TAKE PHOTOGRAPHS.

Behind her are old fragments of colour, the white-red borders on the painted stone he can see even in this moonlight. From the promontory they watch the start of the fireworks. Some of the extravagant explosions are cut short, crashing too soon into the water, or they skitter dangerously like flung lit stones towards the rest house.

He turns to her. She is wearing his jacket over her ruffled shirt.

And she realizes there is an emotional seriousness in this distant man. She needs to step backwards out of the maze they have innocently entered. He is content to be near her, the beauty of this ear and earring, then a comparison with the other side of her head, the way the moon is over them and also in water, the way the water holds the night lilies and their reflection. The false and true alternatives surround them.

She takes his hand and brings it to her forehead. 'Feel that. Do you feel that?' 'Yes.' 'That's my brain. I'm not as drunk as you, so I am smarter than you. Or even if you were not drunk I might be clearer about this than you. A little.' Then a smile from her that will make him forgive anything she says.

She talks to him, more strongly than what the scar on her wrist suggests, her shirt open in a billow at the neck.

'You look, at some moments, like my brother's wife.' He laughs.

'You are going to be my husband's brother, then. That's how I'll treat you. That is a kind of love.'

He leans back against the pavilion of stone, someone or other's cosmic mountain, and she moves forward, he thinks it is to him, but she is only returning his black jacket.

He remembers swimming later that evening, entering the dark water naked and climbing out onto the abandoned firework raft. He sees a few silhouettes in the glassed room over the water. The Queen of England came to this rest house years ago, when she was young. He sits out there clearing his head of the way she disappeared into the throng with the subtlest of courtesies. The way . . .

A year from now he will return to Colombo and meet his future wife. *Gamini?* A woman named Chrishanti will say, approaching him. *Chrishanti.* He knew her brother at school. It is another fancy-dress party. Neither of them is wearing a costume, but they are both disguised by the past.

There were some passengers on the train squatting in the aisles with wrapped bundles, pet birds.

I was the one she should have loved, Gamini said.

Anil sitting beside him assumed she was to get a confession. The mercurial doctor about to expose his heart. That category of seduction. But there was nothing he did or said during the remaining journey—to the ayurvedic hospital he had offered to show her—that used the reins of seduction. Just his slow drawl as the train swept unhesitatingly into the darkness of tunnels and he would turn from looking at his hands towards his reflection in the glass. That was how he told her, looking down or away from her, and she seeing him only in a wavering mirror image lost when they moved back into light.

I saw her often. More than most people knew. With her job at the radio station, my strange hours, it was easy. And we were 'related.' . . . It wasn't a courtship. That suggests two people in a dance. Well, maybe one dance at my wedding, I suppose. 'The Air That I Breathe.' Remember that song? A romantic moment. It was a wedding after all, you could embrace each other. I was getting married. She was married already. But I was the one she should have loved. I was already on speed, in those days, when I would see her.

Who are you speaking of, Gamini?

I'm always awake. I'm good at what I do. So when she was brought in to Dean Street Hospital, I was there. She had swallowed lye. Suiciders decide on that method of death because, since it's the most painful, they might stop themselves doing it. The throat is burned out, then the organs. She was unconscious, even when she woke she didn't know where she was. I ran her through into Emergency with a couple of nurses.

With one hand I was giving her painkillers and with the other using ammonia to snap her awake. I needed to reach her. I didn't want her to feel alone, in this last stage. I overloaded her with painkillers but I didn't want her asleep. It was selfishness on my part. I should have just knocked her out, let her go. But I wanted her to be comforted by me being there. That it was me, not him, not her husband.

I held her eyelids up with my thumbs. I shook her until she saw who it was. She didn't care. I'm here. I love you, I said. She closed her eyes, it seemed to me in disgust. Then she was in pain again.

I can't give you any more, I said, I'll lose you completely. She put her hand up and made a gesture across her throat.

The train was sucked into the tunnel and they moved within it, shuddering in the darkness.

Who was she, Gamini? She could not see him. She touched his shoulder and could feel him turn towards her. He brought his face close to her. She could see nothing in spite of the muddy flicker of light now and then.

What would you do with a name? But it wasn't a question. He spat it out.

The train came into daylight for a few seconds, then slid into the darkness of another tunnel.

All the wards were busy that night, he continued. Shootings, others to be operated on. There are always a lot of suicides during a war. At first that seems strange, but you learn to understand it. And she, I think, was overcome by it. The nurses left me with her and then I was called into the triage wards. She was full of morphine, asleep. I found a kid in the hall and I got him to watch her. If she woke he was to come and find me in D wing. This was three a.m. I didn't want him falling asleep, so I broke a Benzedrine and gave him half. He found me later and told me she was awake. But I couldn't save her.

There was a train window open and the sound of the clatter doubled. She could feel the gusts.

What would you do with her name? Would you tell my brother? Someone kicked her ankle and she drew in her breath.

When Leaf left Arizona Anil didn't hear from her for more than six months. Although during every moment of her farewell she had promised to write. Leaf, who was her closest friend. Once there was just a postcard of a stainless-steel pole. Quemado, New Mexico, the postmark seemed to read, but there was no contact address. Anil assumed she'd abandoned her, for a new life, for new friends. *Watch out for the armadillos, señorita!* Still, Anil left a snapshot on her fridge of the two of them dancing at some party, this woman who had been her echo, who watched movies with her in her backyard. They'd sway in the hammock, they'd consume rhubarb pie, they'd wake up at three in the morning entangled in each other's arms, and then Anil would drive home through the empty streets.

The next postcard was of a parabolic dish antenna. Again no message or address. Anil was angry and threw it away. A few months later, when working in Europe, she got the phone call. She didn't know how Leaf had found her.

'This is an illegal call, so don't say my name. I'm cutting into someone's line.'

(As a teenager Leaf had made long-distance calls on Sammy Davis Jr.'s stolen phone number.)

'Oh Angie, where are you! You were supposed to write.'

'I'm sorry. When's your next break.'

'In January. A couple of months. I may go to Sri Lanka after that.'

'If I send you a ticket, will you come and see me? I'm in New Mexico.'

'Yes. Oh yes . . .'

So Anil returned to America. And she sat with Leaf in a doughnut shop in Socorro, New Mexico, an hour away from the Very Large Array of Telescopes, which minute by minute drew information out of the skies. Information about the state of things ten billion years ago, and as many miles out. It was here, in this place, that they caught up with the truth in each other's lives.

Originally Leaf had said she had bad asthma, that was why she had moved into the desert for a year, disappearing from Anil's life. She had got involved with Earthworks and was living at *The Lightning Field* near Quemado. In 1977, artist Walter De Maria had planted four hundred stainless-steel poles high in the desert on a flat plain a mile long. Leaf's first job was to be a caretaker of the lodge. Powerful winds swept in from the desert and she got to witness storms, because during the summer the poles drew lightning onto the plain. She stood among them, within the electricity, the thunder simultaneous around her. She had just wanted to be a cowboy. She loved the Southwest.

Now Leaf met Anil near the Very Large Array—the telescope assembly that picked up languages of data out of the universe above the desert. She was living alongside these receivers of the huge history of the sky. Who was out there? How far away was that signal? Who was dying unmoored?

Well, it turned out Leaf was.

They sat facing each other during the meals they had together every day at the Pequod. Anil felt the giant telescopes in the open desert belonged to the same genre as Leaf's beloved drive-ins.

They talked and listened to each other. She loved Anil. And she knew Anil loved her. Sister and sister. But Leaf was ill. It would get worse.

'What do you mean?'

'I just keep . . . forgetting things. I can diagnose myself, you see. I have Alzheimer's. I know I'm too young for this, but I had encephalitis as a kid.'

No one had noticed her illness when they had worked in Arizona. Sister and sister. And she had left without telling Anil why she was really leaving. With all the solitary energy she could draw on, she had gone east to the New Mexico deserts. Asthma, she said. She was starting to lose her memory, fighting for her life.

They sat at the Pequod in Socorro, whispering into the afternoons.

'Leaf, listen. Remember? Who killed Cherry Valance?'

'What?'

Anil repeated the question slowly.

'Cherry Valance,' Leaf said, 'I . . .'

'John Wayne shot him. Remember.'

'Did I know that?'

'You know John Wayne?'

'No, my darling.'

My darling!

'Do you think they can hear us?' Leaf asked. 'That giant metal ear in the desert. Is it picking us up too? I'm just a detail from the subplot, right.'

Then a splinter of memory returned and she added, awfully, 'Well, you always thought Cherry Valance would die.'

· · ·

And did she? Sarath had asked, when Anil told him about her friend Leaf.

'No. She called me that night when I had fever, when we were in the south. We always would phone each other and talk till we fell asleep, laughing or crying, trading our stories. No. Her sister watches over her, not far from those telescopes in New Mexico.'

Dear John Boorman,

   I do not have your address but a Mr. Walter Donohue from Faber & Faber has offered to forward this to you. I write on behalf of myself and my colleague Leaf Niedecker about a scene in an early film of yours, Point Blank.

   At the start of the film, the prologue as it were, Lee Marvin is shot from a distance of what looks like four or five feet. He falls back into a prison cell and we think he might be dead. Eventually he comes to, leaves Alcatraz and swims across the So-and-so Straits into San Francisco.

   We are forensic scientists and have been arguing about where on his body Mr. Marvin was shot. My friend thinks it was a rib glance shooting and that apart from the rib break it was a minor flesh wound. I feel the wound to be more serious. I know many years have passed, but perhaps you could try to remember and advise us of the location of the entry wound and exit wound and recall your discussions with Mr. Marvin as to how he should react and move later on in the film when time had passed and his character had recovered.

Sincerely,
Anil Tissera

A rainy-night conversation at the *walawwa*.

'You like to remain cloudy, don't you, Sarath, even to yourself.'

'I don't think clarity is necessarily truth. It's simplicity, isn't it?'

'I need to know what you think. I need to break things apart to know where someone came from. That's also an acceptance of complexity. Secrets turn powerless in the open air.'

'Political secrets are not powerless, in any form,' he said.

'But the tension and danger around them, one can make them evaporate. You're an archaeologist. Truth comes finally into the light. It's in the bones and sediment.'

'It's in character and nuance and mood.'

'That is what governs us in our lives, that's not the truth.'

'For the living it is the truth,' he quietly said.

'Why did you get into such a business?'

'I love history, the intimacy of entering all those landscapes. Like entering a dream. Someone nudges a stone away and there's a story.'

'A secret.'

'Yes, a secret . . . I was selected to go and study in China. I was there a year. And all I saw of China was this one area about the size of a pasture. I didn't go anywhere else. That's where I stayed and where I worked. Villagers had been cleaning a hillock and had come across earth of a different colour. Something that simple, but teams of archaeologists came. Under the different-coloured grey earth they found stone slabs, under these they found timbers—huge timbers that had been cut and stripped and nestled together like a great floor in some mead hall. Only of course, it was a *ceiling*.

'So it was, as I said, like an exercise in a dream where you are made to go deeper and further. They brought in cranes to lift the timbers out and underneath them they discovered water—a water tomb. Three giant pools. Floating there was a lacquered coffin of an ancient ruler. Also in the water were coffins with the bodies of twenty female musicians along with their instruments. They were to accompany him, you see. With zithers, flutes, pan-pipes, drums, iron bells. They were delivering him to his ances-tors. When they removed the skeletons from the coffins and laid them out there was no damage to any of the bones to reveal how the musicians had been killed, not one fractured bone.'

'Then they were strangled,' Anil said.

'Yes. That's what we were told.'

'Or suffocated. Or poisoned. A study of the bones could have told you the truth. I don't know if there was a tradition of poi-soning in China at that time. When was it?'

'Fifth century B.C.'

'Yeah, they knew poisons.'

'We soaked the lacquered coffins with polymer so they wouldn't collapse. The lacquer had been made out of sumac sap mixed with coloured pigments. Hundreds of layers of it. Then they discovered the musical instruments. Drums. Mouth organs made from gourds. Chinese zithers! Most of all—bells.

'By now historians had arrived too. Taoist and Confucian scholars, specialists in musical chimes. We pulled sixty-four bells up out of the water. Till now no instruments from this period had been found, though it was known that music had been the most significant activity and *idea* of this civilization. So you would be buried not with your wealth but alongside music. The great bells removed from the water turned out to have been made with the most sophisticated techniques. It seemed each region of the country had its own method of bell-making. In those regions there had been, literally, wars of music. . . .

'Nothing was as important. Music was not entertainment, it was a link with ancestors who had led us here, it was a moral and spiritual force. The experience of breaking through barriers of slate, wood, water, to discover a buried women's orchestra had a similar mystical logic to it, do you understand? You must understand their state of acceptance somehow of such a death. The way the terrorists in our time can be made to believe they are eternal if they die for the cause of their ruler.

'Before I left they had an event where everyone who had worked there came to hear the bells being struck. It was at the end of my year. It took place in the evening and, as we listened, we felt them physically, lifting into the darkness. Each bell had two notes to represent the two sides of the spirit, containing a balance of opposing forces. Possibly it was those bells that made me an archaeologist.'

'Twenty murdered women.'

'It was another world with its own value system that came to the surface.'

'Love me, love my orchestra. You *can* take it with you! That kind of madness lies within the structure of all civilizations, not just in distant cultures. You boys are sentimental. Death *and* glory. A guy I know fell in love with me because of my laugh. We hadn't even met or been in the same room, he'd heard me on a tape.'

'And?'

'Oh, he swooned over me like a married man, made me fall

in love with him. You've heard the story. How smart women become idiots, ignore everything they should keep on knowing. By the end I wasn't laughing too much. No bell-ringing.'

'Was he in love with you before he met you, do you think?'

'Well, that's interesting. Perhaps it was the habit of my voice. I think he'd listened to the tape two or three times. He was a writer. A writer. They have time to get into trouble. I had been asked to chair a talk at a conference given by a teacher of mine, Larry Angel. A lovely, funny man, so I was in fact laughing a lot at the way he thought and put things together with his nonlinear mind. We were onstage sitting at a table and I introduced him, and I guess my microphone was on and I was chuckling as he gave the lecture. The old guy and I always had a good rapport. Favourite-uncle atmosphere, slightly sexual but definitely platonic.

'I guess the writer, my eventual friend, also had a nonlinear mind, so he was getting the jokes. He had ordered the tape because he was interested in researching burial mounds or something, a rather serious subject, and he wanted information, and details. That was our meeting. In proxy. Not a big moment across the universe . . . We were on a high wire for three years during our relationship.'

*

Their first adventure together: Anil drove her unwashed white car that smelled of mildew to a Sri Lankan restaurant. It was just a few months after Cullis had heard her on the tape. They were driving through early-evening traffic.

'So. Are you famous?'

'No.' He laughed.

'A little?'

'I'd say about seventy people who are not relatives or friends would recognize my name.'

'Even here?'

'I doubt it. Who knows. What is it, Muswell Hill?'

'Archway.'

She opened the window and yelled.

'*Hey, listen, everybody*—I've got the science writer Cullis Wright in my car! Or is it Cullis Wrong? Yes, it's him! He's with me today!'

'Thank you.'

She rolled up the window. 'We can check the gossips tomorrow, to see if you were busted.' She rolled down the window and this time used the horn to gain attention. They were stuck in traffic anyway. Maybe from a distance it looked like a fight. An angry woman half out of the car gesturing towards someone within, trying to get passersby on her side.

He nestled back into the passenger's seat, watching her loose energy, the ease with which she swept her skirt up to her knees and leapt out of the car once more after pulling the hand brake with a grunt. She was now waving her arms, banging on the dirty roof of the car.

He would remember other moments like this later—times when she tried to strip off his carefulness, tried to unbuckle his worried glance. Making him dance on one of the dark streets of Europe to a small cassette player she pressed against his ear. 'Brazil.' *Remember this song.* He sang the words with her on that Paris street, their feet dancing over the painted outline of a dog.

He sat there, pressed against the back of his car seat, traffic all around him, watching her torso through the car door as she yelped and pounded on the roof. He felt he had been encased in ice or metal and she was banging on its surface in order to reach him, in order to let him out. The energy of her swirling clothes, the wild grin as she entered the car again and kissed him—she could have broken him free. But as a married man he had already pawned his heart.

She left him eventually in the Una Palma motel room in Borrego Springs. Left nothing of herself for him to hold on to. Just the blood as black as her hair, the room as shadowed as her skin.

He lay in the dark room watching the twitch of his arm muscle flick the knife into movement. He drifted, a boat without oars, into half-sleep. All night he could hear the faint whir of the hotel clock. His fear was that the beating in his blood would stop, that the noise on the roof of the car as she reached for him would end. Now and then a truck hushed by, twisting light. He fought sleep. Usually he loved the letting go. When he wrote, he slipped into the page as if it were water, and tumbled on. The writer was a tumbler. (Would he remember that?) If not, then a tinker, carrying a hundred pots and pans and bits of linoleum and wires and falconer's hoods and pencils and . . . you carried them around for years and gradually fit them into a small, modest book. The art of packing. Then he would be off scouring the wetlands again. How to make a book, Anil. You asked me *How,* you asked *What's the most important thing you need?* Anil, I'll tell you. . . .

But she was on the night bus climbing out from the valley, locked for warmth in her grey ferren—half cloak, half serape. Her eyes inches away from the window, receiving the moments of lit trees. Oh, he knew that look in her, realigning herself after a fight. But this was to be the last time. No second chances. She knew and so did he. Their life of sparring love, tentative abandonment, the worst and best of times, all the memory of it balanced as on a clearly lit lab table in Oklahoma, the bus stirring its way up into the mist, passing the small towns in the mountains.

Anil's body hunched into itself as it became colder. Still, her eyes did not blink, she would not miss any movement this last night with him. She was determined to underline their crimes towards each other, their failures. It was just this she wanted to be certain about, although she knew that later there would be other versions of their fatal romance.

Apart from the driver she was the only sentinel. She saw the jackrabbit. She heard the thud of a night bird against the bus. No lights on within this floating vessel. She would be cleaning up her desk for five days, and then leave for Sri Lanka. She had somewhere in her bag a list of every phone and fax number where he could reach her on the island for the next two months. She had planned to give it to him. She had circled around his fucked-up life, his clenched fears, the love and comfort he was scared to take from her. Still, he had been like a wonderful house to her, full of unusual compartments, so many possibilities, strangely rousing.

The bus climbed above the valley. Like him she couldn't sleep. Like him she would continue the war. How would he sleep in the night with her name between him and his wife? Even the tenderest concerns between this couple would contain her presence, like a shadow. She didn't want that anymore. To be a mote or an echo, to be a compass unused except to give his mind knowledge of her whereabouts.

And whom would he talk to if not her at midnight through several time zones? As if she were the stone in the temple grounds used by priests as the object of confession. Well, for now, they both had no destiny. They only had to escape the past.

Anil was one unable to sing, but she knew the words and the pace of phrasing.

> *Oh, the trees grow high in New York State,*
> *They shine like gold in autumn—*
>
> *Never had the blues whence I came,*
> *But in New York State I caught 'em.*

She said the lines in a whisper, head down, to her own chest. Autumn. Caught 'em. How the rhyme snuggled into its partner.

The Life Wheel

Sarath and Anil had identified Sailor at the third plumbago village. He was Ruwan Kumara and he had been a toddy tapper. After breaking his leg in a fall he had worked in the local mine, and the village remembered when the outsiders had picked him up. They had entered the tunnel where twelve men were working. They brought a *billa*—someone from the community with a gunnysack over his head, slits cut out for his eyes—to anonymously identify the rebel sympathizer. A *billa* was a monster, a ghost, to scare children in games, and it had picked out Ruwan Kumara and he had been taken away.

They now had a specific date for the abduction. Back at the *walawwa* they planned the next step. Sarath felt they should still be careful, have more evidence, or all their work would be rejected. He proposed that he go to Colombo and search for Ruwan Kumara's name in a list of government undesirables; he claimed he could get hold of such a thing. It would take two days and then he would be back. He would leave her his cell phone, though she would probably not be able to contact him. So he would call her.

But after five days Sarath had not returned.

All her fears about him rose again—the relative who was a minister, his views on the danger of truth. She moved around the *walawwa* furiously alone. Then it was six days. She got Sarath's cell phone working and called Ratnapura Hospital but it seemed that Ananda had left, had gone home. There was no one to talk to. She was alone with Sailor.

She took the phone and went out to the edge of the paddy field.

'Who is this?'

'Anil Tissera, sir.'

'Ah, the missing one.'

'Yes sir, the swimmer.'

'You never came to see me.'

'I need to talk to you, sir.'

'What about.'

'I have to make a report and I need help.'

'Why me?'

'You knew my father. You worked with him. I need someone I can trust. There is maybe a political murder.'

'You are speaking on a cell phone. Don't say my name.'

'I'm stranded here. I need to get to Colombo. Can you help?'

'I can try to arrange something. Where are you?'

It was the same question he had asked once before. She paused a moment.

'In Ekneligoda, sir. The *walawwa*.'

'I know it.'

He was off the phone.

A day later Anil was in Colombo, in the Armoury Auditorium that was a part of the anti-terrorist unit building in Gregory's Road. She no longer had possession of Sailor's skeleton. A car had picked her up at the *walawwa* but Dr. Perera had not been in it. When she arrived at the hospital in Colombo he had met her, put his arm around her. Then they'd eaten a meal in the cafeteria and he had listened to what she had done. He advised her to take it no further. He thought her work good, but it was unsafe. 'You made a speech about political responsibility,' she said. 'I heard a different opinion then.' 'That was a speech,' he replied. When they returned to the lab, there was confusion as to where the skeleton was.

Now, standing in the small auditorium that was half filled with various officials, among them military and police personnel trained in counter-insurgency methods, she felt stranded. She was supposed to give her report with no real evidence. It had been a way to discredit her whole investigation. Anil stood by an old skeleton laid out on a table, probably Tinker, and began delineating the various methods of bone analysis and skeletal identification relating to occupation and region of origin, although this was not the skeleton she needed.

Sarath in the back row, unseen by her, listened to her quiet explanations, her surefootedness, her absolute calm and refusal to be emotional or angry. It was a lawyer's argument and, more important, a citizen's evidence; she was no longer just a foreign authority. Then he heard her say, 'I think you murdered hundreds of us.' *Hundreds of us.* Sarath thought to himself. Fifteen years away and she is finally *us.*

But now they were in danger. He sensed the hostility in the room. Only he was not against her. Now he had to somehow protect himself.

Between Anil and the skeleton, discreetly out of sight, was her tape recorder, imprinting every word and opinion and question from officials, which she, till now, responded to courteously and unforgivingly. But he could see what Anil couldn't—the half-glances around the hot room (they must have turned off the air-conditioning thirty minutes into the evidence, an old device to distract thought); there were conversations beginning around him. He shrugged himself off the wall and moved forward.

'Excuse me, please.'

Everyone turned to him. She looked up, her face amazed at his presence and this interruption.

'This skeleton was also located at the Bandarawela site?'

'Yes,' she said.

'And how much earth was found over it?'

'Three feet approximately.'

'Can you be more precise?'

'We cannot. I really don't see its relevance.'

'Because sections of the hill outside the cave, where this one was found, had been worn down by cattle, trade, rains . . . isn't that correct? Can someone turn on the damn air-conditioning in here, it's difficult for us all to think clearly in this heat. Isn't it true that in the old nineteenth-century burial grounds, murder sites as well as graves were often—in fact in nearly every case—found with less than two feet of earth over them?'

She was becoming agitated and decided to be silent. Sarath could sense them focusing on him, turning in their seats.

He walked down to the front of the auditorium and they let him approach her. He faced Anil now across the table, leaned forward and with a set of tongs pulled out the piece of stone imprisoned within the rib cage.

'This stone was found in the ribs of the skeleton.'

'Yes.'

'Tell us what happens in ancient customs. . . . Think carefully, Miss Tissera, don't just theorize.'

There was a pause.

'Please don't speak like that. Patronizing me.'

'Tell us what happens.'

'They bury bodies and they place a stone on the earth above it, usually. It acts like a marker and then it drops when the flesh gives way.'

'Gives way? How?'

'One minute!'

'How many years does that take?'

Silence.

'Yes?'

Silence.

He spoke very slowly now.

'A minimum of nine years usually, isn't it? Before the stone falls through, into the rib cage. Right?'

'Yes, but—'

'Right?'

'Yes. Except for fire corpses. Burned ones.'

'But we're not even sure of this, because most of them were burned in the last century, these ones in the historical gravesites. As you know, there was a plague there in 1856. Another in 1890.

Many were burned. The skeleton you have here is likely to be a hundred years old—in spite of your fine social work about its career and habits and diet. . . .'

'The skeleton I *could* have proved something with has been confiscated.'

'We seem to have too many bodies around. Is this one less important than the confiscated one?'

'Of course not. But the confiscated one died less than five years ago.'

'Confiscated. Confiscated . . . Who confiscated it?' Sarath said.

'It was taken while I met with Dr. Perera in Kynsey Road Hospital. It was lost there.'

'So you lost it, then. It was not confiscated.'

'I did not lose it. It was taken from the lab when I was speaking with him in the cafeteria.'

'So you misplaced it. Do you think it's possible Dr. Perera had something to do with that?'

'I don't know. Perhaps. I have not seen him since.'

'And you wished to prove that skeleton was a recent death. Even if we now do not have the evidence.'

'Mr. Diyasena, I'd like to remind you that I came here as part of a human rights group. As a forensic specialist. I do not work for you, I'm not hired by you. I work for an international authority.'

He turned and directed his words to the audience.

'This "international authority" has been invited here by the government, has it not? Is that not right?'

'We are an independent organization. We make independent reports.'

'To *us*. To the government *here*. That means you do work for the government here.'

'What I wish to report is that some government forces have possibly murdered innocent people. This is what you are hearing from me. You as an archaeologist should believe in the truth of history.'

'I believe in a society that has peace, Miss Tissera. What you are proposing could result in chaos. Why do you not investigate the killing of government officers? Can we get the air-conditioning on, please?'

There was a scattering of applause.

'The skeleton I had was evidence of a certain kind of crime. That is what is important here. *"One village can speak for many villages. One victim can speak for many victims."* Remember? I thought you represented more than you do.'

'Miss Tissera—'

'Doctor.'

'All right, "Doctor." I have brought here another skeleton from another burial site, an earlier century. To establish the difference, I would like you to do a forensic study of it for me.'

'This is ridiculous.'

'This is not ridiculous. I would like to have evidence of the difference between two corpses. *Somasena!*'

He gestured to someone in the back of the hall. The skeleton, wrapped in plastic, was wheeled in.

'A two-hundred-year-old corpse,' he said out loud. 'That's what we assume, anyway, the boys in archaeology. Perhaps you can manage to prove us wrong.'

He was tapping his pencil against her table, like a taunt.

'I need time.'

'We give you forty-eight hours. Leave the skeleton you were talking about and go with Mr. Somasena to the lobby, he will escort you. You will have to sign back all your research before you leave. I must warn you of that. This skeleton will be waiting for you in the front entrance in twenty minutes.'

She turned from him and collected her papers.

'Leave the papers and the tape recorder, please.'

She was still for a moment, then removed the tape recorder from the pocket where she had just put it, and left it on the table.

'It belongs to me,' she whispered. 'Remember?'

'We'll get it back to you.'

She started walking up the steps to the exit. The officials hardly looked at her.

'Dr. Tissera!'

She turned at the top of the stairs and faced him, certain it would be for the last time.

'Don't attempt to return for these things. Just leave the building. We'll call you if we want you.'

She stepped through the door. It closed behind her with a pneumatic click.

Sarath remained there and spoke quietly, out into their midst.

With Gunesena he wheeled the two skeletons on the trolley through the side door. It opened onto a dark passageway that would take them towards the parking lot. They stood still a moment. Gunesena said nothing. Whatever happened, Sarath did not want to return to the auditorium. He felt for a switch. There was the crackle of neon trying to catch, that stuttering of light he was used to in buildings like this.

A row of red arrows lit the passageway, which inclined upwards. They pushed the trolley with the two skeletons in the semi-darkness, arms turning crimson every time they passed an arrow. He imagined Anil two floors above him, walking angrily, slamming each door she walked through. Sarath knew they would halt her at each corridor level, check her papers again and again to irritate and humiliate her. He knew she would be searched, vials and slides removed from her briefcase or pockets, made to undress and dress again. It would take her more than forty minutes to pass the gauntlets and escape the building and she would, he knew, be carrying nothing by the end of the journey, no scraps of information, not a single personal photograph she might foolishly have carried with her into the Armoury building that morning. But she would get out, which was all he wished for.

Since the death of his wife, Sarath had never found the old road back into the world. He broke with his in-laws. The unopened letters of condolence were left in her study. They were, in reality, for her anyway. He returned to archaeology and hid his life in his work. He organized excavations in Chilaw. The young men and women he trained knew little about what had occurred in his life and he was therefore most comfortable among them. He showed them how to place strips of wet plaster on bone, how to gather and file mica, when to transport objects, when to leave them in situ. He ate with them and was open to any question in regard to work. Nothing was held back that he knew or could guess at in their field. Everyone who worked with him accepted the moats of privacy he had established around himself. He returned to his tent tired after their day of coastal excavations. He was in his mid-forties, though he seemed older to the apprentices. He waited until the early evening, until the others had finished swimming in the sea, before he walked into the water, disappearing within its darkness. At this dark hour, out deep, there were sometimes rogue tides that would not let you return, that insisted you away. Alone in the waves he would let go of himself, his body flung around as if in a dance, only his head in the air rational to what surrounded him, the imperceptible glint of large waves that he would slip beneath as they rose above him.

He had grown up loving the sea. When he was a boy at school at St. Thomas's, the sea was just across the railway lines. And whatever coast he was on—at Hambantota, in Chilaw, in Trincomalee—he would watch fishermen in catamarans travel out at dusk till they faded into the night just beyond a boy's vision. As if parting or death or disappearance were simply the elimination of sight in the onlooker.

Patterns of death always surrounded him. In his work he felt he was somehow the link between the mortality of flesh and bone and the immortality of an image on rock, or even, more strangely, its immortality as a result of faith or an idea. So the removal of a wise sixth-century head, the dropping off of arms and hands of rock as a result of the fatigue of centuries, existed alongside human fate. He would hold statues two thousand years old in his arms. Or place his hand against old, warm rock that had been cut into a human shape. He found comfort in seeing his dark flesh against it. This was his pleasure. Not conversation or the education of others or power, but simply to place his hand against a *gal vihara,* a living stone whose temperature was dependent on the hour, whose look of porousness would change depending on rain or a quick twilight.

This rock hand could have been his wife's hand. It had a similar darkness and age to it, a familiar softness. And with ease he could have re-created her life, their years together, with the remaining fragments of her room. Two pencils and a shawl would have been enough to mark and recall her world. But *their* life remained buried. Whatever motives she had for leaving him, whatever vices and faults and lack he had within him that drove her away had remained unsought by Sarath. He was a man who could walk past a stretch of field and imagine a meeting hall that had been burned to the ground there six hundred years before; he could turn to that absence and with a smoke smudge, a fingerprint, re-create the light and the postures of those sitting there during an evening's ceremony. But he would unearth nothing of Ravina. This was not caused by any anger towards her, he was just unable to step back to the trauma of that place when he had talked in darkness, pretending there was light. But now, this afternoon, he had returned to the intricacies of the public world, with its various truths. He had acted in such a light. He knew he would not be forgiven that.

He and Gunesena pushed the trolley against the incline. There was hardly any air in the tunnel. Sarath put on the brake.

'Get some water, Gunesena.'

Gunesena nodded. There was irritation in the formal gesture. He went off, leaving Sarath in the half-dark, and returned five minutes later with a beaker of water.

'Was it boiled?'

Again Gunesena nodded. Sarath drank it and then got off the floor where he had been sitting. 'I'm sorry, I was feeling faint.'

'Yes, sir. I had a tumbler too.'

'Good.'

He remembered Gunesena drinking the remnant of cordial, Anil holding the bottle, the night they had picked him up on the Kandy road.

They continued a while longer with the trolley. Pushed the double swing doors and broke out into daylight.

The noise and sun almost made him step back. They had come out into the officers' parking lot. A few drivers stood in the shade of the one tree. Others remained within their cars, the air-conditioning purring. Sarath looked towards the main entrance but couldn't see her. He was no longer sure she would make it out. The van that was to carry the skeleton they were going to give Anil pulled up beside them and Sarath supervised the loading. The young soldiers wanted to know everything that was going on. It had nothing to do with suspicion, they were just curious. Sarath desired some pause or quiet but he knew he would not get it. The questions were personal not official. Where was he from? How long had he been . . . ? The only way he could escape them was to answer. When they began asking about the figure on the trolley, he waved his hands in front of his face and left Gunesena with them.

She hadn't come out of the building. He knew, whatever had happened, he couldn't go in looking for her. She would have to go through the hurdles of insult and humiliation and embarrassments on her own. It was almost an hour since he had last seen her.

He needed to keep busy. Beyond the fence a man was selling sliced pineapple so Sarath bought some through the barbed wire and sprinkled the salt-and-pepper mixture on it. A rupee for two slices. He could go into the lobby, out of the sunlight, but he didn't know whether he could trust her not to lose her temper and endanger herself more.

An hour and a half now. When he turned and looked back for the fourth time he saw her at the doors. Just standing there, not moving, not knowing where she was or what she was supposed to do.

He came towards her, his fist clenched, his mind swirling.

'Are you all right?'

She looked down, away from him.

'Anil.'

She pulled her arm from him. He noticed she was carrying no briefcase. No papers. No forensic equipment. He put his hand on her chest to feel for the small test tubes in the inner pocket of her coat but they were not there. She didn't react to that. Even in her state she did at least understand what he was doing.

'I told you I would return to the *walawwa*.'

'You didn't.'

'Everyone pays attention. My brother told you that. People knew you were in Colombo the moment you got here.'

'Damn you.'

'You have to leave now.'

'No, thanks. No more help from you.'

'Take the skeleton I've given you and get in the van. Go back to the ship with Gunesena.'

'All my papers are in that building. I have to get them back.'

'You'll never get them back. Do you understand? Forget them. You will have to re-create them. You can buy new equipment in Europe. You can replace nearly everything. It's just you who has to be safe.'

'Thanks for your help. Keep your fucking skeleton.'

'Gunesena, get the van.'

'Listen . . .' She swung her look towards him. 'Tell him to take me home. I don't think I can walk there. I really don't want your fucking help. But I can't walk. I was . . . in there . . .'

'Go to the lab.'

'Jesus, keep your—'

He slapped her hard. He was aware of people on the periphery, her gasp, her face as if it contained fever.

'Go with the skeleton and work on it. You don't have long. Don't call me. Get it done overnight. They want a report in two days. But get it done tonight.'

She was so stunned by his behaviour she climbed slowly into the van, which had drawn up beside her. Sarath watched her. He handed Gunesena the pass through the window. He saw her lowered burning face as the van curled out of his sight.

There was no vehicle for him. He went past the guards at the gate, out onto the street, waved down a *bajaj* and gave the driver the address of his office. You could never settle back and relax in a *bajaj;* if you lost concentration you were in danger of falling out. But sitting forward, his head in his hands, he tried to lose touch with the world around him as the three-wheeler struggled through the traffic.

Anil climbed the gangplank, then walked along the upper deck. A harbour in the afternoon. She could hear whistles and horns in the far reaches of the port. She wanted openness and air, didn't want to face the darkness in the hold. Farther down the quay she saw a man with a camera. Anil stepped back so he would be out of sight.

She knew she wouldn't be staying here much longer, there was no wish in her to be here anymore. There was blood everywhere. A casual sense of massacre. She remembered what a woman at the Nadesan Centre had said to her. 'I got out of the Civil Rights Movement partly because I couldn't remember which massacre took place when and where. . . .'

It was about five now. Anil found the arrack bottle and poured herself a glass, and walked the narrow steps down into the hold.

'Everything all right, miss?'

'Thank you, Gunesena. You can go.'

'Yes, miss.' Yet she knew he would stay with her, somewhere on the ship.

She turned on a lamp. There was the other set of tools, which belonged to Sarath. She heard the door close behind her.

She drank more arrack and spoke out loud, just to hear the echo in the dim light so she would not feel alone with the ancient skeleton she had been given. She cut the plastic wrapping with an

X-acto knife and rolled it down. She recognized it immediately. But to be certain moved her right hand down to the heel and felt the notch in the bone that she had cut weeks earlier.

He had found Sailor. Slowly she directed another lamp onto him. The ribs like struts on a boat. She slid her hand between the arched bones and touched the tape recorder that was there, not believing this now, not yet, until she pressed the button and voices began filling the room around her. She had the information on tape. Their questions. And she had Sailor. She put her hand between the ribs again to press the button to stop it, but as she was about to, his voice came on, very clear and focused. He must have held the recorder close to his mouth as he whispered.

'I'm in the tunnel of the Armoury building. I have just a moment. As you can tell, this is not any skeleton but Sailor. It's your twentieth-century evidence, five years old in death. Erase this tape. Erase my words here. Complete the report and be ready to leave at five tomorrow morning. There's a seven-o'clock plane. Someone will drive you to the airport. I would like it to be me but it will probably be Gunesena. Do not leave the lab or call me.'

Anil made the tape roll back on the rewind. She walked away from the skeleton and paced up and down the hold listening to his voice again.

Listening to everything again.

On Galle Face Green the brothers had talked comfortably only because of her presence. So it had seemed to her. It was a long time later that she realized they were in fact speaking only to each other, and that they were pleased to be doing so. There was a want in each of them to align themselves, she was the beard, the excuse. It was *their* conversation about the war in their country and what each of them had done during it and what each would not do. They were, in retrospect, closer than they imagined.

If she were to step into another life now, back to the adopted country of her choice, how much would Gamini and the memory of Sarath be a part of her life? Would she talk to intimates about them, the two Colombo brothers? And she in some way like a sister between them, keeping them from mauling each other's worlds? Wherever she might be, would she think of them? Consider the strange middle-class pair who were born into one world and in mid-life stepped waist-deep into another?

At one point that night, she remembered, they spoke of how much they loved their country. In spite of everything. No Westerner would understand the love they had for the place. 'But I could never leave here,' Gamini had whispered.

'American movies, English books—remember how they all end?' Gamini asked that night. 'The American or the Englishman gets on a plane and leaves. That's it. The camera leaves with him.

He looks out of the window at Mombasa or Vietnam or Jakarta, someplace now he can look at through the clouds. The tired hero. A couple of words to the girl beside him. He's going home. So the war, to all purposes, is over. That's enough reality for the West. It's probably the history of the last two hundred years of Western political writing. Go home. Write a book. Hit the circuit.'

The worker from the civil rights organization came in with the Friday reports of victims—the fresh, almost-damp black-and-white photographs, seven of them this week. Faces covered. The reports were left for Gamini on the table by his window. By the time he got to them the shifts were changing. He turned on the tape recorder and began describing the wounds and how they were probably caused. When he got to the third picture he recognized the wounds, the innocent ones. He left the reports where they were, went down one flight of stairs and ran along the corridor to the ward. It was unlocked. He began pulling the sheets off the bodies until he saw what he knew he would see. Ever since he had picked up the third photograph, all he could hear was his heart, its banging.

Gamini didn't know how long he stood there. There were seven bodies in the room. There were things he could do. He didn't know. There were things he could do perhaps. He could see the acid burns, the twisted leg. He unlocked the cupboard that held bandages, splints, disinfectant. He began washing the body's dark-brown markings with scrub lotion. He could heal his brother, set the left leg, deal with every wound as if he were alive, as if treating the hundred small traumas would eventually bring him back into his life.

The gash of scar on the side of your elbow you got crashing a bike on the Kandy Hill. This scar I gave you hitting you with a cricket stump. As brothers we ended up never turning our backs on each other. You were always too much of an older brother, Sarath. Still, if I had been a doctor then, I could have sewn the stitches up more carefully than Dr. Piachaud. It's thirty years later, Sarath. It's late afternoon—with everyone gone home except me, your least favourite relative. The one you can never relax with or feel secure with. Your unhappy shadow.

He was leaning over the body, beginning to dress its wounds, and the horizontal afternoon light held the two of them in a wide spoke.

There are pietàs of every kind. He recalls the sexual pietà he saw once. A man and a woman, the man having come and the woman stroking his back, her face with the acceptance of his transformed physical state. It was Sarath and Sarath's wife he had witnessed, and then her eyes had looked up at him, in his madness, her hand not pausing in its stroke of the body within her arms.

There were other pietàs. The story of Savitra, who wrestled her husband away from Death so that in the startling paintings of the myth you saw her hold him—joy filling her face, while *his* face looked capsized, in the midst of his fearful metamorphosis, this reversal back into love and life.

But this was a pietà between brothers. And all Gamini knew in his slowed, scrambled state was that this would be the end or it could be the beginning of a permanent conversation with Sarath. If he did not talk to him in this moment, admit himself, his brother would disappear from his life. So he was too, at this moment, within the contract of a pietà.

He opened his brother's shirt so the chest was revealed. A gentle chest. Not hard and feral like his own. It was the generous chest of a Ganesh. An Asian belly. The chest of someone who in his sarong would stroll into the garden or onto the verandah with his tea and newspaper. Sarath had always sidestepped violence because of his character, as if there had never been a war within him. He drove people around him mad. If Gamini had been the Mouse, his brother was the Bear.

Gamini placed the warmth of his hand against the still face. He had never worried about the fate of his one brother, had always thought he himself would be the fatal one. Perhaps they had each assumed they would crash alone in the darkness they had invented around themselves. Their marriages, their careers on this borderland of civil war among governments and terrorists and insurgents. There had never been a tunnel of light between them. Instead they had searched out and found their own dominions. Sarath in sun-drenched fields looking for astrological stones, Gamini in his medieval world of Emergency Services. Each of them most at ease, most free, when not conscious of the other. They were too similar in essence and therefore incapable of ever giving in to the other. Each refused to show hesitation and fear, it was only strength and anger they revealed when in the other's company. The woman Anil had said, that night on Galle Face Green, 'I can never understand someone by his strengths. Nothing is revealed there. I can only understand people by their weaknesses.'

Sarath's chest said everything. It was what Gamini had fought against. But now this body lay on the bed undefended. It was what it was. No longer a counter of argument, no longer an opinion that Gamini refused to accept. Oh, there seemed to be a mark like that made with a spear. A small wound, not deep in his chest, and Gamini bathed it and taped it up.

He had seen cases where every tooth had been removed, the nose cut apart, the eyes humiliated with liquids, the ears entered. He had been, as he ran down that hospital hallway, most frightened of seeing his brother's face. It was the face they went for in some cases. They could in their hideous skills sniff out vanity. But they had not touched Sarath's face.

The shirt they had dressed Sarath in had giant sleeves. Gamini knew why. He ripped the sleeves down to the cuffs. Below the elbows the hands had been broken in several places.

It was dark now. It looked as if the room were full of grey water. He walked to the entrance and touched the switch, and seven central lights came on. He came back and sat with his brother.

He was still there an hour later when the bodies started coming in from a bombing somewhere in the city.

President Katugala was in a white cotton outfit, looking old, not at all like the giant posters of him throughout the city that had celebrated and idealized him for years. When you looked at the real image of the man, the lean face below the thinning white hair, there was a compassion for him, no matter what he had done. He looked weary and scared. He had been tense during the previous days, as if there was some kind of foreshadowing in his mind, as if some mechanism he had no control of had been put in motion. But it was now National Heroes Day. And the one thing the Silver President did every National Heroes Day was to go out and meet the people. He could never give up a political rally.

The week before, there had been warnings from the special forces of the police and army for him *not* to go among the crowds. He had in fact promised he would not do so. But around three-thirty in the afternoon, it was discovered the President was out meeting the people. The head of Katugala's special unit, with a few other officials, leapt into a jeep and went looking for him. They located him reasonably quickly in the crowded Colombo streets and had just reached him and were standing behind him at the moment the bomb went off.

Katugala was wearing a loose white long-sleeved jacket and sarong. He was wearing sandals. He had a watch on his left wrist. He stopped by Lipton Circus and made a short speech from his bulletproof vehicle.

R—— wore denim shorts and a loose shirt. Underneath these was a layer of explosives and two Duracell batteries and two blue switches. One for the left hand, one for the right, linked by wires to the explosives. The first switch armed the bomb. It would stay on as long as the bomber wished. When the other switch was turned on, the bomb detonated. Both needed to be activated for the explosion to occur. You could wait as long as you wanted before turning on the second switch. Or you could turn the first switch off. R—— had more clothing on above the denim shorts. Four Velcro straps held the explosives pack to his body, and along with the dynamite there was the great weight of thousands of small ball bearings.

After Katugala finished speaking at Lipton Circus, he travelled in the bulletproof Range Rover towards the large rally on Galle Face Green. A year earlier a fortune-teller had said, '*He will be destroyed like a plate falling to the ground.*' Now he made his way along the dual carriageway. But he kept climbing out from his vehicle and greeting the crowd. R—— threaded his way on a bicycle through the chaos of people, or maybe he was walking, wheeling it. In any case, Katugala was now among the people; he had stopped again because he saw a procession of slogan-waving supporters coming onto the street from a side road. He tried to help supervise it. And R——, who would kill him, who had infiltrated the outer circle of Katugala's residential staff so that he was well known by them, R—— came slowly towards him, riding or walking his bicycle.

There are a few photographs of Katugala taken during the last half-hour of his life that exist only in a file belonging to the army. A couple of pictures were taken by the police from a high building, some by journalists, which were later confiscated and never returned, never published in the newspapers. They show him in his white outfit, looking frail, beginning to appear concerned. Mostly he looks old. Over the years no unflattering pictures of him were published in the newspapers. But in these photographs what you notice first is his age—emphasized by the fact that behind him is his platonic form on a giant cardboard cut-out, where he looks vibrant, with thick white hair. And behind him you can also see the armoured vehicle that he has left for the last time.

Katugala's plan, in his last minutes, was to get the procession of supporters from *his* constituency to join the crowd on Galle Face Green. He had begun walking back to his vehicle, changed his mind and returned to choreograph the procession once more; this was how he came to be caught with his bodyguards between two very different processions—his supporters and the general populace celebrating National Heroes Day. If someone had said the President was in their midst, most of those in the crowd would have been surprised. *Where is the President?* At street level, in the crowd, the only presidential presence was a giant cardboard cut-out of him carried like a film prop, bobbing up and down.

No one knows really if R—— came with this new procession, as seems most likely, or whether he was at the junction where the group met the larger crowd. Or he could have been waiting near the vehicle. In any case, he had been waiting for this day, when he was sure he would be able to get to Katugala on the street. There was no way R—— could have entered the presidential grounds with explosives and ball bearings strapped to him. The bodyguards were unforgiving. There were never exceptions. Every pen in every pocket was examined. So R—— had to approach him in a public place, with all the paraphernalia of devastation sewn onto himself. He was not just the weapon but the aimer of it. The bomb would destroy whomever he was facing. His own eyes and frame were the cross-hairs. He approached Katugala having already switched on one of the batteries. One blue bulb lighting up deep in his clothing. When he was within five yards of Katugala he turned on the other switch.

At four p.m. on National Heroes Day, more than fifty people were killed instantly, including the President. The cutting action of the explosion shredded Katugala into pieces. The central question after the bombing concerned whether the President had been spirited away, and if so whether by the police and army forces or by terrorists. Because the President could not be found.

Where was the President?

The head of the President's unit, who half an hour earlier had been told that Katugala was out meeting the crowds, who had leapt into the jeep and made his way towards the Silver President, had just reached him and was insisting that he return to the armoured vehicle and be driven back to his residence. When the bomb went off he was left miraculously untouched. The direct spray of ball bearings entered and were held within the body of Katugala or went through him and fell in a clatter to the tarmac in the few feet behind him. But the sound of the blast drowned out the clatter. And it was the awfulness of the noise that most remember, those who survived.

So he was the only human left standing in the silence that contained the last echoes of the bomb. There was no one within twenty yards of him save the Gulliver-like replica of Katugala, rays of sun coming through the cardboard, which the ball bearings had reached and gone through.

Around him were the dead. Political supporters, an astrologer, three policemen. The armoured Range Rover just a few yards away was undamaged. There was blood on the unbroken windows. The driver sitting inside was unhurt except for damage to his ears from the sound.

Some flesh, probably from the bomber, was found on the wall of the building across the street. The right arm of Katugala rested by itself on the stomach of one of the dead policemen. There were shattered curd pots all over the pavement. Four p.m.

By four-thirty every doctor who could be located had reported for duty in the emergency hospitals in Colombo. There were more than a hundred injured on the periphery of the killing. And soon rumours rose in every ward that Katugala too had been in the crowd when the bomb went off. So each hospital waited for the possibility that his wounded body would be brought in. But it never arrived. The body, what remained of it, was not found for a long time.

The general public first became aware of the assassination when phone calls started coming in from England and Australia, people saying they had heard Katugala was dead. And then the truth slipped across the city within an hour.

Distance

The 120-foot-high statue had stood in a field of Buduruvagala for several generations. Half a mile away was the more famous rock wall of Bodhisattvas. In noon heat you walked barefoot and looked up at the figures. This was a region of desperate farming, the nearest village four miles away. So these stone bodies rising out of the earth, their faces high in the sky, often were the only human aspect a farmer would witness in his landscape during the day. They gazed over the stillness, over the buzz-scream of cicadas which were invisible in the parched grass. They brought a permanence to brief lives.

After the long darkness of night the rising sun would first colour the heads of the Bodhisattvas and the solitary Buddha, then move down their rock robes until finally, free of forests, it swathed down onto the sand and dry grass and stone, onto the human forms that walked on bare burning feet towards the sacred statues.

Three men had travelled all night across the fields carrying a thin bamboo ladder. Some quiet talk, a fear of being witnessed. They had made the ladder that afternoon and now they propped it against the statue of the Buddha. One of them lit a beedi and put it in his mouth, then climbed up the ladder. He tucked the roll of dynamite into a stone fold of cloth on the statue and ignited the fuse with the cigarette. Then he jumped down and the three of them ran and turned at the noise and held hands and lowered their heads in a crouch as the statue buckled and the torso leapt towards the earth and the great expressive face of the Buddha fell forward and smashed into the ground.

The thieves pried the stomach open with metal rods but found no treasure, and so they left. Still, this was broken stone. It was not a human life. This was for once not a political act or an act perpetrated by one belief against another. The men were trying to find a solution for hunger or a way to get out of their disintegrating lives. And the 'neutral' and 'innocent' fields around the statue and the rock carvings were perhaps places of torture and burials. Since it was mostly uninhabited land, with only a few farmers and pilgrims, this was a place where trucks came to burn and hide victims who had been picked up. These were fields where Buddhism and its values met the harsh political events of the twentieth century.

The artisan brought to Buduruvagala to attempt a reconstruction of the Buddha statue was a man from the south. Born in a village of stonecutters, he had been an eye painter. According to the Archaeological Department, which oversaw the project, he was a drinker but would not begin drinking until the afternoons. There was a small overlap of working and drinking but it was only in the evenings that he was unapproachable. He had lost his wife some years earlier. She was one of the thousands who had disappeared.

Ananda Udugama would be on the site by dawn, would peg the blueprints into the earth and assign duties to the seven men who worked with him. The workers had dug out the base, which held the lower legs and thighs of the statue. These had not been damaged. They were pulled out and stored in a field where there were bees and left there until the rest of the body was reconstructed. A quarter of a mile away, and simultaneously with the reconstruction of this large broken Buddha, another statue was being built—to replace the destroyed god.

It was assumed that Ananda would be working under the authority and guidance of foreign specialists but in the end these celebrities never came. There was too much political turmoil, and it was unsafe. They were finding dead bodies daily, not even buried, in the adjoining fields. Victims picked up as far away as Kalutara were brought here, out of family range. Ananda appeared to stare past it all. He gave two of the men on his team the job of dealing with the bodies—tagging them, contacting civil rights authorities. By the time the monsoon came the murders had subsided, or at least this area was no longer being used as a killing field or a burial ground.

Later it came to be seen that the work done by Ananda was complex and innovative. All through the various seasons of heat, the time of monsoons and their storms, he oversaw the work in the mud trench, which resembled a hundred-foot-long coffin. It was a structure in which the found fragments of stone would be dropped. Inside it was a grid divided into one-foot squares, and once the stones were identified as to what likely part of the body they came from, by someone at the head of the triage, as it were, these were placed in the appropriate section. All this was tentative, approximate. They had pieces of stone as big as boulders and shards the size of a knuckle. This distinguishing took place in the worst of the May monsoons, so fragments of rock would be tossed into square pools of water.

Ananda brought in some of the villagers to work, ten more men. It was safer to be seen working for a project like this, otherwise you could be pulled into the army or you might be rounded up as a suspect. He got more of the village involved, women as well as men. If they volunteered, he put them to work. They had to be there by five in the morning and they packed it in by two in the afternoon, when Ananda Udugama had his own plans for the day.

The women distinguished the stones, which slid wet from their hands into the grid. It rained for more than a month. When the rain stopped, the grass steamed around them and they could finally hear one another and began to talk, their clothes dry in fifteen minutes. Then the rain would come again and they were back within its noise, silent, solitary in the crowded field, the wind banging and loosening a corrugated roof, trying to unpeel it from a shed. The distinguishing of the stones took several weeks, and by the time the dry season came most of the limbs had been assembled. There was now one arm, fifty feet long, an ear. The legs still safe in the field of bees. They began to move the sections towards each other in the cicada grass. Engineers came and with a twenty-foot drill burrowed through the soles of the feet and moved up the limbs of the body, till there was a path for metal bones to be poured in, tunnels between the hips and torso, between the shoulders and neck to the head.

During the months of assembly, Ananda had spent most of his time on the head. He and two others used a system of fusing rock. Up close the face looked quilted. They had planned to homogenize the stone, blend the face into a unit, but when he saw it this way Ananda decided to leave it as it was. He worked instead on the composure and the qualities of the face.

On the horizon the other statue of the Buddha rose gradually into the sky, while Ananda's reconstruction stretched out along a sandy path. The path sloped, the head remaining the lowest part of the body—essential for the final stage of knitting it together.

Five cauldrons of boiling iron hissed under the slight rainfall. The men brought out the prepared corrugated troughs and poured the iron along them and watched it disappear into the feet of the statue, the red metal sliding into the path drilled within the body—giant red veins slipping down the hundred-foot length. When it hardened it would lock all the limbs together. Then it rained again, this time for two days, and the village workers were sent home. Everyone left the site.

Ananda sat in a chair next to the head. He looked up at the sky, into the source of the storm. They had built a walk ledge ten feet off the ground with bamboo. Now this forty-five-year-old man got up and climbed up onto the ledge to look down at the face and torso, which held inside it the cooling red iron.

He was there again the next morning. It was still raining, then it suddenly stopped, and the heat began to draw out steam from the earth and the statue. Ananda kept pulling off and drying his wired-together spectacles. He was on the platform most of the time now, wearing one of the Indian cotton shirts Sarath had given him some years back. His sarong was heavy and dark from the rain.

He stood over what they had been able to re-create of the face. It was a long time since he had believed in the originality of artists. He had known some of them in his youth. You slipped into the old bed of the art, where they had slept. There was comfort there. You saw their days of glory, then their days of banishment. He had always liked them and their art more during their years of banishment. He himself did not create or invent faces anymore. Invention was a sliver. Still, all the work he had done in organizing the rebuilding of the statue was for this. The face. Its one hundred chips and splinters of stone brought together, merged, with the shadow of bamboo lying across its cheek. All its life until now the statue had never felt a human shadow. It had looked over these hot fields towards green terraces in the distant north. It had seen the wars and offered peace or irony to those dying under it. Now sunlight hit the seams of its face, as if it were sewn roughly together. He wouldn't hide that. He saw the lidded grey eyes someone else had cut in another century, that torn look in its great acceptance; he was close against the eyes now, with no distance, like an animal in a stone garden, some old man in the future. In a few days the face would be in the sky, no longer below him as he walked on this trestle, his shadow moving across the face, the hollows holding rain so he could lean down and drink from it, as if a food, a wealth. He looked at the eyes that had once belonged to a god. This is what he felt. As an artificer now he did not celebrate the greatness of a faith. But he knew if he did not remain an artificer he would become a demon. The war around him was to do with demons, spectres of retaliation.

It was the evening before the Nētra Mangala ceremony of the new Buddha statue and offerings were being brought from the nearby villages. The figure stood upright, high above the fires, as if leaning into the darkness. By three in the morning the chants had altered into the recitation of *sloka*s alongside quiet drums. Ananda could hear the recitations of the *Kosala-bimba-varnanāva,* could also hear the night insects chirping beside the paths of light that radiated from the statue, like spokes into the fields, leading to bonfires where children and mothers slept or sat waiting for morning. The drummers returned from their performance sweating in the cold dark, their feet lit by the oil lamps as they came along the paths.

The work on the statues had ended days apart, so there seemed suddenly to be two figures—one of scarred grey rock, one of white plaster—standing now in the open valley a half-mile away from each other.

Ananda was sitting in a teak chair, being dressed and painted. He was to perform the eye ceremony on the new statue. The darkness around him had removed centuries of history. In the time of the old kings, such as Parakrama Bahu, when only kings performed the ceremony, there would have been temple dancers who danced and sang the Melodies, as if this were heaven.

It was almost four-thirty when the men pulled two long bamboo ladders out of the dark fields and within the ring of bonfires lifted them against the statue. When the sun rose it would be seen that they rested on the giant figure's shoulders. Ananda Udugama and his nephew were already climbing the ladders up into the night. Both were robed, Ananda with a turban of fine silk on his head. Both carried cloth satchels.

In the coldness of the world, halfway up, it seemed that only the fires below connected him to earth. Then, looking into the dark, he could see the dawn prizing itself up out of the horizon, emerging above the forest. The sun lit the green bamboo of the ladder. He could feel its partial warmth on his arms, saw it light the brocade costume he wore over Sarath's cotton shirt—the one he had promised himself he would wear for this morning's ceremony. He and the woman Anil would always carry the ghost of Sarath Diyasena.

He reached the head a few minutes before the precise hour for the eye ceremony. His nephew was there, waiting for him. Ananda had climbed this ladder a day earlier and so knew he would be most comfortable and efficient two rungs from the top. He used a sash to tie himself to the ladder and then his nephew passed him the chisels and brushes. Below them the drumming stopped. The boy held up the metal mirror so that it reflected the blank stare of the statue. The eyes unformed, unable to see. And until he had eyes—always the last thing painted or sculpted—he was not the Buddha.

Ananda began to chisel. He used a coconut husk to clean the grit from the large trough he had cut, which to those below would be only a delicate line of expression. There was no talking between him and the boy. Every now and then he would lean forward into the ladder and put his arms down to let the blood back into them. But the two worked at a fast pace, because soon there would be the harshness of sunlight.

He was working on the second eye, sweating within the brocade costume though it was still just dawn heat. Only the sash held him safe on the ladder. There was plaster dust everywhere— on the cheeks and shoulders of the statue's head, on Ananda's clothes, on the boy. Ananda was very tired. As if all his blood had magically entered into this body. Soon, though, there would be the evolving moment when the eyes, reflected in the mirror, would see him, fall into him. The first and last look given to someone so close. After this hour the statue would be able to witness figures only from a great distance.

The boy was watching him. Ananda nodded to acknowledge he was all right. They still did not speak. He had probably about another hour to go.

The noise of his hammering stopped and there was just the wind around them, its tugs and gusts and whistles. He handed the tools to his nephew. Then he drew from a satchel the colours for the eye. He looked past the vertical line of cheek into the landscape. Pale greens, dark greens, bird movement and their nearby sounds. It was the figure of the world the statue would see forever, in rainlight and sunlight, a combustible world of weather even without the human element.

The eyes, like his at this moment, would always look north. As would the great scarred face half a mile away, which he had helped knit together from damaged stone, a statue that was no longer a god, that no longer had its graceful line but only the pure sad glance Ananda had found.

And now with human sight he was seeing all the fibres of natural history around him. He could witness the smallest approach of a bird, every flick of its wing, or a hundred-mile storm coming down off the mountains near Gonagola and skirting to the plains. He could feel each current of wind, every lattice-like green shadow created by cloud. There was a girl moving in the forest. The rain miles away rolling like blue dust towards him. Grasses being burned, bamboo, the smell of petrol and grenade. The crack of noise as a layer of rock on his arm exfoliated in heat. The face open-eyed in the great rainstorms of May and June. The weather formed in the temperate forests and sea, in the thorn scrub behind him in the southeast, in the deciduous hills, and moving towards the burning savanna near Badulla, and then the coast of mangroves, lagoons and river deltas. The great churning of weather above the earth.

Ananda briefly saw this angle of the world. There was a seduction for him here. The eyes he had cut and focussed with his father's chisel showed him this. The birds dove towards gaps within the trees! They flew through the shelves of heat currents. The tiniest of hearts in them beating exhausted and fast, the way Sirissa had died in the story he invented for her in the vacuum of her disappearance. A small brave heart. In the heights she loved and in the dark she feared.

He felt the boy's concerned hand on his. This sweet touch from the world.

Acknowledgments

I would like to thank the doctors and nurses, archaeologists, forensic anthropologists, and members of the human rights and civil rights organizations with whom I met in Sri Lanka and in other parts of the world. This novel could not have been written without their generosity and their knowledge and experience in archaeological sites, in hospitals of chaos and dedication, in archives of terrible sadness. This book is for these people and these organizations. It is especially for Anjalendran, and Senake, and Ian Goonetileke.

*

Thanks to the following for the help they gave me during the research and writing of this book: Gillian and Alwin Ratnayake, K. H. R. Karunaratne, N. P. Sumaraweera, Manel Fonseka, Suriya Wickremasinghe, Clyde Snow, Victoria Sanford, K. A. R. Kennedy, Gamini Goonetileke, Anjalendran C., Senake Bandaranayake, Radhika Coomaraswamy, Tissa Abeysekara, Jean Perera, Neil Fonseka, L. K. Karunaratne, R. L. Thambugale, Dehan Gunasekera, Ravindra Fernando, Roland Silva, Ananda Samarasingha, Deepika Udagama, Gunasiri Hewepatura, Vidyapathy Somabandu, Janaka Weeratunga, Diluni Weerasena, D. S. Liyanarachchi, Janaka Kandamby, Dominic Sansoni, Katherine Nickerson, Donya Peroff, H. Rousseau, Sara Howes, Milo Beech, David Young and Louise Dennys.

Also: the Kynsey Road Hospital, the Base Hospital Polonnaruwa, the Karapitiya General Hospital, the Nadesan Centre, the Civil Rights Movement of Sri Lanka, Amnesty International and the Conference on Human Rights organized by the Colombo Medical Faculty and the Colombo University Centre for the Study of Human Rights in May 1996.

*

The following works were invaluable in the writing of this book: *The National Atlas of Sri Lanka* (Survey Department, 1988); *Cūlavaṃsa*; *Asiatic Art in the Rijksmuseum, Amsterdam*, ed. Pauline Scheurleer (Rijksmuseum, 1985); *Bells of the Bronze Age*, a documentary film produced by *Archaeological Magazine*; *Mediaeval Sinhalese Art* by Ananda K. Coomaraswamy (Pantheon Books, 1956), especially his writing on 'eye ceremonies'; *Reconstruction of Life from the Skeleton*, ed. Mehmet Yaşar İşcan and Kenneth A. R. Kennedy (Wiley, 1989), especially Kennedy's work on markers of occupational stress; 'Upper Pleistocene Fossil Hominids from Sri Lanka' by Kennedy, Deraniyagala, Roertgen, Chiment and Disotell, *American Journal of Physical Anthropology* (1987); *Stones, Bones, and the Ancient Cities* by Lawrence H. Robbins (St. Martin's Press, 1990); pamphlets on war surgery, especially "Injuries Due to Anti-Personnel Landmines in Sri Lanka" by G. Goonetileke; 'Senarat Paranavitana as a Writer of Historical Fiction in Sanskrit' by Ananda W. P. Guruge, *Vidyodaya Journal of Social Sciences* (University of Sri Jayawardenapura); *Witnesses from the Grave: The Stories Bones Tell* by Christopher Joyce and Eric Stover (Little, Brown, 1991); 'A Note on the Ancient Hospitals of Sri Lanka' (Department of Archaeology); 'Restoration of a Vandalized Bodhisattva Image at Dambegoda' by Roland Silva, Gamini Wijeysuriya and Martin Wyse (Konos Info, March 1990); P. R. C. Peterson's memoir of his years as a doctor in Sri Lanka, *Great Days! Memoirs of a Government Medical Officer of 1918*, compiled and edited by Manel Fonseka; reports from Amnesty International, Asia Watch, the Commission of Human Rights.

*

The epigraph is made up of two poems from the essay 'Miner's Folk Songs of Sri Lanka' by Rex A. Casinader, *Etnologiska Studier* (Goteborg), no. 35 (1981).

The partial list of the 'disappeared' is drawn from Amnesty International reports.

The line by Robert Duncan is from *The HD Book*, chapter 6, "Rites of Participation" (*Caterpillar*, October 1967).

Lines from Victor Hugo's *Les Misérables* and from Alexander Dumas's *The Man in the Iron Mask* appear on page 54.

Italicized sentences from H. Zimmer's *The King and the Corpse* (Bollingen Series XI, Princeton University Press, 1956) appear on page 56.

The italicized line on page 135 is from *Plainwater* by Anne Carson (Knopf, 1995).

The italicized remark on page 43 is from *Great Books* by David Denby (Simon and Schuster, 1996).

The remark on Jung on page 230 is by Leonora Carrington during an interview with Rosemary Sullivan.

Thank you to David Thomson for his genealogical unearthing of American western heroes.

A special thank you to Manel Fonseka.

Much forensic and medical information was also drawn from interviews with Clyde Snow in Oklahoma and Guatemala; Gamini Goonetileke in Sri Lanka; and K. A. R. Kennedy in Ithaca, New York, as well as from many persons listed above.

*

Thank you to Jet Fuel. To Rick/Simon and Darren Wershler-Henry and Stan Bevington at Coach House Press. To Katherine Hourigan, Anna Jardine, Debra Helfand and Leyla Aker. Also to Ellen Levine, Gretchen Mullin and Tulin Valeri.

And finally, thanks to Ellen Seligman, Sonny Mehta, Liz Calder. And Linda, Griffin and Esta.